BECOMING BOBBIE

BECOMING BOBBIE

R. J. STEVENS

KENSINGTON BOOKS
http://www.kensingtonbooks.com

KENSINGTON BOOKS are published by

Kensington Publishing Corp.
850 Third Avenue
New York, NY 10022

All Kensington Titles, Imprints, and Distributed Lines are available at special quantity discounts for bulk purchases for sales promotions, premiums, fund-raising, and educational or institutional use.

Special book excerpts or customized printings can also be created to fit specific needs. For detail, write or phone the office of the Kensington special sales manager: Kensington Publishing Corp., 850 Third Avenue, New York, NY 10022, attn: Special Sales Department, Phone: 1-800-221-2647.

Kensington and the K logo Reg. U.S. Pat & TM Off

ISBN: 0-7394-3865-4

First printing: August 2003
10 9 8 7 6 5 4 3 2 1

Printed in the United States of America

For Lindsey, my Stella.

Thank you to my family, who never told me that I couldn't, and put up with more than I'd like to admit, and to my friends, including the personnel of South Barry County, and Christian County Ambulance, you all have been great to me. Thank you to all the great musicians I mentioned here, and more, you've always been an inspiration to me. Janet King and JoKay Smith, two of the best teachers I'm honored to call friends. Thanks to Alison Picard and John Scognamiglio, for having faith in both Bobbie and me, and helping me stumble through this.

Special thanks goes out to Melissa Etheridge, for *Your Little Secret*.

Terrie, as always, you are my constant.

Chapter One

I guess you're here for the story. This is my story, but I really don't think it's much of one. I'm not a writer, I'm not even much of a storyteller, but Stella thinks that I need to be. She asked me to write it down, partly because she thinks someone out there might want to read it, but mostly because I can't tell it and keep it all straight. The memories just seem to get jumbled up.

It's a funny thing about memories . . . you bury them. Really. You lock them tight into a little box, and bury it somewhere deep within your mind. I don't think you mean to, at least I never meant to, but somehow those memories get buried just the same. You bury them so deep that you think you've forgotten them. But you haven't. Sometime, somewhere, something happens to trigger them.

For some people it's something big that triggers those memories, but it doesn't have to be. It could be something small. Like someone from your high school walking up to you on the street. Or old pictures found in a scrapbook you forgot you had. Anything, a smell, a sight, a taste. For me it was a song. Several of them, actually.

Oh, there were so many things I thought I'd put behind me, I thought I'd forgotten. Really forgotten, as if they never happened at all. I think that sometimes people can get so caught up in the present that it seems as if there were never anything else. That's what happened to me, I guess. That is, right up until I listened to a CD a few years ago.

And somehow, listening to that music, all those memories suddenly came flooding back. The box splintered open and all those buried memories came out in a rush. Not nice and neat, in a little package, but all disjointed and fragmented, like chunks tossed about after an explosion. There was no order, no continuum. Talking about those pieces of memories made no sense. Even thinking about them made no sense. They were so fragmented that I couldn't wrap my mind around one whole memory. I just had flashes of everything, like a slide show in high speed, out of order. I had to sit down and sort through those chunks of my life, like I expect people do after a fire, picking up each piece and examining it before putting it in some sort of order.

And it took me a long time to sort through it all. A really long time. I had to sit down with all those shards of memory, like so much broken pottery, and piece them together slowly, unable to fit one piece in until its surroundings were there. It turned into a terribly long process.

I tried to talk about it a time or two, while I was putting it back together, but it kept getting jumbled. I'd skip around in time, mix up things. So Stella asked me to start at the beginning and write it all down. And she asked me to be honest.

That's going to be the hardest part, I think, the honesty. To admit your mistakes to the world at large is one thing, but to admit them to someone you love . . . that's tough. But I'll do my best. This shouldn't take long.

I guess I really have to start with me. I was born an only child, in a small town in Mississippi, the spring after what Don McLean would later refer to as "the day the music died." Things were kind of crazy then, especially in the Deep South.

During the first decade of my life, the country was in turmoil. Those who weren't Caucasian were marching for equality, teenagers were fighting their parents for the right to play rock and roll music, and roughly half the country was trying to live on peace and love. And drugs. Mostly drugs. The peace and love thing didn't work out, but a lot of people thought it did, for a while at least. Maybe it was all the drugs giving the illusion of peace and love. I don't know, I was pretty young. The teenagers won their battle, rock and roll was here to stay. And Equal Rights became a reality. Well, at least on paper.

Anyway, late in the winter that year, the music died in a plane crash. And I was born that spring. My mother named me Barbara Ann, which would have been bad enough all by itself, but it was made much worse because of that song (you know the one, it's probably playing in your head right now). But my father always called me Bobbie, and that wasn't so bad. And after I was eleven or so, if he was in a particularly playful mood, he called me Bobbie McGee.

My father probably could have called me anything, I wouldn't have minded. I was truly a daddy's girl. Not the kind that wears frilly dresses and ribbons, no, that wasn't me at all. I was more like the kind that idolizes her father and follows him everywhere.

My early childhood (and really, a good portion of my life) was consumed by three things: my father, cars, and music. And the last two centered on the first.

My father was a mechanic. What's referred to as a "shade tree mechanic." He worked on cars in the front yard, and at other people's houses, even on the side of the road. Anywhere he was needed. He always seemed to be working on something. If it wasn't a car, he was tinkering around with something in the house, but mostly cars. Everyone brought their cars to him. Everyone. And he fixed them all.

Oh, I wanted to be just like him. And I was well on my way at a very early age. He was tall, broad shouldered, and strong. I thought he was the strongest man on earth. And the tallest. When he lifted me up, I felt as if I were flying. His dark brown hair matched my own, and his eyes were brown, also like mine. I guess I look a lot like him. I can say that now, and not feel any resentment.

So, he was my hero, and I wanted to be just like him. I followed him everywhere. He took me with him when he worked on cars, even when I was too small to do any more than hand him tools. He'd be under some car, and I'd be sitting in the dirt beside him, or even crawling under the car with him, asking a million questions. He was always so patient, explaining everything to me while I watched his big rough hands work their magic on those cars.

I loved the cars. There weren't any economy cars back then. No, they were all big, heavy, and solid. The muscle cars. Oh, I loved the lines on the muscle cars! The steel curves and big fins, the way they looked rolling down the highway. And the engines. The sound of a well-tuned engine running perfectly. The sheer power of it. And all the intricate little parts that worked together perfectly to make it whole. I wanted to know everything about them, just like my father did. It was incredible to me.

And always, behind it all, was the music.

My father kept the radio on all the time. The music played like a constant backdrop to my life. That was when popular music was all rock and roll. There weren't so many subcategories to keep up with. It wasn't separated into contemporary, metal, alternative, light, or anything else. The songs weren't pigeonholed. If it didn't twang, it was rock and roll. Even if it did twang, it got played on the rock stations too, if it was especially good. And I loved it all, from the psychedelic rock to the blues, from the folk to the Motown. All the great stuff played on the radio, and my father would softly sing along as he worked. He knew every song. The music and the work, the cars and my father. They all intertwined in my mind, and I loved them equally.

Even when I was just three and four years old, I was right there beside him. We'd spend all day working on those cars, just Dad and me, getting covered in grease and dirt. The radio would be on, playing everything from "The Twist" to "Wipe Out," the Shirelles to the Drifters.

Dad and I talked about the cars, the music, plans for the next day. We worked together until darkness began to fall; then he'd pick me up, spin me around, and set me up high on his shoulders. Singing the last song that we had heard, I'd duck under the doorway as he carried me into the house.

My mother was always so mad at the sight of us, coming in so filthy. She'd scrub me until I was squeaky clean, yelling at him the whole time, making him promise never to do that again. He would always solemnly promise her, wink at me, and we'd be back under a car the next day.

I spent all day every day with my father until The Beatles hit the States, and Roy Orbison sang to a "Pretty Woman." That's when things started to change. I had to start going to school.

My days were taken up with school. I hated school. Not the work, that wasn't too tough for me, but the time it took. I didn't want to be there, I wanted to be outside, working. I wanted to be working with my hands. I wanted to learn about cars, not reading, not math. I sat there in those classes just itching to be out. And every day after school I'd find my father and help him.

He taught me everything he knew about cars. And that was a lot. I worked side by side with him from the time I could walk until Woodstock.

Then things changed again. It was a brand-new decade, surfer music was dying out, rock and roll got harder, and Dad began trusting me to do some things by myself. He'd give me a job to do and walk away. And I found that I could do it. By the time The Beatles broke up, I had rebuilt my first big block on my own. By the time Don McLean sang about that fateful plane crash, I'd built my first motorcycle from spare parts and junkyard offal, and rebuilt more motors than I could remember.

Dad would always walk up at the end of a job and watch as I put the last parts together, or stand back as I fired it up for the first time, and grin. "I knew you could do it, Bobbie McGee, I knew you could. I knew it back when you were two. You're gonna be better at this than your old man." He said it every time, exactly the same way. Sometimes I can still hear an echo of those words in my mind, after a challenging job is done.

I was doing it all, everything that needed doing to a car. I could do the bodywork, but I really loved working with the engines.

With a machine, there's always a reason for everything. It's always logical. You can run down each part and find the one that isn't working properly. You can take it apart and see what makes it work, or why it won't. You can fix what's broken. Knowing that parts can be replaced, that things could be fixed, felt stable to me. Solid. I felt like I had complete control over it. Unlike my life.

Not that there weren't stable things in my life, there were. My father was so central in my world, and he was always there. And my mother. *That* was stability.

She was a stay-at-home mom. She was a petite woman (not like Dad, who towered over her) but she ruled the house. Without ever wearing pants. Not one time. I don't think she owned any pants. Or any shoes without heels. Or any clothing that didn't involve the latest fashion in hemlines. Her hair was always put up neatly, also in the latest fashions. And I never came home to find her gone.

She was a good mother, hell, she was practically June Cleaver. But I wasn't anything like her. I was only into cars and music. I refused to wear dresses, my hair was disheveled, my face was usually dirty. And I wasn't even growing up to look like her. I was shaping up to look like my father, tall, slim, broad shouldered. Just looking at me sometimes drove her crazy.

Mom was so set in her beliefs. She thought that ending segregation was the "downfall of our great country." When it wasn't, she decided that the rising women's liberation would be.

"Women shouldn't act like that, they're asking for trouble. Any girl that demands to be equal to men will never get a good husband."

I rejected all of her beliefs. It drove her nuts.

She couldn't believe that she had produced a girl that didn't act like her, didn't think like her. She thought that girls were supposed to grow up without ever getting dirty, find nice boys, settle down, and stay home to raise the next batch of kids *just like them*. She hated anything that didn't match her views. She even hated rock and roll.

We didn't agree on much.

But she was stable, never changing.

So I had some stability in my life, but no control. Other than my parents, the rest of my life was unstable. Completely out of control. We moved a lot during my childhood. I mean *a lot*. So much that in school I wasn't just a new kid, I was the Professional New Kid. You know the type, they never go to the same school two years in a row, if they go to the same one all of one year. I never did. I didn't end a year in the same school I started in until . . . well, until my world turned upside down and fell apart. But I'll get to that.

Anyway, I think I kind of floated through my early childhood, that whole part of my life. On the radio I heard about the freedom rallies, the marches for equal rights, news of the war, sit-ins to protest this and that. On television I saw these things unfold before me. I went all over the South and the Midwest, and saw the world changing around me. But I wasn't really a part of it. I was wrapped up tight in my own little world. I didn't participate.

I don't think I could participate in the world. I was never anywhere long enough to even get into extracurricular activities in school. Not that I really wanted to. You see, Professional New Kids either get really good at fitting in and making friends quickly, or they get really good at being alone and uninvolved. I was the loner type. I didn't make friends, I didn't really even try. I didn't think I needed to. The cars were my friends. The music on the radio was my friend. I had Bob

Dylan, The Rolling Stones, Van Morrison, and Credence Clearwater Revival, among others. And girlfriends? I had Aretha Franklin, Carol King, Diana Ross. And oh, I had Janice Joplin. What more could a girl want?

I had my very own motorcycle, I could fix it and practically anything else. I had music. I had Dad. I didn't need to make friends, I had all the friends I needed.

Then came high school, and the little world that I had wrapped myself up in came unraveled. I never expected it, never even guessed that it could fall apart so quickly. Or so often.

By the time I started high school, we lived in a little town in Missouri. That's when I found out why we moved so often. I had asked Mom about that a few times, she always told me that we had to go where the work was. I thought mechanic work was everywhere, and I mentioned that to her. She just shook her head and told me that I didn't know everything. She was right, I didn't know. But I found out the real reasons behind our frequent moves that year.

Not that I was trying to find out, I wasn't. I was just doing my homework.

It was my ninth grade year. I was fourteen. Nixon was trying to end a war that was never declared a war, and causing all kinds of havoc in the White House. There was a new guy on the radio that I was falling in love with, named Bruce Springsteen. Elton John was walking a "Yellow Brick Road," Pink Floyd was on the "Dark Side of the Moon," Deep Purple had "Smoke on the Water," and I had an American civics class.

We were studying the war, I think everyone was. There was so much controversy over it that it stayed at the top of everyone's mind. My civics teacher gave us the assignment to do a report on someone we knew with a military background. We had almost a week to get it done.

Did I mention that I was kind of a loner? I was so much of one that I couldn't do my report. I didn't know anyone.

Well, I put off my report until the last day. I spent the week helping my dad instead. He had a big job, some fairly wealthy man in town had a Cadillac collection he was trying to restore. So I spent my time doing that with Dad.

The day before my report was due, Dad was out of town when I got home from school, getting parts for those Caddies. So it was purely by chance that I did that report at all. I had decided that I couldn't, and mostly put it out of my mind. Well, without Dad around, I didn't have anything to do, so I was poking around in the attic. I found an old trunk up there with some stuff of my father's in it. All kinds of stuff.

I didn't know that he had been in the navy until I found that trunk. It had all kinds of paperwork in it, and his dog tags. So I gathered it all up and wrote my paper on him.

Dad didn't get back that night until late, and I was already in bed. So I didn't get a chance to talk to him. Things would have been a lot different if I had.

I guess my report was pretty thorough, because my civics teacher recognized him. I didn't know my civics teacher was an old navy man himself, and he had even been in the same company as my father. Now what are the odds?

I also didn't know my father was AWOL.

Now, I'm not much on the military myself, but I understand that you take some sort of vows when you go in. And I think that if you make promises, you should keep them. I think that if you want out, there are ways to do it without running.

Don't get me wrong, I loved my father. He wasn't a bad guy, he just made some really bad choices. And the military is really serious about that sort of thing. *Really serious*. I found that out when the military police showed up at our house the very day after I turned in that paper. They took Dad away, right then. I didn't even get to say good-bye.

I know, you're thinking that I sound pretty flippant about the whole thing. I'm really not. I just think that he was wrong. I know that he probably wouldn't have gotten caught if it wasn't for me, but he didn't tell me. I felt so betrayed by that. I had thought that I knew him so well, and I found out, purely by accident, that his whole life was a lie.

That was my first Great Revelation. I think there are a set of lessons in each person's life. Some are small lessons, things that everyone learns just by growing up, and some are those huge, earth-shaking realizations that make you change your life, or at least your mind. An epiphany. A sudden awakening to the real world. I've kept track of those lessons, I call them my Great Revelations. And that was my first. You never know anyone as well as you think. Never. No matter how much you love someone, no matter how well you *think* you know them, you never really do. People wear masks, and rarely do you ever see the real person behind those masks. Just when you think you have seen, when you think you've figured someone out, they show you a side you never thought existed.

And consequently, if everyone wears masks, no one can ever know the real you beneath yours either.

Do I sound a bit jaded? I probably am. Or at least I was then. I hope that I have grown past that now, but I'm sure I hadn't then. I thought that I handled losing my father well, but when I look back, I find that I didn't. I withdrew further into myself. My grades in school fell. Not much, but a little. I started smoking. I started drinking. I got angry.

Angry with myself, for getting Dad caught. Angry at my father, for doing something that could get him taken from me, and for not telling me that he could be taken. At my teacher for turning Dad in, at my mother just for being who she was. At the whole world. I was just angry.

I mentioned that I had never been one to make friends. Well, I got worse. Not only did I not try, I wouldn't let anyone else try to be my friend either. I pushed them away with a huge attitude and cutting remarks. I lashed out at everyone that tried to get close to me. I was "expressing my anger in unproductive ways." At least that's what that shrink said, the one that Mom sent me to after Dad was gone. The one that I refused to talk to. He was probably right, I was expressing all kinds of anger, in all kinds of ways.

Mom and I moved again soon after Dad was taken away. We went as far away from there as the state of Missouri and Mom's limited bank account could take us, which put us in a little town just outside of Kansas City.

We never got along well after that. We had never really agreed on much anyway, but we had managed all right until then. I guess Dad had always been there to buffer our clashes. Or maybe I just got to that stage where I didn't care what she said, I was going to do what I wanted anyway. Maybe it was all that unproductive anger I was expressing. I don't know. I just know that we didn't have much of a relationship by that point. And it didn't get any better.

She got married again, very quickly, to a guy named Dan. And *that* didn't help our relationship any. I shouldn't have been surprised, I should have known she would do that. She was the kind of woman that is defined by her status. And to her, that meant her husband. She could never have stood the stigma of being a single parent. And I don't think she could have stood being alone.

Dan was an okay sort of guy, I guess. He was an accountant, and almost the perfect characterization of one. He was short and small, wore wire-rimmed glasses, and looked . . . well, bookish. Really. But he treated Mom well, and I guess he made her happy. As happy as a woman like her could be anyway.

Dan never had much use for me, unless the car was broken down. He couldn't even change a tire. Other than the tools (which I kept), I was the only thing of my father's that Mom didn't sell. Or burn. I guess my being there reminded Dan that he wasn't the first. I think he hated that.

Anyway, we moved. So it was sometime around the end of October, my tenth grade year, and I once again changed schools. Mom told me that she was done moving, that we'd stay in that school until I graduated. I didn't think about that the first day I went. Maybe I should have.

You see, I had never been someone that made good first impressions. (I can sense the shock from you.) Really. I never thought to try for that good first impression because I never stayed anywhere long. Why try so hard? Who cares what people think about you if you're only going to be around them for a short time, then never see them again? I know I didn't care.

Being the Professional New Kid that I was, I figured that there were two ways to start a new school. You could walk in all meek and mild like a mouse, trying to make friends and fit in, or you could storm in like a hurricane and to hell with what anyone thought of you. I never was much of the mouse type.

So I came stomping into the classroom in my ripped, grease-stained jeans and my boots. Not cowboy boots, motorcycle boots. Black leather, square toes, just enough heel to catch the pedals, worn thin and faded from working and walking. I had Led Zepplin on my T-shirt and my hair pulled back in a ponytail. (My hair was long and dark, I hated it. I'd have cut it, but Dad always told me not to, so it spent most of its time in a ponytail.) I didn't wear any makeup that day, or any other day for that matter. I still don't. Not only did I dress that way, I didn't have any of my mother's "feminine curves" (much to her dismay). I had my father's tall broad build and average features. I probably could have passed for a boy easily. As it was, I looked for all the world like the tomboy that I was. It didn't surprise me when a boy in the back of the room made a rude noise. I guess he wasn't real surprised when I flipped him off.

I wasn't a big hit with the in crowd.

Well, my mother hadn't lied. She told me that she was done moving, that that was the last school I'd be enrolled in.

I should have thought more about that first impression. But I didn't, I stormed in there and flipped someone off.

So I started off on a bad note. That was nothing new, but this time it lasted. Always before, I left the school before it got too bad. I just kind of floated through it until the next move. It wasn't a bad plan, but it didn't work when I stayed in the same school.

Well, it worked at first. I just went about my business, ignoring everyone else, and they mostly returned the gesture. I sat in the back of the classes, I kept quiet, I made average grades. I found that the very stupid and the very intelligent tend to call attention to themselves, but average people with average grades go unnoticed, for the most part. So I did that. But I made a mistake. I enrolled in shop class.

You have to understand, things were a bit different then. Billy Joel was the "Piano Man," McCartney & Wings were the "Band on the Run." Everyone wore bell-bottom jeans and there was a huge women's movement going on, but there were still a lot of things that girls weren't "supposed" to do. And shop class was one of those things. We could burn our bras, but we couldn't learn to check the oil in our cars. Well, I guess you're figuring out that I never really conformed to the general population standards very well. I didn't care what anyone else thought. I wanted to take shop. So I did.

I was the only girl in that class and the guys didn't like it much. I didn't do anything to them, I didn't even ace the class. I figured it was something I could cruise through without much effort, and that's what I was doing. I didn't say much, I didn't tell them they weren't teaching me anything. I just kept quiet and did what I had to do to get by. For a while.

Then the guys started teasing me. Now, being the somewhat antisocial person that I was, teasing never had bothered me much. But that time it really got to me. I don't know why, it was just razzing, you know stupid comments.

"Hey, Bobbie, shouldn't you be in home ec?"

"Hey, don't you know girls can't take shop?"

"Maybe she's not really a girl, I can't tell."

"Yeah, maybe it's just one of them longhaired hippies."

"Could be, with a name like Bob."

"Hey, Bob, are you a girl, or just a queer?"

You know, just stupid stuff that schoolkids do. But it really started to bother me. So I decided to shut them up by showing them up.

I brought my grade up higher than theirs. I began speaking up, answering the teacher's questions, letting them all know that I knew what I was doing. I figured that they would leave me alone if I was better than them.

I was wrong, being better than them didn't help me at all. In fact, the teasing got worse. The guys teasing me seemed angry, their remarks sounded like threats. Maybe they weren't, but they sounded that way to me. I guess they weren't as serious as I thought, at least not until after Christmas. That's when I got jumped.

I'd like to say that it wasn't my fault, but if I'm going to be honest (and I told Stella that I would) I have to take some of the credit. Maybe most of it. I had a chip on my shoulder. No, if I'm honest, I had a boulder up there. My attitude was so big, and so bad. The teasing got worse. It became so bad to me that I decided to do something about it. I thought I'd show them up again. That wasn't a smart move at all.

We were rebuilding a car for that year's project. A '67 Ford Mustang. Just a common rebuild, it didn't have any major problems. By the time school let out for Christmas vacation, the motor was all in pieces. And laid out nicely, I might add. The body was sanded down, ready for some light work and paint. It was all laid out there for me, I really couldn't resist. I didn't take a vacation that year.

I broke into the school and spent my holidays working. I did all the work on that car. The whole thing, from the transmission to the carburetor to the bodywork. It was a lot of work, and I didn't have much time, but I got it all done. I would have liked to soup it up, put in a bigger cam, maybe a four-barrel carb, but I didn't have the time or parts. I had to rush as it was to get it painted. And oh, I painted it. Pink.

Well, we came back to school just after the new year. A couple of things happened then. First, we had lost a teacher over the break, I don't remember why, but she was replaced with a "permanent substitute" (whatever that means) for the rest of the year. Her name was Miss Claraday. She was teaching literature.

I noticed Miss Claraday on that first day back because she watched me. Closely. Constantly. And she seemed a lot younger than the other teachers. Her blond hair didn't show any gray, and I didn't notice any wrinkles, which seemed (up until her) to be a prerequisite to work at that school. I couldn't figure out why she was watching me, but she was. And she seemed to look right *into* me somehow. It made me uncomfortable, but I didn't dwell on it long. I knew I had other things to worry about.

Because that was the day everyone found out about the car. With that pink paint job, I couldn't really deny that I had been the one that had done it. Well, that, and the fact that no one else in the class could have done it.

We walked into shop that afternoon and everyone saw the car. The teacher was mad enough, but the guys in class . . . they were way beyond mad. I really thought a couple jaws were actually going to hit the floor. The looks on their faces were priceless. Then they turned to me.

The hospital bill when they finished with me was close to priceless as well.

Oh, the guys didn't do it right there. That would have been too easy. And I don't think the teacher, even as angry as he was, could have allowed it. No, they didn't do it right there. They let me stew for almost a week.

And stew I did. I was completely paranoid. I jumped at every footfall, I was suspicious of every brush against me in the hall. I started every time someone glared at me. And glare they did. Constantly.

And the new teacher was watching me. By the second day, I thought she knew what I had done and was waiting for me to do something else wrong. Her gaze was so piercing, as if she could see right through me, as if she could tell what I was thinking. I was so nervous around her, I just knew she was out to get me.

I was so wrong about her.

But I wasn't wrong about the guys from shop class. They were after me and I knew it. I expected it. I just couldn't avoid it.

They caught me walking home from school one day. It was early the next week, I'm not sure what day, things were pretty fuzzy for me for the next couple of days or so. Anyway, there were three of them. I didn't even see it coming. I'd like to say that I won the fight, or at least held my own, but I'm being honest here. I did get in a few good licks, and they knew I was there, but that's all. I don't think any of their injuries needed medical attention. Mine on the other hand . . . I ended up with two broken ribs, a fat lip, and one hell of a shiner on my left eye. I was bruised all over, and sore for weeks. They kicked my ass.

Those guys were so angry, I think they might have killed me that day if Miss Claraday hadn't interrupted them. She was driving by when she saw us fighting in the ditch next to the road. By that time they had me on the ground, hitting, kicking, I don't know what all. The next thing I knew, a woman yelled and they took off running.

Miss Claraday came over to help me up. Like I said, I was on the ground, and she held her hand out to me. I took it without thinking; then I looked up at her. Now *that* I remember. As if it were yesterday.

I looked up at her. I don't think I had ever looked at anyone that way before. It was as if I was seeing not just her, but a *person* for the first time in my life. I mean, I had looked at people, but I had never really seen a person like I saw her that moment. But I saw her.

She stood in that ditch, her high heels sinking in the soft ground, her tweed skirt hiked up, showing a pair of smooth, tanned thighs. Her wavy blond hair was pulling out of the bun she had put it in that morning, curly little tendrils of it were clinging to her neck. Her face was perfect, small boned, and symmetrical, her skin smooth and without flaw. Her full, soft lips were pressed into a frown and she had a little worry furrow between her eyebrows. Her arm was extended out to me, and when I followed it down I realized my hand was in hers.

"Hey, are you okay?" The furrow between her brows deepened a little.

I had a sudden rush of feelings, all new and confusing. And I felt a flush crawl up from my collar and redden my face. I tried to speak, but all that came out was a mumble. "Yeah, I'm okay."

Her white blouse gaped a little between the buttons as she pulled me to my feet. "You don't look okay. I think you might be hurt, and you're all red."

I dropped her hand. "No, I'm all right." It was a lie. My ribs were killing me.

She glanced at my hand, then looked around. "Well, at least let me give you a ride home."

"No, thanks, Miss Claraday." I was straining not to cry when I spoke. I needed a ride. I had my left arm pressed against my ribs and the pain was intense. I needed a ride badly, I wasn't even sure I *could* walk home. But I was willing to try before I was willing to let her know that.

Besides, I wanted a ride home. Or anywhere, just to sit in the car next to her. I wanted a closer look at those thighs. I wanted to be closer to her, but I didn't understand why. I began to shake, I'm not sure if it was from nerves or pain.

She looked worried. "You don't look so good. Let me give you a ride."

"I'll be all right."

Miss Claraday reached out again and put her hand on my shoulder. "Bobbie, right?"

I nodded.

"Look, Bobbie, let me give you a ride home. It's not out of my way or anything, I passed you this morning on the way to school. I think I live just a few blocks down from you. And it's the least I could do. Come on, get in the car."

She slid her hand down my arm to my hand and led me to her car. I stumbled after her, trying to concentrate on the pain, or anything but the feeling of her hand in mine, trying to control my shaking. She helped me into the car and I sat back.

I held my arm to my ribs, trying not to cringe at the pain, trying to look nonchalant about the whole thing. She got in behind the wheel and looked at me. I glanced sideways at her (which was difficult, because my left eye was quickly swelling shut) and grinned through the pain.

"Hey, you wouldn't happen to have a smoke on you, would you?"

She tilted her head and smiled, a smile that started at one corner of her mouth and eased across her face, lighting up her eyes as it passed, then slowly tugged up the other corner of her mouth. As if she were just hearing something funny that she knew no one else could hear. A secret smile.

"Now, Bobbie, I couldn't give you cigarettes. You're under age."

"Shit, you can't be much older than me." I was trying to sound, I don't know, somehow bigger.

She shook her head, pulled out a tissue, and dabbed at the blood on my face. "Were those boys your friends?"

I flinched. Her dabbing at my face hurt. "Friends, that's funny. Not hardly. They're just pissed about the car."

"The shop car?"

"Yeah."

She stopped dabbing my face. "That was you!" She

laughed and leaned over me to drop the tissue into a small bag hanging from her glove box, glancing up sideways into my face.

"I heard about that, the rumors said it was you, but I wasn't sure. It wasn't the smartest thing to do, but it took some guts."

I thought she looked impressed, but maybe it was just wishful thinking. I shrugged. It hurt. "I guess."

She pulled back onto the road and drove slowly. "So why'd you do it?"

"Do what?" I was so caught up in watching her that I forgot what we were talking about.

"The car. Why'd you fix it up like that?"

I sighed. It hurt my ribs. "I don't know. It's hard to explain."

"Try."

"Well, it just got to be too much. I just got fed up with them."

"Them?" She turned onto my street.

"The guys in that class. They're just always on my case, you know?" I shook my head. "No, you wouldn't know."

She nodded and gestured toward the houses on the street. "Which one is it?"

I pointed to my house.

"This one?"

I nodded and she pulled over. I started to get out.

"Bobbie."

I turned back to her. I had to turn all the way, because my eye was completely shut. She looked at it and I saw a flash of something across her face, something I couldn't identify.

"It'll get better. I just know it will." She patted my knee quickly. "You hang in there, okay?"

"Yeah, sure."

I got out of the car and leaned over just before I closed the door. "Um, thanks for the ride." (Writing it now sounds just as lame as saying it then did.)

She smiled again, that secret smile that spread so slowly across her face. "Anytime. I'll see you tomorrow."

I stood there as she pulled away, thinking about that agonizingly slow but God-I-want-it-to-last-forever secret smile, and memorizing her car (it was a '69 Chevy, green with white interior, and it had a small dent in the passenger door). I wanted to be sure I'd recognize it when I saw it in her driveway.

Chapter Two

I didn't see Miss Claraday the next day. I didn't see anyone except my mother, and I only saw her from one eye. The only one not swelled shut.

Mom had me bundled off to the emergency room almost as soon as I walked into the house. I think that was the only time she ever did anything without telling Dan first. She drove like a banshee all the way to the hospital, complaining the whole trip. She went on and on about "those hoodlums" and how much the "school board's gonna hear" about them. I couldn't stand to hear it, so I thought I'd shut her up. I told her what I'd done to the car. I had been hoping it would shut her up. It didn't work. Her complaining just got worse.

The school board didn't hear a thing. As soon as I told her about the car, Mom started in on me. At first it was just about "one more stupid stunt" that I managed to pull off. "Just like your father!"

And that hurt! I didn't want her to say I was like him. But at the same time, I did. I guess I was going through a real love-hate thing with him. After all, he had been the center of my life, of course I loved him. But he had deserted me. I didn't know where he had been taken, but I was sure he could have called, or written, or *something*. Even prisoners had rights of communication with the outside world. But as far as I knew, he hadn't even tried to contact me. And I needed him. I needed him when I was working on cars and found a problem I didn't know about. I needed him when I fought with Mom, when she didn't understand why I wasn't the clone of her that she seemed to want me to be. Mom told me that the military wouldn't tell her where Dad was, that if there was to be any contact it would have to come from him. I never questioned her. She was my mother, why would she lie to me? *She* hadn't deserted me, *she* wouldn't lie to me. I didn't think about her divorcing him before she married Dan. Now I realize that she must have known where he was, maybe even had contact with him. But she told a different story, and I never doubted her. So Dad was the only one left to doubt.

But at the same time, I didn't hate him. I loved him. But sometimes I wished I could hate him. I think it would have been easier than missing him so much. I don't know if you know what it's like to miss someone so much, but be so angry at them at the same time. And I was angry at him. He left me. And left me with this mother that I'm not sure I even liked much. I mean, I loved her, and I'm sure she loved me, but I don't think we liked each other at all. But this is where he left me, so now I had to deal with it.

So, I was still so angry with him; any allusion to me being like him hurt. But at the same time it filled me with a sense of . . . revenge. As if my being like him was the ultimate slap in the face to Mom and Dan. Like they got what was coming to them without me having to feel guilty. I knew that in Mom's opinion, that was the worst thing she could say to me, and I think a little part of me just giggled inside when she did. After all, I couldn't help the way I was, could I? (Maybe I should have talked a little to that shrink. I'm starting to wonder just how messed up I was!)

So it was the "stupid stunt" lecture. But soon it turned into an all-out lament about "normal girls." As in: "Normal girls wouldn't do this sort of thing" and "I was a normal girl, why aren't you?" There was so much more, but I won't bore you with all the details. Besides, there are some memories better left buried. Deeply buried.

It was a *very* long trip.

I didn't get back to school for several days. I don't know if you've ever had broken ribs, but I can tell you that it's not a bit of fun. I spent the first two or three days lying in bed with nothing to do but hurt. I tried to sneak a carburetor into my room, and some other small parts to work on, but Mom caught me. That was a whole other "just like your father, bringing those dirty parts in my house" lecture. I didn't try that again. So I had nothing to do but lie around and hurt. I was bored out of my mind. I only had myself for company. You would think, being the loner that I was, that I wouldn't have minded much. But I did. I hated it.

Then a strange thing happened. At least, I thought then that it was strange.

I guess it was the Friday after my little fight, and Mom was out doing something. I don't remember what, but I'm sure it was grocery shopping or some other such domestic thing. I was up and moving around. I know, I wasn't supposed to be, but I was bored and terribly restless. The doorbell rang, and that gave me a reason to be up anyway, so I answered it. I opened the door and found myself face-to-face with Miss Claraday.

"Hello, Bobbie, how are you?" She gave me a big smile that left me stumbling for words.

"Um, uh, hi." I stood there for a minute, feeling (and no doubt looking) like an idiot. She tilted her head down and raised her eyebrows, looking pointedly behind me, reminding me of my manners.

"Oh, I'm sorry." I stepped aside to let her in the door. She smiled at me again. It wasn't that oh-so-slow secret smile I wanted so badly to see, but it was beautiful anyway.

"I brought you some homework." She held a stack of books out to me. "I didn't think you wanted to fall too far behind. I got something from all of your classes, except shop, of course."

"Um, thanks."

I took the books and stood there a minute, staring at her. I couldn't think of a single reason she would bring anything to me, or care at all. I couldn't think of anything to say. She reached out and touched my arm.

"How are you, Bobbie? Really?"

I turned away from her and put the books down. "Oh, I'm healin' up okay." I shrugged. "You know, just sore."

"And *you*? Your body can heal a lot faster than your heart sometimes."

I refused to look at her. I was afraid I'd tell her that my heart hurt. I wanted to tell someone, anyone. And I felt myself wanting to tell her. Tell her that I was sad, I was lonely, that I was desperate to get near her, that I thought I might be losing my mind. I blinked quickly, pushing back tears that wanted to spill.

"Aw, my heart's fine."

She nodded. "Okay, I just wanted to be sure. And bring you those books."

"Okay. Thanks."

She moved back to the door and opened it herself. She started to walk out and paused, looking back at me. "Get better, okay? Come back to school."

She closed the door behind her before I could even answer her. I stared at that closed door wondering why I was shaking. Why all these new emotions were bombarding me, why I wanted to open the door and run after her.

It took a few more days and another trip to the doctor before I could go back to school. Miss Claraday stopped in again somewhere in there, but I was in bed and didn't see her. Mom gave her my completed work and got some more for me to do. And I did it too. I had to, I didn't have anything else to do and I was bored out of my mind. Mom wouldn't let me do anything. So I did the homework. By the time I did get back to school, I was nearly caught up in every class, except shop. I received an F in that one for my "inconsiderate attitude."

I was healing though, at least physically, and by the time that I got back to school the guys that jumped me didn't have a mark on them. One had had a broken nose (a lucky punch from me obviously, because I'd been swinging blind), but he was healed by the time I got back. I never got to see it. And Miss Claraday acted the very same in class. She watched me, but didn't say anything. I didn't say anything to her, either.

I didn't walk to school after that fight. Ever again. My mother drove me back and forth until I could ride my bike. It was February by then.

I mentioned my bike, didn't I? It was a little red Honda that I had put together myself. It wasn't fancy, but it got me around. Even before I had a license to ride it. Anyway, as soon as I felt like I could ride it (and got up the nerve), I climbed aboard and searched out Miss Claraday's house.

I'm not sure what I thought I was going to do when I found it. Whatever I thought, I was wrong. I couldn't do anything. I couldn't say anything. I couldn't even get off my bike.

The house wasn't too hard to find, it was two blocks down and one and a half blocks over from my house. I pulled over to the corner where I had a clear view of the house (but I was kind of hidden by a tree) and sat there. I knew it was her house because her car was in the drive. So was she.

It was a sunny day, unseasonably warm for February, and she was washing her car. She had on this tank top, wet and clinging to her body, and jean shorts cut really short (a couple of years later those shorts would be called Daisy Dukes, but at that moment, I didn't know what to call them). Her hair was pulled back and somehow piled up on the back of her head, the afternoon sun was slanting down through the trees, touching each curl with gold. She had some soap suds on her face and her shorts rode up every time she bent over the bucket. She wasn't even as tall as me, but in those shorts, oh! Those legs looked a mile long.

I was in awe.

I don't know how long I sat there, watching her wash that car. Long enough for her to finish. I began to feel things, feelings that I had never known existed, and couldn't possibly put into words. I couldn't even put them into thoughts. I had never really been sexually interested in anyone before. I don't think I had ever been interested in anyone for any reason before. I knew at fifteen, almost sixteen, most other kids were thinking about sex (or doing it), but I hadn't ever thought about it much. I wasn't interested in anything unless it had tires and an engine.

Until that moment. Everything in my world changed as I watched her wash that car. I saw things in a different light. I felt things I hadn't imagined before. I thought of things I had never considered. I wanted things I had never wanted. I wanted *her*.

That thought scared the hell out of me. I had no idea what I would do with her, and I wasn't sure I even wanted to know. But, God, I wanted her.

Just when I thought I couldn't stand to watch her anymore, but I couldn't stand to turn away, she turned the water off, emptied her bucket of suds, and went inside. I shook loose from whatever trance I had been in and went home.

I lay in bed awake most of that night, trying to understand. I had all these new feelings, emotional and physical, running through my heart and body. I was shaking. I was hot, I was cold, I had chills running up and down my spine. I couldn't think, and I couldn't stop thinking. I was confused. I was caught somewhere between fear and need.

It was the first huge decision in my life, and I made it that night. I decided that I had to find a lover.

So there I was, fifteen years old, and suddenly I wanted sex. And not just sex, I wanted a *lover*. Someone that I could spend time with, share with. Experiment with. Oh, just someone to talk to.

I started watching people. At school, in stores, people passing in cars. For the first time in my life I wasn't looking at the cars, but at the people in them. I watched the way they interacted with each other, and found myself wondering if they were having sex. I knew about sex, of course, but I hadn't ever really thought about it much. It hadn't interested me before. Now it did. Suddenly, I wanted to know everything.

I listened to the girls in the locker room and the bathroom, how they talked about boys. I couldn't imagine that I could enjoy what they described, but I had no idea what I'd do with a woman either. And none of them mentioned women. Except one girl, once she whispered something about some woman her father knew. I don't remember what she said, but I remember the look of disgust on her face, and the way she whispered like it was some nasty secret that couldn't be said aloud.

So I had no idea what to do with a woman. It wasn't that I wouldn't be able to touch a woman, I just couldn't wrap my mind around that image at all.

So, in need of a lover, I looked around me. I looked at school. And I found . . . no one. Not one single person interested me (except Miss Claraday, and I couldn't put my mind there either. I just couldn't), so I knew that I had to go elsewhere. And that had to wait.

The wait seemed like forever, but it was really only a couple of weeks. Then March rolled around. My sixteenth birthday. Oh, the freedom! I could go anywhere, do anything, meet anyone!

Not quite.

I found that at the end of Nam, when Abba rivaled KC & The Sunshine Band for radio play, a sixteen-year-old girl really didn't have much freedom. I just couldn't go much of anywhere. There weren't just parties on the street waiting for me, looking to fill my needs. I went into the city, but didn't find much there either. Then it occurred to me. Bars! That's where people went to find each other. I looked older than I was. It could work.

It didn't. I was carded everywhere I went. So I was moping along down the street in the city one night, when I walked into this store. It was a head shop. You know, selling drug paraphernalia under other pretenses. Only back then there wasn't really much pretense. I could have bought nearly anything I wanted in there. Anyway, there was a guy there that was making fake IDs.

Wow! That ID gave me the freedom I'd been looking for. I started hitting the bars. I didn't pay much attention, just went into whatever place came up. Boy, that was another stupid move.

The first bar I ever walked into was this biker joint. I stepped through the door and every face turned toward me. Black Sabbath blared out of the jukebox, and the smoke was almost too thick to see through. Every person there seemed to be large, rough, and tattooed. Two men got up and started my way. I backpedaled out of there and walked several blocks before I stopped and leaned against the wall, breathing hard. It scared the hell out of me.

I almost gave up and went home right there. But I found that I was standing beside another bar. I could hear Chubby Checker through the door, so I went inside. That was quite a bit better, the crowd there was better, a lot of mixed races and different classes of people. I hung out awhile and had a couple of beers before I decided it still wasn't what I was looking for.

I tried a lot of different places. I remember walking into one bar and sitting down before I realized that I was the only one in the whole place not wearing a cowboy hat. I made a beeline out of there and never looked back. That's when I started paying better attention to signs, and the kind of people walking into the places. Not that I had a problem with any type of person in particular, I was just looking for somewhere I'd fit in. It was April before I found it.

It was a little place right downtown, I must have ridden by it a hundred times without noticing. There was so much mixed company there, I don't think I had ever seen that much diversity in one room before. I didn't look completely out of place there. I liked it.

I met a guy there that first night I went. His name was Eric, and he was wonderful. He bought me a couple of drinks and we danced most of the night. We danced to everything from Bad Company to REO Speedwagon. And oh, could Eric dance! He was fantastic. He danced, he sang along to every song, and he laughed a lot. He was genuinely having a good time, and it was infectious.

Eric was tall, handsome, nice, everything you're told you should want in a man. My mother would have been proud, had I ever told her about him. But I didn't. He sort of reminded me of my father. Is that terribly Freudian? Maybe it is, I don't know. But I liked Eric.

He kissed me that night. It was my first kiss. Okay, so there weren't any fireworks and the earth didn't move, but it was new and exciting. And he knew how to kiss. Soft, tender, sweet. That was Eric.

He took me out to his car parked behind the bar. I guess he did that often, because he seemed to know exactly what he was doing. And he did all the right things.

So there I was, in the backseat of Eric's car. He said all the right things, he kissed just the right way, his hands were gentle and sweet. I was ready. Or so I thought.

Then I saw it. *Him.* I freaked.

The realization of what I was doing hit me. It was like a slap in the face, waking me up. I suddenly was completely repulsed. The thought of letting him inside me, *anywhere* inside me, even the thought of touching him, made me sick. I mean *sick*.

I opened the door, leaned over, and threw up.

Eric was incredible. He stood there in that parking lot, patting me on the back while I threw up, talking to me.

"It's all right, it's all right. A little too much to drink, that's all. You'll be okay."

I shook my head and wiped my mouth. "It's not the alcohol. At least, not all of it."

I rubbed my face and started to cry. I hadn't cried in so long, and when it started, I couldn't stop it.

Eric helped me up and sat me down in the front seat of his car. He crouched down and took my hands. "What is it, Bobbie? Was it too much for you? Too fast?"

I laughed, a little hysterically, I'm afraid, then shook my head. I couldn't stop crying. He pulled a handkerchief out of his pocket and handed it to me. He stayed right there beside me, holding my hand, and waited for me to get myself under control. When I was down to a few sniffles I looked at him.

"I'm sorry."

He smiled. "It's all right. Are you okay?"

I nodded and shrugged.

"I don't mean to pry, sugar, but what was that all about?"

"I don't know, I just . . . I just . . ."

I choked up and wiped my eyes again.

Eric touched my face. "You're not ready for this, are you?"

I shook my head.

"That's okay, really."

"No, it's not. I am ready. I came here looking for a lover. That's what I want. I just don't want . . ."

I trailed off, trying to find the right words.

Eric raised his eyebrows. "And what about this bothers you? Is it me?"

I shook my head. "No, it's not you, it's just . . . me. I think I just wasn't ready for . . ." I glanced at his crotch, trying to find a decent word.

"Well, I've had a lot of reactions to that, but never puking!" He smiled. "Okay, let's go back a little. Why'd you pick me?"

"Because you're . . . you're sweet, and gentle, and . . . and . . ."

"Feminine?"

"No! No, Eric, nothing like that."

"Are you sure?"

He laughed and stood up, slowly turning around in the dim lights of the parking lot. When he had turned all the way around, he gave a little bow and crouched down in front of me again.

"What do you see?"

And there it was. I hadn't noticed before, I thought he reminded me of my father, and in his attitude he did. But his looks . . . that was a different story altogether. His hair was just long enough to rest on his shoulders, which were narrow. His waist was slim, his butt nicely rounded. I was bigger than him, except in height. His delicate face was cleanly shaved. In the dim lights of the parking lot, and the flashing lights of the bar, he could have been mistaken for a tall, slim woman. Even his hands, lean and long, with their clean nails and smooth palms, were effeminate. I looked at him again, searching for words. He smiled and touched my face.

"It's okay. It's not the first mistake that's ever been made. You need to find yourself a nice woman somewhere, and figure it out from there."

"I don't know. God, Eric, I'm so sorry."

He waved his hand at me. "Don't be. I'm just glad you were with me. A lot of guys wouldn't have taken it so well. Look." He reached around me to rummage in his glove box, finding a pen and paper. He began writing. "Here's my phone number. You call me when you're ready to figure out who you really are, okay?"

I nodded and took the number, figuring I'd never use it.

"Really, call me. I'll take care of you. And if a girl answers, don't worry, that'll be my sister, Jean. Or her girlfriend."

I guess I looked pretty relieved, because he laughed and hugged me.

"You call me."

I promised to call him and went home. That was another night that I lay awake in bed, unable to sleep. I had a lot of those over the next week or so. I watched people. I thought about sex. I tried to look at the boys, but the image of Miss Claraday washing her car kept getting in the way.

I finally had to admit to myself what I had probably known all my life and just never thought about. What I'm sure you've figured out already. My second Great Revelation. I was gay.

I called Eric.

We met at his house. It took almost everything I had in me to walk up and knock on that door. Eric answered my knock with a grin and a hug.

"I'm glad you came. Come on in, let's talk."

I followed him into his house, relieved that he was alone. He sat me down and offered me a drink. I accepted.

"So, how have you been?"

I shrugged. "Okay, I guess. A little confused."

"Well, honey, I've got just the thing for you. I know this place downtown, it's really laid-back and comfortable. The ladies are very friendly, and there are very few men to confuse you."

"Okay."

I guess I didn't sound convinced, because he sat down and looked at me. "Bobbie, I know this is probably scary and confusing, but I want you to know that it's okay. I'm here for you."

I looked at him, then back down at the drink in my hands. "Why? Why do you care at all?"

He patted my hand. "You remind me a little of my sister, Jean. She and I are very close. She's gay, and when she went through something like you are now, no one was there for her. She tried to ignore it, she wanted to be the good girl that Mom always wanted. But she was miserable. I didn't know what she was going through, I was off in that damn war. I wish someone would have been there for her, but no one was. When she said no to a man, he raped her."

He shook his head, I could have sworn that his eyes were wet. "I don't ever want another woman to go through what Jean did. I couldn't be there for her then, but I can try to be here for you now."

I was amazed at this man, his sensitivity. I think a little of that deep ache that I had for my father departed as I watched him.

He shrugged. "I don't know. Maybe it's a karmic thing. I have to help someone the way I should have helped my sister."

"Why me?"

He winked at me and grinned, a complete change of mood. "I like you. And I *love* women, why wouldn't you?"

I grinned back at him. "Maybe I do!"

"Okay, so, wanna go to this place and find out? I'd be happy to take you."

He put me at ease so well, how could I say no? "Yeah, okay. You're sure you're not uncomfortable hanging out with me?"

"Nah, I go with sis all the time. I'll even stay sober and drive you back. We've got a spare room, you can crash here if you want."

"Now *that's* an offer I can't refuse! When do we go?"

"In just a minute. I want to show you something first." He left the room and came back with three or four books. "You like to read?"

"Sure," I said. And I do, sort of.

"I told Jean about you, and she wanted me to give you these."

He handed the books to me. They had titles like *Am I Gay?* and *The Joy of Lesbian Sex*. I blushed, Eric laughed.

We pulled up to this little bar about twenty minutes later. There was no name on the outside, but Eric walked up and rang the doorbell. A small woman with short brown hair opened it up and invited us in. She gave Eric a big hug and squealed when he kissed her cheek. He introduced me to her as his friend and took me over to the bar. I ordered something strong and we found a table.

It was a small bar, packed with women. Women of every color, shape, and size. I was amazed. Here was this place, just *filled* with people like me. My God, they looked so natural, so comfortable with themselves and each other. *And they were like me.*

Okay, they weren't exactly like me. You see, back then, most lesbians seemed to be categorized. You were either butch, or you were femme. And it showed. Most of the women were either dressed in men's suits, or in heels and skirts. There I was with my jeans and motorcycle boots, my T-shirt and long hair. I didn't really fit into either category, but I was all right with that. I had never really fit in anywhere else, and this was closer than anything I'd experienced before.

I sat at that table and watched those women for a long time. I was stunned. There they were, loving each other, laughing, drinking, joking. And dancing. Just to watch them was an incredible experience for me. It was beautiful. So I sat and drank, and watched. But Eric was all over the place, greeting everyone, flirting (harmlessly, of course, I don't think there was a straight woman in the place), and having such a good time. His attitude was infectious, and I found myself on the dance floor with him. I relaxed.

Then a young woman with a pretty face asked me to dance. It must have been six or seven songs before we even left the floor. It felt so right to me. Dancing with guys had always been fun, but this felt *right*. I started asking other women to dance.

When I left that little bar that night, I had four phone numbers in my pocket. I never did call any of them, but I kept those numbers for years afterward.

True to his word, Eric drove me back to his house. I was so happy, I could have kissed him. In fact, I did. On the cheek. I went into his spare room and sat on the edge of the bed, thinking. Somehow, even though I didn't find the lover I'd been looking for, I was no longer alone. There were other people in the world like me. I wasn't the only one, and I didn't have to be afraid. It was like waking up and discovering that I could really be who I was without fearing rejection.

And there was Eric. Maybe for the first time in my life, I had a friend.

Chapter Three

When I got home after staying out all night, Mom was waiting for me at the door. She was really pissed. I suppose she had a right to be. I didn't think so then, but I've grown up a little since.

She grounded me. But that wasn't so bad. I wasn't allowed to go anywhere (except school), but I talked to Eric almost every day on the phone, and even talked to Jean a few times.

Jean was great, really sweet, and she was very open about herself and her girlfriend. It was interesting to me, to hear someone talking candidly about being gay. I had never talked to anyone that was gay as far as I knew, much less someone so open and willing to share her life with a stranger. Talking to her reinforced my belief that I was okay, that there wasn't anything *wrong* with me. She confirmed to me that sexuality is a part of ourselves, and we shouldn't try to deny any part of our nature. As I think back now, I realize that she made a real impact on my life.

And, during that time that I was grounded, I read. A lot. Those books that Jean had passed on to me. I read them, each one, cover to cover. I devoured the information like a starving animal will devour tidbits of food, even from a hand it doesn't know. I wanted to know everything. And I learned (in theory, anyway) almost everything I wanted to know. But what I really wanted was experience. I decided, no, I was *de-*

termined, to go back to the bar, on my own. I knew that Eric would go with me, or even Jean, but I thought I needed to be by myself to find that lover I was looking for.

So I sneaked out. Late at night, I sneaked out of my house and rode into the city. It really wasn't difficult, Mom and Dan were in bed by ten-thirty every night. Sneaking out isn't too tough when you know the routines of your parents. I got pretty good at it.

On those late nights, I rode into the city and went to the bar. I mostly just sat and watched those women. I watched them alone and together, I watched them play out that part of their lives in front of me. I imagined them out in the world, no one knowing what I knew about them, no one caring like I did, no one feeling for them, loving them just for being. But I did, I loved them all.

I watched because it felt so great to see other people like me. All those women, there because they felt the same as me. They were beautiful to me, each and every one of them. I could just go there and suddenly I didn't feel so alone in the world.

And I watched because I was so worried about getting caught dancing with someone else's girlfriend. The last thing I wanted was to break up a happy home, or get my ass kicked. So I loved them and all they stood for, but from a distance, from my own vantage point not quite in the middle of them, but trying to be a part of it all.

By the time that Mom finally cut me loose from my grounding, I found that lover I'd been looking for.

Mom cut me loose and I went back to the bar. Nothing new, I'd been going anyway. But instead of just watching, I finally got up the nerve to ask a woman to dance with me. Maybe it was getting there earlier, feeling like I had time. Maybe I just had to be out with my mother's knowledge before I had the nerve, I don't know. But I finally got that nerve, and I asked a girl to dance.

Her name was Jennifer. She was small, shorter than me,

with light, curly brown hair and big shy brown eyes. Her face was pretty, small featured, and round. And she had all the curves that I didn't have. She looked very feminine, and I liked that. She looked like the exact opposite of me, and I liked that even more. I found it sexy and intriguing.

We danced, Jennifer and I. We danced for hours, letting the music move our bodies to the beat, holding each other and swaying gently to the slow songs. She sat at my table and I bought her drinks. Again, I had the sensation that this was *right,* dancing with a woman, being with her. This was where I belonged.

Jennifer asked me to follow her home. She lived in a small apartment by herself. She unlocked the door, took my hand, and led me inside. Her hand felt so small and tender in mine, like a fragile little bird. I was frightened that I would crush it. I started to shake.

Jennifer kicked off her shoes, making her even shorter, reached up, and put her arms around my neck. Her fingers slid into my hair and pulled it out of its ponytail as she pulled my face down to hers. I was shaking harder.

"Um, Jennifer. I need to tell you . . ."

"Shhh," she said. "Just kiss me."

I leaned into her kiss. Our lips met, softly at first. She pressed her body to mine, I could feel every curve of her against me. My shaking turned into an all-over tremble. That's when the fireworks went off inside my head. And I knew. I guess I had always known, but that first kiss clenched it home for me. I knew from that moment that this was what I had been looking for, this was right for me. I was gay, I wanted the touch of a woman, I wanted to touch her. I knew I wanted a lover, and I knew it would never be a man.

The kiss became harder, hotter, then ended. But I didn't want to stop. My lips found her neck and I kissed her there, and began moving down. She pushed me back.

"Hey, hey, take it easy. We've got all night."

I pulled back from her, afraid I'd screwed up already. "I'm sorry. I just . . ."

"It's okay." She touched my face, ran her fingers through my hair. Her hands were so small, so soft. Not like mine, mine are big and rough, scarred, callused, and hard.

"You're a virgin, aren't you?"

I nodded, shaking even more.

"Bobbie, how old are you?"

I shifted my eyes. I never was much good at lying. "Twenty-one."

Jennifer laughed. "I doubt it. But that's okay. Just tell me you're an adult."

"Oh, yeah, of course." That wasn't really a lie. I *felt* like an adult.

She smiled, I couldn't tell if she was relieved, or if she was humoring me. "Okay. I can be your experiment, as long as I get to play too."

I leaned down and kissed her again. "I don't know what I'm doing."

She smiled up at me. "Do whatever you feel like doing. If I don't like it, I'll let you know."

People say that you never forget your first. I know I never will. The feel of her body against mine, the silkiness of it, the way she felt under my hands, all curves and softness, her skin smooth and dreamy. I could never forget that.

I finally understood. I understood what it meant when the girls in the locker room talked about heat and passion. I understood what the big deal about sex was. I got it. It all made sense to me. The heat, the fire, the intensity. It was finally all there for me.

My little world *rocked*.

I was so nervous that first night, but Jennifer was incredible. She was patient, understanding, kind. She didn't seem to mind my fumbling, my shaking. She took it all in stride and didn't even seem to notice.

And she was *vocal*. Very.

She wasn't kidding when she said that she'd let me know if she didn't like it. She let me know everything. She knew exactly what she wanted and wasn't shy about telling me. She said things to me that I had never heard a woman say before. It was shocking to me, and exciting all at the same time.

I'll never forget that first orgasm either. It hit me like a wave, and I rode it all the way in. My body shook, my fingers clenched, my toes curled. Though my eyes were clenched tightly shut, I saw stars. The earth shook.

And Jennifer laughed.

She wasn't laughing at me. I think it was more like laughing out of pure joy. Like she lived to please, to feel that response. She was still laughing when she took my face in her hands and kissed me.

I felt so wonderful, I wanted to make her feel that way, too. I wrapped my arms around her and rolled us both over.

She put her hand on top of mine and guided it. I touched her, she showed me what she needed, told me what she wanted. It didn't take long for her to reach orgasm. She came quickly, thrusting her hips and sinking her nails into my back. And I understood her laughter. I understood why she so enjoyed my reaction. I understood because watching her, feeling her reaction to me, set something off inside me that I had never even imagined existed. I wanted to feel that again. I wanted to do anything to make her feel that, to make her react like that again. *Anything*.

I kissed her, and moved down, wanting to taste her. She caught my chin in her hand.

"No. I don't want you to do that. Not now."

I slid back up to her face. "Why?"

"Oh, I want you to lick me, Bobbie. And lots of other things. There's so much for us to do. Just not now. I don't think you're ready for that yet. Later, okay?"

I nodded and laid my head on her shoulder. We rested, touching each other. I reveled in the feel of her, the way she lightly rubbed her fingertips across my skin, leaving fire trails over my body. Her kisses, soft on my skin, sweet on my lips. I was aroused fully for the first time in my life. I was happily exhausted, like I had never been before. I didn't think a feeling like that existed until that night. I felt *alive*.

*   *   *

I wanted to spend the night with Jennifer, maybe spend forever with her, but I knew that I couldn't. I knew that if I stayed out all night again, I'd never see the light of day. So I got up and dressed, and she walked me to the door, naked. She was so open, so unashamed of herself and her sexuality, and that made me want to stay even worse. She hugged me and kissed me good-bye, writing her phone number on my hand. It was almost rubbed off by the time I got home, so I made sure to write it down and put it in my wallet (yes, wallet. I've never even owned a purse, much to Mother's dismay) before I went to bed.

I expected that to be another sleepless night, reliving the experience over and over in my head, but I think I was asleep before my head hit the pillow.

Chapter Four

I called Jennifer the next day. I was going to wait, I think I was supposed to wait, but I couldn't. I wanted to see her again. But I was nervous. I think I dialed her number six or seven times before I let it ring. Then I was holding my breath while it rang, wondering what I'd say if she picked up. She did.

"Hello?"

"Um, Jennifer?" I twirled the phone cord around my finger, trying so hard not to sound as nervous as I felt.

"Yes?"

"Hi." I didn't know what to say. "It's Bobbie." I was afraid she'd just hang up.

"Oh, hi! I didn't expect to hear from you so soon. How are you?"

"Pretty good. I just wanted to call and tell you that I had a really great time last night. I'd love to see you again, maybe Friday night?"

"What did you have in mind?"

I hadn't expected that. I was prepared for her to say no, I was praying she'd say yes, but I wasn't sure how to respond to that.

"Um, I don't know. I'd like to take you out to dinner, and maybe a movie."

"You wouldn't rather just come over here?"

"Well . . ." I had thought of that, but I didn't think she had.

She laughed. "I'd love to go out with you. I'm free Friday night, and dinner sounds great. But I'd rather skip the movie and just come back here for dessert."

I guess she could hear the smile in my voice. "Dessert sounds better than dinner."

"So, you liked it, huh? Decide women are for you?"

"Oh, yeah! Women are definitely for me." I was thinking of the feel of her, the fireworks shooting off in my head. She interrupted the memory.

"Where are you?"

"I'm at home."

"Yes, but where? Are you alone?"

"I'm in my bedroom."

"Do you live alone?"

"No, but there's no one else here now."

"Good. I want you to do something for me."

"Okay."

"What are you wearing?"

"Um, a sweat suit. Why?"

"I want you to reach down and touch your pussy."

I was shocked. I thought that was a word that boys used when they didn't approve. I didn't expect any self-respecting woman to use it, especially one who loved it so much.

"Are you serious?"

Her voice dropped. I could almost see her eyes, big and dark, looking at me. "Very. I want you to do it."

"Are you playing with me?" I began to shake as if she were right there in the room with me.

"As much as I can over the phone. Now reach down. . . ."

There was more to that conversation, but I don't think I can remember it all. Besides, I don't think it's relevant to this little story. And no matter what I promised, there are just some things I'm not ready for the world at large to know (sorry, Stella).

*   *   *

After seeing Jennifer the first time, and before I could see her again, I had to go back to school. That was so hard for me. I had to sit there with all those people, all those children, for a whole week. In my opinion, they were children, and I wasn't anymore. I didn't feel like I belonged there with them. I belonged . . . I don't know, somewhere else. All I wanted to do was see Jennifer, touch her, feel her against me. It felt like such a long time that I had to wait. And my mind began to wander.

I started looking at other girls. I watched them and began to imagine how it would feel to be with them, how they would feel lying next to me. I was fantasizing all the time, about all kinds of things. I couldn't concentrate. I couldn't eat. What little sleep I got was filled with dreams and images too graphic to set down here, but I will say that they usually started out with a car in the driveway. A green Chevy with a small dent in the door, being washed in the afternoon sun.

That's when I started skipping lit class.

I didn't know what else to do. I couldn't sit in that classroom and watch Miss Claraday teach. I couldn't think about literature with her standing there, or sitting at her desk in her skirt, one knee primly crossed over the other. And I couldn't think about Jennifer when she was around, or any other girls for that matter. I couldn't think about anything.

Not knowing what else to do, I skipped class. I did the work, and I put it in her mailbox, but I didn't set foot in her classroom.

I thought it was a good plan, but I didn't quite get away with it all week. Miss Claraday wouldn't let me.

It was Thursday, and I was under Mom's car. I was changing the oil, in anticipation of borrowing it the next night. So, there I was, on a creeper under the car, little transistor radio blasting away, my mind on nothing but the car and the music. I was putting the oil plug back in when I heard someone tap on the fender. I rolled out with nothing more on my mind than wiping the oil off my hands and found myself looking directly up Miss Claraday's skirt.

She stepped back, but not quickly enough. My blank mind suddenly filled with images that I couldn't even begin to sort through. I started coughing, afraid I had swallowed my tongue. She waited until I got myself under control, then looked down at me.

"Bobbie, I think we need to talk."

I stood up and leaned under the hood, trying to ignore the sudden rush of heat through my body, and the tangle of thoughts in my head, the shaking in my hands.

"About what?" I tried to concentrate on pouring the oil in the car, anything to keep my mind off her, and the glimpse I'd just gotten. *God,* I thought, *one more image I'll never get out of my head.*

She stepped closer to the car and looked around my shoulder. "What's wrong with it?"

"Huh?" I was truly lost.

She pointed at the engine. I noticed her hands then, lean and shapely, with long fingers and conservative, painted nails. They were beautiful. I closed my eyes, but I could still see them, imagine them touching me.

"The car. Is there something wrong with it?"

"Oh, that." I shook my head. "No, nothing wrong, just a routine oil change. You need one?"

She shook her head. "No, I came by for something else."

I opened another can of oil (they were in cans back then, you had to puncture the top with the funnel) and tipped it in, concentrating so I wouldn't spill it. "Yeah? What can I do for you?"

"You can come to class."

I watched the oil pour in. "Haven't you got my homework?"

"That's not the point. You can't just skip class and put the assignments in my mailbox. It doesn't work that way."

"Why not? My grades aren't good enough for you?"

I hadn't meant for that to come out sounding so mean. I cursed myself under my breath and kept my head down, trying to keep my eyes off her. She was so beautiful, she took my breath away.

"Bobbie, it's got nothing to do with grades. You need to be there for the lectures. You need to be in class."

"Why? If my grades are good enough, then why—"

"Again, it's not the grades. It's integrity. Respect. Honesty, both for you and for me." She leaned her elbows on the fender and looked up at me. "So far, I've been able to cover for you. I haven't counted you absent at all, but people are going to notice soon." She glanced down at her hands. "Do you realize I lied to the superintendent today? I told him you were in the bathroom. How long do you expect me to keep this up?"

I shrugged. She was covering for me, even lying. Teachers didn't do that. Maybe she did like me after all. I couldn't ever remember anyone doing anything like that for me before. It made me nervous. "Don't keep it up. I never asked you to."

But that wasn't what I wanted to say. I wanted to tell her that I was crazy about her. That I couldn't get her off my mind. That I couldn't be in her class because . . .

"It's me, isn't it?"

I jerked my head up, knocking it on the hood. For just a moment, I thought I'd said something out loud. But when I looked at her, I realized that she was caught up in a whole other kind of thought. I tried to rub away the pain in my head and cursed myself for looking so foolish around her. "What are you talking about?"

"You have a problem with me. You must, you aren't skipping any of your other classes. Do you want to transfer to another English class?"

"No." And even if I had, there really wasn't another to transfer to. It was a small school. "I just don't want to go anymore."

"Is it the way I teach? I know I'm not ahead of you, you've

been making straight A's all week. Maybe I'm going too slow for you. Are you bored?"

"No." I shook my head and closed my eyes. If only she knew how much I was *not* bored. But I couldn't say that. I could only tell her a lie. "It's not you. It's just me. You wouldn't understand."

She looked at me softly, almost apologetically. I couldn't look away. She suddenly looked so much older to me than she had just a few weeks before. I wondered what could be such a strain for her. How much stress she was under.

She reached out, as if to touch me, then put her hand back down. She spoke in a softer voice then. Friendly, but a little sad.

"Bobbie, I wish I wasn't your teacher. Because I'd like to be your friend. I'm not so old that I don't remember what it was to be your age, to go through what you're going through. I understand a lot more than you think."

I wanted so badly to tell her, to let her know. I wanted to tell her that she was a great teacher, I was just not a student that could take her teaching. I wanted to tell her everything, that I was gay, that I had a huge crush on her, that I was just too sensitive to her beauty to be anywhere near her. I wanted to tell her that every word she said, every move she made, confused me. That I thought I loved her.

I opened my mouth, thinking I would do just that, afraid I would, when she averted her eyes and pressed her lips together, hardening her face. She looked like a teacher again, and sounded like one.

"I expect to see you in class tomorrow, or I will turn you in for skipping. I *will* see you in class tomorrow."

I stood there with my head down under the hood of that car, trying to think of some way to explain it to her. I wanted her to know that she was a fine teacher, I just couldn't sit in that room and watch her teach. I wanted to say anything, do anything, just to make her face soften like that again, just to make her smile that secret smile at me. That slow, secret smile. . . .

When I finally turned around, still not sure what to say, she was gone.

Friday morning I stood outside Miss Claraday's room almost until the bell rang, wanting to go in (if only to please her), yet fighting the urge to run away. I took a deep breath and pushed open the door.

She was standing at the front of the room with an open book. There was a stack of copies of that book on her desk. I slid into my seat in the back corner and didn't take my eyes off her.

As soon as the bell rang, Miss Claraday said, "Walt Whitman" and began to read.

I know she had to have read for a while, I remember the way her voice carried the words, the way it flowed like a song through my head, but I don't know how long she read, or really what that poem was about. I only remember one line, the last line of that poem. She didn't read that line. She locked her eyes to mine, paused ever so briefly, and recited it from memory.

> *But I walk or sit indifferent, I am satisfied,*
> *He ahold of my hand has completely satisfied me.*

Everyone in that room was silent. I don't know what the rest of them were thinking, but I was sitting there, that last line sinking into my head, into my heart. My eyes felt like they were opened a little. Not much, not enough to see the whole picture, but I thought I caught a glimpse of something previously out of my vision.

Miss Claraday snapped that book closed loudly, breaking that heavy silence that had come over the room, pulled her eyes from mine, and looked over the class. A few kids started to shift uncomfortably in their seats. She took a deep breath and turned, gathering up that big stack of books and starting around the room. She started talking about Walt Whitman, and walked to each desk, laying a copy of that book on each one. When she set that copy on my desk, there was a piece of paper marking the poem she had just read. A small piece of paper with four words handwritten on it.

You are not alone.

Chapter Five

Iborrowed my mom's car to take Jennifer out. I picked her up at her apartment and took her to dinner. We went to this little Italian place with really good food and really bad lighting. And we turned more than a few heads. You have to understand, this was, what? More than twenty-five years ago. I don't think people were really used to seeing two women going out in public together. At least not in the Midwest. Not back when Bob Dylan was "Tangled up in Blue" and the Doobie Brothers were telling us to "Listen to the Music."

And Jennifer wasn't . . . discreet. At all.

All through dinner she played with my leg under the table and played with my mind above it. She did everything she could to distract me, to make me think of sex and her. And oh, boy, it worked. I don't remember what she was eating, but I do remember the way she looked at me and licked the fork, like it was the best thing she had ever run her tongue across, or like she just enjoyed running her tongue across something. And I remember the way she batted her eyes and mouthed "fuck me" when I was trying to order. I think I was almost as uncomfortable as the waiter.

I made it through that dinner, though I'm not sure how. And then we went back to her place. I barely made it in the door before she turned around and kissed me. I kissed her back and had to push her farther in to close the door. She wasn't waiting. She pushed me to the floor, and before I could even think, she had me undressed, right there on the living room floor, and was going down on me. It all happened before I could protest, or even think. But when her mouth touched me . . . I had never imagined anything like that.

Okay, maybe I'd imagined it, but I hadn't gotten far enough to imagine the feeling. The completely different feeling from anything else I had ever experienced.

Jennifer was skilled in pleasing women. I mean really *skilled*. She knew exactly what to do, where and how to do it to get the response she wanted. And I did respond, oh, did I ever! I was writhing on the floor, moaning and begging her to stop, and not to stop. I didn't know what I wanted. I had imagined this, but I hadn't imagined what it would *feel* like. I didn't have anything to compare it to, I couldn't even fathom what it was until then. I wanted it to last forever, but I was afraid that if it didn't end soon I would die. Really die. Like I would explode, or maybe just have a heart attack. But eventually it did end, and I didn't die either, obviously.

Jennifer picked herself up off the floor and stripped. Not slowly, no, she just stood and stripped off her clothes without any ceremony at all. She stepped over and sat down on the edge of the couch, leaning back, with a hand down, touching herself.

I managed to pull myself to my knees and crawl over to her. That's a lesson I learned that day. It wasn't a Great Revelation, but it was a lesson just the same. A good woman can not only bring you to your knees, she can keep you there, and even make you crawl.

Anyway, I crawled over to her. I touched her legs. I kissed her knees, her thighs, and kissed them again. I moved up, but slowly, very slowly, almost putting off what I knew I was about to do.

I was afraid. Afraid of so many things that I couldn't even form into thoughts, much less words. And when I finally got there, *right there,* I panicked. All my fear jumped up into my throat and nearly choked me. I don't know if anyone else in the world has had that problem (probably not, I really should have talked more to that shrink!), but I did. I mean, I really panicked. I was breathing so hard, and felt like I couldn't catch my breath. My heart was pounding so hard I could hear it. I shook all over. All kinds of thoughts flew through my mind.

What was I doing? I mean, I knew what I was doing, but was it really what I wanted? Or was it what I thought was expected? What if I didn't like it? I mean, yes, I was a lesbian, but did that mean I had to like everything about it? And was this necessarily a part of it? Or did I just think it had to be? And if I didn't like it, did that change who and what I thought I was? What if I even hated it? What if I liked it, even loved it, but was terrible at it? And could I explain that to Jennifer? What would she say if I was really bad? Or if I couldn't do it at all?

I paused for a moment, my mouth dry, my tongue feeling huge and wooden, my heart pounding right through my chest, all these questions and thoughts spinning round and round, and laid my head against her inner thigh. I couldn't speak.

Jennifer reached down and ruffled my hair. I looked up at her and she smiled so softly. "You okay?"

"Yeah." I was surprised to find that it was only a whisper.

"Scared?"

I nodded my head against her thigh. "I think."

"Hey." She touched my face, cupped my chin in her tiny hand. "Don't think. Whatever happens, it's all right."

I looked up at her and swallowed. She smiled down at me again.

"Really, it's all right. I understand. We can stop any time you want. No pressure, no expectations. If you want to stop now, just say the word. 'Kay?"

That did it. She was so kind, so understanding. I wanted to please her. I wanted to put my fears to rest. I wanted to make her feel . . . like she had made me feel. As if she would die if I stopped. I lifted my head and kissed her. I inhaled the fragrance of her, a dark, pleasantly mysterious scent. I found it wonderful and intriguing. I breathed her in deeply, closing my eyes and really feeling the scent. Then I did it. I pushed all those whirling thoughts out of my mind and took the dive, so to speak.

I shouldn't have worried. I did like it. A lot. And I wasn't nearly as bad as all my doubts and fears had me believing I would be.

Okay, so I wasn't great either. I'd like to say that I was, and that I had no doubts, that I was naturally a fantastic lover. But that honesty thing keeps getting in the way. Besides, who would I be trying to kid? I made love like I did everything else. I was clumsy and slow. But Jennifer was a wonderful teacher.

I think I was lucky to have my first lover so patient and understanding. Like I said, I was clumsy and slow, I fumbled around a lot. And maybe I was a little dense. Sometimes she had to give me a little push in the right direction. Then I was always either too nervous or too fired up to get anything right. I'd start, and I'd fumble.

But Jennifer would stop me with a touch of her soft little hand, and calm me down. She never got short or frustrated with me, no matter how bad I was, no matter how much she wanted me, *needed* me, to get it right. And we were always able to laugh.

Yeah, she was a good lover, and she taught me well. She taught me so much, and I did love to learn! I was lucky to have her for my first.

Jennifer and I dated for the rest of that school year, and into the summer. Well, I say dated, but I guess we didn't really go out on dates much. We spent a lot of time together, and had a lot of good times, and a lot of sex. Mostly sex. I wanted to do everything, and Jennifer was always accommodating. She loved to see me explore and discover. Or maybe she just loved sex. I don't know, but it worked out well for both of us at the time.

And we did other things, too. We spent hours talking and laughing, and I think we saw every gay movie ever put out. Which at that time was about three.

Mom never knew about Jennifer. I never told her. I just knew, instinctively maybe, or just feared, that she wouldn't understand. So I didn't tell her. I was gone so much, and she'd get so angry about it. So instead of telling her that I had someone I was going to see, I'd just wait and sneak out at night. And when summer came, I stayed gone even more.

When I wasn't with Jennifer, or working on cars to earn money, I was hanging out in libraries. I found books.

I said when Jean gave me those first couple of books that I liked to read, sort of. And that's the way I felt then. But when I started going to libraries, when I found books, I found a brand-new interest in reading. Did you know that there are *thousands* of writers out there that are gay? I was unaware. Well, there weren't that many then, but there are now.

I found every book that I could, from love stories to history. I read them all. I was devouring it, drinking it in as if I had been dying of thirst all my life and had just found water. And in a way, that's exactly how it felt. I had been parched all my life, and I found a fountain that could quench that thirst, fill that hunger for . . . something. Something that I could connect with. I devoured it, reading so quickly, taking in so much information that it would sometimes take days to process it all.

I found gay life outside of the little space I'd been in. There were other people out there, other than the people I'd seen in the bar. People with lives different from mine. Some of those people were real, some were only a writer's illusion, but they were *there*. And I found them, in the history books, in the storybooks, in the writing between the lines.

And I found pride symbols. Wow! I didn't know there were such things until then. I found them fascinating. Not only could a person like me be proud, but we could show it to the world! There were so many different ways to show it, and no one even knew! Every time I saw one of those symbols, I searched out its meaning, its history. I was never brave enough to have anything with one on it, but I learned everything I could about them. I studied them, memorized them, loved them.

This probably sounds crazy to you, but I felt like I was learning my own family history. I was searching out my roots. Like I had found my people. My culture. I finally felt like I belonged somewhere. For the first time in my life, I felt like I had a place to be, to belong. It wasn't a physical place. No, it wasn't really even a place, but a *space*. A space to be, a space in the world, a space among other people. A *place* inside myself. Somewhere that, unlike any physical place that I'd been, felt, at least emotionally, like a home.

Chapter Six

So I guess that brings me up to breaking up with Jennifer. I wish I could say that I dumped her, or that it was all her fault. But I am being honest here (because I promised Stella that I would), so I'll tell you the truth, no matter how much it hurts. Okay, it doesn't hurt, it just makes me look a little psycho. But just a little.

Like I said, we spent the rest of that school year together, and almost all that summer. Right up through the time when America gave us "Sister Golden Hair," the Chi-lites were singing "Oh, Girl," and Dr. Hook was *"Bankrupt."* Then it came crashing down.

We made a mistake, Jennifer and I. I'm sure I told you that we met in a bar. Well, we started going back there. A lot. That was our mistake.

You see, it was there that I found all those women. Jennifer's ex-girlfriends.

I don't know where I had thought she'd gotten all her experience, I guess I was pretty naive about the whole thing. I mean, I knew that there had been other women. I guess I just didn't expect there to have been so many. But there were. It seemed as if they were crawling out of the woodwork.

I could always tell which women she had slept with. When she introduced them to me she would always say, "This is my, uh, friend" and fill in the name. I started to wonder just how many of those "uh, friends" she had. I became insanely jealous.

And in meeting and chatting with those "uh, friends," I found out that Jennifer had cheated on almost every one of them. Or she had simply picked them up and taken them home with her (much like she had done me), and never seen them again.

I'm not sure why it affected me like it did, I guess I loved her. Or maybe I just loved having someone, I don't know. I know I was never *in love* with her, but I did care about her a lot. And the thought of her with all those women drove me nuts. And her history of cheating was worse. I didn't want to be added to that list.

I became terribly possessive of Jennifer. I wanted to spend every moment with her, I hated seeing her even speak to someone else. I badgered her with constant questions.

How long was she with *her?*

What did *they* do together?

Did she love *her?*

And so many more, just like those. I didn't really want the answers, but I asked the questions. And asked, and asked. Until she answered them anyway. And I hated every answer.

I started calling her all the time that I wasn't with her. I showed up at her apartment unannounced, always sure I would catch her with someone else. In her defense, I have to say that I didn't ever catch her with anyone else. But I was so sure I would that I kept trying. It was insane.

The insanity became too much for her. It was really too much for either of us. And she put an end to it.

One day, just before school started again, Jennifer told me not to call her anymore. She said I was driving her crazy. I suppose I was. Oh, she had a bad history, but I was acting obsessed. I think I was. I know it drove me nuts the whole time I was checking up on her, and it drove me nuts not to. I couldn't stop. Yeah, I think I was obsessed. And maybe a little . . . crazy.

But just a little.

Jennifer wasn't mean about dumping me, she just said that she couldn't take it anymore, that it had to end. And I know that it was best for me, too. I hated the way I was acting, and I hated the knowledge that I was driving her nuts, and that I couldn't stop her if she was going to go out with someone else anyway. I knew, somewhere deep inside myself, that it wasn't healthy, that we both needed out.

So she wasn't mean about it, she just ended it. And that was okay for me. It's not like she broke my heart. Yes, I was a little upset, but I wasn't devastated. I understood.

Okay, I didn't understand then, but I did later.

Shortly after Jennifer broke up with me, school started again. There wasn't much time to go to the bar, and I don't think I wanted to for a while. I knew Jennifer went there, and I really didn't want to run into her with the new girlfriend that I was sure she had. So I stayed home. I worked on making my mom happy. She had really been on me about running off to the city all the time, and how she just knew I was on drugs. I didn't bother to tell her the truth (again). I just stayed home. I worked on cars and tucked away some money.

I guess I didn't mention that. That was the only good thing that ever came out of that foolish little prank I pulled with the car in shop class. Yeah, the guys hated me for it, and kicked my ass, but there was an upside in the aftermath. You see, I had done that car right. The shop teacher couldn't complain about that. In fact, he brought his own car to me, and asked for my help with a problem (carburetor, if memory serves me correctly). And after I fixed that, other people started coming around. It was a very small town, with only one garage that did more than fix tires. That one garage was always way behind, so when people found out that I could do the work faster, they brought their cars to me. Some of them were the fathers of those boys that I fought with. That was my only satisfaction in that whole situation. The boys hated me worse than ever, but their fathers depended on my services. And they paid me well. Word of mouth about my abilities got around, and I had all the work I wanted.

So after Jennifer, I went back to school, and back to working on cars. I spent my time that way, and kind of floated through the first part of that school year (like I had so much of my childhood). That was my junior year. I transferred midyear to literature, not by choice, that's just how the school worked. Grammar for the first semester, lit for the second. By the time I transferred, Elton John had an "Island Girl," Little Feat gave us *"The Last Record Album,"* and Miss Claraday had been granted a permanent position with that school.

That put me back in her class. And my mind began to wander once again. It was nearly Christmas, almost a year since I had fixed up the shop car. Bonnie Raitt was on the cover of *Rolling Stone.*

That's when I met Sara.

Sara was new that semester. Her family had moved in from someplace in Colorado. She showed up in homeroom and the teacher had her stand up while she introduced her to the class.

I don't know if you've ever started a new school, or if they did that where you went, but small schools tend to do it. There you are, standing in front of that class, and you feel like you're on display for all the world. And it feels like they are all judging you. It's got to be one of the most embarrassing moments in a teenager's life.

But Sara held her head up and looked around the room defiantly. She looked so sure of herself, so confident. She looked like nothing anyone could say could hurt her, and she just dared anyone to try.

Her hair was lighter brown than mine, cropped short and parted on the side, almost like a boy's. She wore jeans and motorcycle boots, a plain black T-shirt, and no jewelry at all. And she was muscle-bound. I mean wow, as if she had been lifting weights all her life. The look on her face was hard, and she was ready to challenge anyone to anything. I liked that.

And I liked the way she held her head up, like she was daring anyone to say anything to her, like she didn't care what anyone thought of her. She looked tough. I didn't find her attractive, not in the sense that I found Jennifer attractive, or Miss Claraday. But she had a kind of attraction to her, something that I wanted, and I liked her right away. I thought she might be a lot like me. I was right.

After the homeroom bell rang on her first day of school, I caught Sara in the hall and offered to show her around.

She looked at me as if I were insane. "Why?"

I shrugged. "Because I was new here last year, and I know how it feels. Besides, I like the way you look."

I couldn't believe I'd just said that. I guess Sara couldn't either. She looked at me, her eyebrows raised so high they were almost lost in her hair. Then she shrugged.

"Okay, whatever."

I showed her around, we had most of the same classes. The empty seats were usually around me, so I made sure she got close. In science class we had two-person seating to a table, you know those big black slabs they used to use, the ones that wouldn't show any writing on them, they're hard as iron to try to carve on, and they won't burn, no matter what chemicals you pour on them (believe me, I tried). Anyway, I didn't have a partner there, by choice, until Sara. I sat her next to me and the teacher assumed that it was okay.

Then I hung around her, unbidden, and probably unwanted. I'm not sure, but I think being around Jennifer, then without her, made me realize that I wanted some kind of companionship. I didn't ever think Sara and I should be lovers, but I thought we could make good friends.

The problem was that I really didn't know how to make friends. I was following her around, chatting when I could think of anything to say (which wasn't often), and watching her. She responded to me in monosyllables when she responded at all. The rest of the time she just ignored me. I think I was driving her nuts, but I didn't stop. I guess after Jennifer, I was pretty good at driving someone nuts.

It didn't take Sara very long to get fed up with me. Maybe three days or so; then she whirled around suddenly and looked at me. I'm not sure if she was trying to shock me, or maybe get rid of me.

But she stopped me midsentence. "What do you want from me?"

I think I actually drew back a little. I hadn't gotten much response from her before, so I wasn't really expecting one then. Especially not one that sounded so angry.

"I . . . nothing. I don't want anything. I just thought maybe we've got some things in common, you know? Maybe. Maybe we could be friends."

"Friends? Why?"

I shook my head. "I don't know, you're new, you don't have any friends yet. Maybe we've got something in common."

"Something in common?" She looked irritated. "What could we possibly have in common?"

I shrugged. "I don't know, lots of stuff. I like your style. I bet we like some of the same things."

She just looked at me, so I continued. "Maybe cars. Or music. What kind of music do you like?"

Sara suddenly threw up her hands, looking exasperated, and yelled at me. "Girls, okay? What I like is girls! I'm a lesbian!"

I looked at her a moment. I was a little shocked, not that she was gay, but I had never heard anyone ever say it like that before. Then her exasperated look suddenly flashed over to defiance. She looked like she expected me to be disgusted, yell back at her, or maybe even hit her.

Instead, I blinked away my shock and shrugged. "Lesbian, huh? Cool, me too. So, you like music?"

Then it was Sara's turn to look shocked. Have you ever heard the expression "her face fell open"? I found out right then exactly what that means. She looked incredulous.

"Did you hear me? Do you even know what that means?"

"Yeah, I heard you. Lesbian. Girls. I get it." I grinned. "Like I said, I am too. So, music?"

She looked harder at me, as if she was looking for some outward sign. "Really?"

I nodded. "Really. And I think you and I could be friends. You know, if you'd quit trying to ditch me and *talk* to me a little."

Sara laughed.

I laughed.

And I think we became friends that very moment.

Chapter Seven

Sara was my best friend. Okay, she was my only friend. I think I mentioned that I wasn't very popular, didn't I? That's an understatement. But even if I had been, Sara still would have been my best friend. We started talking that day that we came out to each other. Really talking. I'd never been able to talk to anyone like that before, not even Jennifer. I had always held back part of myself, not let anyone see beneath that mask. But I could be open with her. I could tell her about Jennifer, I could tell her about anything.

She understood what it was like to be gay in such a small, narrow place, understood why I wouldn't tell Mom and Dan, she wouldn't tell her parents either. And I could be more open with her than I had with Jennifer because she wasn't my lover. I didn't have to worry about losing her.

And we didn't just talk. We were together all the time. We did everything that best friends are supposed to do. Sleepovers, staying up most of the night giggling, talking about girls and sex, hanging out. We liked the same things, almost. You know, the same kinds of foods, the same kind of clothes, the same music.

The things that we didn't have in common, we shared with each other, and our interests grew. She got me into physical fitness. I was never a weakling, but she taught me how to build on what I had, how to sculpt my body to be what I wanted, and showed me that it could be fun. We started working out together. That was important to both of us. Not only did we want to look good, but building our bodies made us feel safe. As if somehow it made us harder targets for the rest of the world. We needed that.

Bodybuilding wasn't the only physical activity Sara got me into. She loved anything that was a physical challenge. Sports, swimming, running, she loved it all, and we were outside most of the time. I quit smoking then, just to be able to physically keep up with her.

Sara's favorite thing to do was camping. She was really amazing. She knew everything about outdoor survival. She was the kind of person that could be shipwrecked on a deserted island and not only survive, but she'd have built the lap of luxury out there.

When summer slowly rolled around, we started going a lot. We'd go out in the middle of nowhere for days on end, camping all alone. Just getting away from civilization, from all those people that we knew would hate us if they knew us. We'd spend the days hiking, rock climbing, canoeing, anything we wanted. And the nights drinking. Sitting around the fire, talking for hours on end, listening to the radio. That was the country's bicentennial year, Frampton came alive, Fleetwood Mac believed in *Rumours,* and ELO worked their "Strange Magic." We never had a plan, we just threw a bunch of gear in the back of her car and went.

Oh, her car! It was almost *our* car, really. I built it that spring, with her help. It was a '70 Barracuda, rusted and dented all to hell. I remember finding it at a junkyard, wrecked and abused. It was horribly dented, the original yellow paint faded and peeling. The motor was gone, the tires, even the steering wheel. They guy we bought it from must have thought we were nuts for wanting it. Sara bought it for next to nothing. Then we went searching for parts. I found a 426 Hemi to drop in it, bored it out, changed the intake and exhaust manifolds, and threw on a couple of four-barrel carbs. Then I fine-tuned it.

We never did do much with the body, just knocked out the worst dents, sanded down the rust, and spray-painted it. We didn't even do that professionally, just went out to the local auto body shop and bought cans of paint and shot it. Blue. It always looked like shit, but man, that car could *fly!* And did we have some good times!

We raced that old 'Cuda a few times, street racing, but that didn't last long. Word got out about the car, and the fact that I had built it, and we couldn't get any challengers. So we just drove it. We drove everywhere.

There really wasn't anywhere to go, but we went anyway. We drove every road we could find. Most of them went . . . nowhere. But every now and then we'd find something worth seeing. There was a road that came off the park, way back, past where everyone else went. A little narrow dirt road that went back another mile and a half or so, and dead-ended at an old set of railroad tracks that weren't used anymore. And beyond those tracks was an old boxcar, half covered in weeds, slowly but steadily rusting away. If you were really careful you could drive across those tracks and park out behind that old boxcar.

Once we found that place, that's where we went. We'd drive down there late at night, sit on the hood of that car with some cheap wine, or maybe some beer, looking up at the stars and dreaming of something better.

It was one of those nights when she told me why she stayed outside so much. I don't remember the words she said, but I remember the way she looked, and the way it felt to look at her. She sat on the hood of that old blue 'Cuda, with one leg stretched out in front of her and the other foot planted on the hood of the car, her elbow propped on her bent knee, a beer dangling from her hand. She stared off in the distance, I don't think she was really looking at anything.

And I felt so bad for her. I hurt inside, just to watch her trying to be so strong, trying not to care. But I knew that she hurt as she talked.

She talked about her father, and his temper. She never actually said he was abusive, but I got the feeling that he was. She just told me that it was easier to stay outside when he was mad. I didn't question her further, I'm not so sure she'd have told me any more anyway. She was so closed about those kinds of things.

And I talked to her, too. I told her about Jennifer. About my dreams to get out of that place, to go anywhere, as long as it was away from there. She told me about the girls she had known, and I told her about Miss Claraday. Sara was the only person I had even said that name to, much less discussed my fascination for her. I couldn't tell anyone else in the world, but I could tell Sara.

We spent many nights down there past that park. And most of the days we spent driving. We drove for hours, up and down the highways and state roads. We drove sometimes all day, windows down, arms hanging out, the wind blowing through our hair, the radio blasting. Maybe we were going nowhere, but we were *free,* and we could *fly.* And the music, oh, it was so good back then! We knew every song on the radio, and every song Bob Seger and Bruce Springsteen had *ever* done.

No, we didn't just *know* those songs, we *lived* them. We were "Beautiful Losers," a couple of tramps "Born to Run." We were sure that if we could only find "Thunder Road," it would lead us straight to "Katmandu." And we were ready to go. We understood every gut-wrenching emotion those guys sang about, and we basked in the music.

When we weren't driving or hanging outdoors, we were reading. We spent hours in libraries, mostly looking up stuff that I had already found. Sara had hated reading, but I showed her that it could be interesting, if you found the right stuff. I loved watching her, she was drinking in the information as hungrily as I had the year before. She felt a lot like me, I think. Like we had found a place we belonged.

My mom was so happy for a while. She knew that Sara had influenced me to quit smoking. She thought that since I had finally found a friend, I would start acting like a "normal girl," maybe even get a boyfriend. She saw Sara and me reading and discussing books, and decided that I was starting to get serious about learning. She didn't like the way we stayed out all night, but she usually didn't know about it. I either told her that I was spending the night with Sara (which wasn't really a lie, I was with her, just not where Mom thought), or I'd simply sneak out.

It was mostly okay with Mom. She let me go just about anywhere, do just about anything as long as I was with Sara. Mom loved her. Or at least she loved the influence that she thought Sara had over me. But that was before . . . before it all went to hell.

It's always amazed me, how your life can fall apart in an instant.

I guess I need to explain that Sara and I were not lovers. Well, not really. You see, I think I've explained that most lesbians back then were butch or femme. And we were both closer to butch. Not completely, at least I wasn't, but closer than anything else. And neither of us really found the other attractive in that way. I mean, she was attractive, but in a different way. I wanted to be *like* her much more than I wanted to be *with* her, sexually anyway. She was attractive more as a role model for me, and I think she felt the same way about me. We were looking to each other for someone to look up to because there wasn't anyone else. So we weren't lovers.

But there were times . . .

And how do I explain that? Well, we were friends. That was the important part. And there were just times that we needed more. When one of us was feeling especially vulnerable, or was terribly upset, the other was always there to hold her. Because that's what friends do, they comfort each other. A couple of times it just went a little further.

I'm not sure why, maybe we needed extra comforting. Maybe we needed release. We had both been in relationships in the past, and maybe we thought we needed that sexual release. Maybe we just needed to feel close to another human being, and we only had each other. I don't know. Maybe it was wrong, maybe it wasn't. I don't know, I just know that we were young, and we didn't have anyone else to turn to, and a couple of times we turned to each other.

And Sara used to say, "If you can't fuck your friends, who can you fuck?" Okay, maybe it was wrong. If it was, so be it. I can't change it now.

Either way, I don't remember exactly when the sex started. I think it was on one of those long camping trips, after I told her some horrible experience or fear of mine, and she held me until I felt better. Or maybe it was the night she told me about her father, and we cried on each other for so long. It could have been on one of those nights, or any number of other times when it started. I don't remember.

But I'll never forget when it ended.

That's something else that has always amazed me, how some memories are fuzzy or vague, and others are so clear. Crystal clear. In those clear memories, you can recall everything, down to the smallest word in a conversation. There's nothing fuzzy or vague about it, the clarity is astonishing. I think people remember tragedies that way. Like what you were doing when the president was assassinated, or when the news hit that Janis Joplin was dead, or when you found out that some horrible thing had happened to alter your life.

The day it all ended is like that for me.

I can see it clearly in my mind, even today. As if I'm watching it on a movie screen.

It was the tag end of that summer. School had just started, it was our senior year. I was seventeen, Sara was a month or so shy of eighteen. Rock and roll was still alive and kicking, Rod Stewart sang "The Killing of Georgie," The Rolling Stones were *"Black And Blue,"* and disco hadn't quite taken over the world yet. Sara and I were buffed from a summer of fun, and looking forward to the end of that year. Even though school had just started, we could see the end. We would leave that little town and never look back. Things were good.

It was August, and grotesquely hot. Anyone who's been in the South or the Midwest in the late summer knows what it can be like. It was so hot you didn't want to move, and the humidity made the air so heavy. Almost too heavy to breathe.

Sara and I were at her house, or rather, that's where we had started. She lived out of the town proper, on about ten acres of land. We went down to a little creek that ran across the back of her parents' property. The water was too shallow to swim, but there was a spot where we could lie in it, under the shade of a huge old elm tree. The water wasn't cold, but in the shade, with our skin so hot, it felt cool and good. We had a portable radio, a boom box we called it back then. We had just switched over to cassette tapes from eight-tracks, and we were listening to a fairly new one. Bob Seger's *Live Bullet*. We were lying there on the water-smoothed pebbles, listening to the music and talking about girls.

Sara had a crush on a cheerleader from school. I remember her saying how funny it would be if that little cheerleader left her football-playing boyfriend for her. I was laughing.

"She'd never go for you, you know. I heard her talking in the bathroom. She likes men way too much."

"Oh, I think I could change her mind."

"Like she'd give you half a chance. She wouldn't give you the time of day."

"It could happen."

"Not in this town." I looked at her sideways and grinned. "Not in this lifetime." I was teasing her, and she knew it. She gave back as good as she got.

"Maybe not, but at least she's not untouchable. It's not as if she's my teacher or anything. Hell, you might as well be in love with a movie star."

"Hey, that's not even funny!" I splashed her in the face and tried to sound offended, but I was laughing. "At least I'd know what to do with her when I got her. You wouldn't!"

Sara splashed me back. "Oh, yeah?"

"Yeah!"

That started a splashing fight that had us dripping wet and

giggling like crazy. Then she dunked me under and I came up sputtering. She let me go and we lay back down in the shallows to catch our breath. I was still giggling. She turned and looked at me.

"What's so funny?"

"You." I shook my head at her. "You couldn't nail her if you tried."

"Sure I could. I could get anyone if I tried hard enough. I could even get you."

"No, you couldn't."

"Sure I could." She raised her right hand out of the water and wiggled her fingers at me. "I have a special talent that you know nothing about."

"I know everything about you."

"No, you don't. I've still got a few tricks you've never seen."

I laid my head back and sighed. "You aren't that special."

"Really?" Sara rolled over on top of me, grabbed both my hands, and sat up, straddling me. "I'll show you!"

And she proceeded to do just that. I don't think either of us planned it, or even meant for it to happen. But it did. Our wet bathing suits were thrown to the bank and there we were, in the late afternoon, laughter gone, fucking in that cool, shallow water.

I guess Sara's mom had been calling us for a while. We didn't hear her. So she came to find us. We didn't hear her walk up either. We didn't hear anything until she screamed.

And scream she did. My God, have you ever been interrupted by a scream? I hope not, but I can tell you what happens. First, you jump. Then your head turns, of its own will, toward the scream. And then you freeze, no matter what position you're in, no matter how incriminating, you are frozen in place. You can't move. You can't speak. You can't breathe. You can't think. All you can do is stay exactly where you are. Frozen, staring, your heart beating uncontrollably, somewhere in the vicinity of your throat.

Sara's mom turned around and ran back toward the house. Sara and I looked at each other. I could see the fear in her, and I'm certain it was just as plain on my face.

Her mom called my mom before we could even get our bathing suits back on.

Well, there wasn't much explaining to do. I don't think we could have, even if Sara's mom had given us the chance. Which she didn't. After all, in that situation, what's left to explain?

I followed Sara to her house, and her mom stopped me at the door (by slamming it in my face). She wouldn't let me in, she wouldn't let Sara out. She opened the door one more time, threw out my jeans and my boots, and slammed it again. I stood there for a minute, then picked my jeans and boots up off the ground and put them on. I climbed on my bike and headed home, without even a shirt. I looked back and saw Sara in the window, her mother screaming in her face, her father reaching for her. We didn't even get to say good-bye.

Mom called Dan at work and he made it home before I did. By the time I got there, they were both waiting for me. Mom started yelling before I could even get the front door closed.

Oh, she screamed and ranted on about Sara, how terrible she was, how she had corrupted me. I couldn't stand it. I yelled back at her. I told her that I was gay, I had been all my life, and I was fucking girls before I ever met Sara.

That didn't help. In fact, I'm pretty sure it actually made things worse.

Mom kept yelling. She told me how disgusting I was, what a deviant I was, how I had ruined her life.

I tried to explain to her that being gay was healthy and normal for me. I was born that way and it was okay. I told her that it had even been removed from the abnormal psychology books as a diagnosis (that was accepted in most states, anyway, just not the one we lived in). I tried to explain everything, but she wouldn't listen. Neither would Dan. He sat there with a smirk on his face, as if the last thing that had belonged to my father had just gone up in smoke.

I think that's when I missed Dad the most. I thought he would have understood. Even if he didn't, I was sure that he would have loved me anyway. He would have at least tried. After all, he called me Bobbie McGee. I'd listened to that song a million times. Bobbie McGee was a man. Did he know?

I remembered messing up once, I hadn't scraped the heads clean enough before attaching the new gaskets, costing him a new gasket set and a couple of hours' more work. I think I had cried over that, but he never yelled at me. He had me help him fix it, and told me that it was okay, nobody was perfect, and I could mess up every day and he'd love me anyway. And I could remember being even younger, maybe four or five, and him telling me that I was different. I was different from other little girls. Most other little girls didn't like to work on cars, most of them were more like Mom. But he said that it was okay because that made me special. I was more special than other little girls, and little boys, too. Maybe he had known somehow, way back then. Maybe he was trying to tell me that it was okay, that he loved me anyway.

Or maybe my memory was playing tricks on me and that never really happened. It was just wishful thinking. But he told me he loved me all the time when he was around. And I knew that he did. The way he looked at me, I couldn't mistake that. He would have at least *tried* to keep loving me.

I guess I picked the wrong time to tell that to Mom and Dan. That gave them someone else to blame.

Oh, yes, Mom decided right then that it was all Dad's fault. He had treated me too much like a boy, let me do, even encouraged me to do all those masculine things. He should have sent me back into the house where a girl belonged. Then he left. He wasn't around enough for me to realize that a woman needed a man. Oh, he probably even encouraged me to look at girls when I was too young to realize that he was brainwashing me, turning me into the son he'd always wanted.

And the mere mention of Dad made Dan glare. And he glared at me as if he wanted to rip my head off then and there.

I do have to give them credit, though. As much as I'm sure they wanted to, neither of them struck me. I don't know if it was because they were nonviolent, or if they weren't sure they could. After all, I was big, like my father, tall, broad shouldered, I was bigger than either of them. And I was hard as nails back then. Mom was such a petite woman, and Dan was a wimp. A small man, with a small view on the world.

Either way, they didn't hit me. Instead, they grounded me for life.

I was sure Sara was going through the same thing, or something a lot like it, at her house. I thought that would be the worst of it, that nothing could top what she and I had just been through. I was so wrong. That great afternoon that suddenly turned into a nightmare was only the beginning. We still had to go back to school.

I'm sure the whole thing would have stayed in the privacy of our own homes if it had been up to our parents. They were so horrified, they wouldn't have told a soul. But Sara's little sister had a different plan.

She heard her mother yelling at Sara, put it all together, and told practically the entire school before the next day. I don't know if it was intentional maliciousness on her part, or if she just didn't realize how severe the consequences could get. I'd like to believe the latter. Either way, she told everyone she knew. And they told everyone else.

By the time I got to school Monday morning, there were already nasty notes in and on my locker, and obscenities written (and drawn) on the bathroom walls. There were a lot of sideways glances, other kids moving away from me in the hall and in classes, and a few snide remarks. And I knew it was only going to get worse.

That wasn't the best day for me, but at least I made it to school. Sara didn't. Not for the first half of that week. And when she did come back, she had bruises all over her.

I tried to talk to Sara when she got back to school. I wasn't allowed. I couldn't get near her, not even in the hallway between classes. No one would let me near her, the other students stood in the way and wouldn't move. When I tried to force my way to her, the teachers stepped in.

And the snide comments got worse. People began to get bolder. They got louder. The words cut deeply, but there was so much that was worse. If they would have just shunned us, just stayed their distance, it would have been okay. But they didn't. They got bold enough to make sure my life was miserable. The girls would squeal and slap at me if I got too close in the hall, or reached around them to get to my locker. The guys would brush hard against me as they walked by, or knock me aside with their shoulders.

I was constantly replacing tires on my bike because they were slashed, and painting over the terrible words spray-painted on and scratched into it. I guess Sara would have been doing the same if she had been allowed to drive, but she wasn't. Her parents brought her and picked her up every day.

Then the other kids got even bolder. The comments and cutting words turned into all-out verbal abuse. Then came the physical attacks. They attacked me every time they caught me alone, whether in the bathroom, on the way home from school, in the gym trying to change clothes. I didn't always know who it was, they came from behind more often than not. I was fighting several times every week. I felt like I was fighting for my life.

It was almost unbearable. I can't even begin to explain it to you. Unless you've been through it (and I pray that you haven't), I can't make you understand what it was really like.

Yes, I could tell you about the girls locking me out of the locker room, or in the bathroom. I could tell you about the conversations about the dykes and deviants, shouted loud enough for me to hear. I could tell you about the things those kids said to me, about me, around me. The words they used to describe me and all of my "kind." I could tell you about some of the fights I got in, some of the beatings I took. The football player that knocked me off my bike on the street. The two guys that decided to show me what a real man was, and beat me when they couldn't rape me. The constant verbal harassment. And the way the teachers turned away. They never saw any of it, they never heard anything. That's enough by itself to drive a person insane.

Oh, yeah, I could tell you some of it, some of those memories that I thought were locked safely away forever, those things I wanted so badly to forget. But I can't make you understand what it was like for me. What it *felt* like. It was too horrible for words.

At that time, I had never heard the term "hate crime" before, I'm not even sure it had been coined yet. But I know what it was. I know what it *felt* like. Sara and I lived it every day.

That was my third Great Revelation. People can be more cruel than even the wildest imagination will let you believe.

I began to understand why people stayed in the closet. Closets are dark and confining, but in their own way, they're *safe*. I began to understand the lying, the elaborate webs of deception people spun to stay in that closet. The way someone might do almost anything to stay in the safety of that dark closet. I understood fear. And I began to understand the concept of suicide.

I even began to consider that as an option. I couldn't see a way out. When someone finds themselves in pain, they turn to the people that love and understand them. The people that accept them. I think everyone does that, it's human nature. For me, there was only one person like that. One person that understood, that accepted me just the way I was, that loved me. Sara.

But I couldn't get near her. I couldn't get close to her at school. The other kids, even the faculty, made sure of that. I couldn't get out of my house long enough to go see her. Oh, I could have sneaked out in the night, but she wouldn't have known to meet me. And her family wouldn't let me even close to her house, nor would mine let her close to ours. I couldn't even reach her by phone, our parents kept that guarded, too. I began to think the whole world was working together to keep us apart. And not just keep us apart, but to keep us isolated. To make sure neither of us had *anyone*.

My life was in a downhill spiral, I could feel the darkness of the world closing in around my heart and mind.

Yeah, okay, I toyed with the idea of suicide. Not seriously, not like I made a plan or anything, but I thought about it. I thought about how much easier it would be if I just wasn't there anymore. If I could just blink out of existence. Nothing seemed to be getting better, and I had to have a release. Everyone seemed to be against me. I needed someone, anyone. I was more alone than I had ever been.

I think things would have just continued to get worse until I actually did it if Miss Claraday hadn't stepped in, saving me for the second time.

Chapter Eight

The year had turned while I was lost in my dark thought, and the new one came in without any changes in my life. And I couldn't see any on the horizon. But Miss Claraday had plans that I was unaware of. She saved me, again.

It happened when I was sitting in lit class, near the end of the hour. Miss Claraday was passing back out book reports. She didn't stop at my desk, didn't even hesitate, just twitched the corner of her mouth up as she set mine on my desk. I flipped it over and found a handwritten note stapled to it.

Can you come to my house after school Friday? I think I may be able to help.

That's all it said, no signature, nothing else.

Of course, I couldn't go. I was grounded for life. I gathered my stuff slowly, waiting until the bell rang and everyone started out of the room, then spoke above the noise.

"Miss Claraday? Can I speak to you about this grade?"

"Sure, Bobbie."

I walked up to her desk, not sure what I was going to say. "Um, I really can't have this grade. Can I make it up another time?"

I didn't even know what the grade was, I hadn't looked at it. I was trying to tell her that I couldn't go, and praying she knew what I meant. A guy brushed by me and mumbled, "That's not all she wants to make up, Teach."

I closed my eyes and prayed she hadn't heard that. But she had. She turned and looked sharply at the boy, shutting him up immediately. Then she glanced at me before she flipped open her grade book.

"Well, I don't know, let's see what you've got . . ." She was stalling for time until the other kids cleared out of the room, and I knew it. As soon as the last one was gone she looked at me.

"You don't have to accept my help if you don't want it."

I did want her help, and now I didn't even care if she knew. "No, ma'am, that's not it at all. I'm grounded, I can't go anywhere."

"How long are you grounded?"

"Forever."

She gave me a doubtful look.

"Really. For life. I could sneak out, but not until after eleven."

She shook her head. "I don't want to get you into any more trouble . . ."

She looked startled when I laughed. "Honestly, Miss Claraday, I don't think it's possible for me to be in any *more* trouble."

And it was then that, oh joy! she gave me one of those secret little smiles of hers. "Okay, after eleven it is then."

"But if anyone sees me . . ." I shrugged. "I don't want *you* to get into trouble."

I was sincere about that. I knew what I was going through, could guess what Sara had to deal with. But I couldn't imagine what would happen to her if people saw us together late at night. She nodded gravely.

"Well, what do you suggest?"

"We could drive. That late at night, no one would notice who was in the car with you."

She nodded. "All right, where do I pick you up? Not in front of your house."

"No. On the corner. I could meet you there."

"The corner?"

"Yes, not the one closest to my house, the one on the other end of the street, just rounding the corner. The streetlight there is out, no one will notice you."

She raised an eyebrow and looked at me. I shrugged. "It won't be the first time I've been out past curfew."

The corner of her mouth twitched up again and she nodded as the tardy bell rang. I was late for my next class. "All right, I'll be there at eleven. You know my car?"

I grinned at her, the first time I had had a reason to grin since . . . well, since Sara and I had been caught. "Sixty-nine Chevy, two-door, green. By the sound of it, I'd say she's got a 350 under the hood."

Miss Claraday smiled at me and shook her head as I headed out the door. I hurried to my next class, thankful that the hallways were empty. I was laughing a little to myself. I think I had surprised her with my instant plan. I know it surprised me.

I'm sure that I've mentioned that I had plenty of practice sneaking out of my house. You know that scene you see in the movies, where the girl climbs down the trellis? Trust me, that doesn't work. It's not sturdy enough to hold the weight. I've lived in enough houses to know that for a fact. But the house I was living in then was only one story, so it wasn't difficult at all. It even had a big, low window. It was so perfect, almost as if if was meant to be used as a sneak-out method. I climbed out the window that night, like I had a million times before, and walked to the corner.

Miss Claraday was there, pulled off the road under the broken streetlight, engine idling, lights off. I opened the door and climbed in.

She looked at me and smiled, pulled back onto the road, and started driving. I fidgeted with my hands for a minute before speaking.

"Hi." My own voice sounded awkward to me, so loud in the silence.

"Hi," she said back. "Where do we go now?"

I shrugged. "I know a spot, there's a road at the back of the park that'll take you out there."

"No one will be there?"

I shook my head. "Only me, and I'm here."

She nodded and turned the car toward the park. I pointed the way down the little dirt road and across the tracks. She went over the tracks slowly and pulled up as far as she could, until the car was completely hidden by that old boxcar, and shut the car off. The silence settled over us, near deafening.

"Relax, Bobbie. I promise not to bite."

It was only a whisper, but I jumped. I realized I'd been fussing at my hands. My knuckles were skinned and I was rubbing them on my jeans. I guess I was really nervous. Miss Claraday smiled gently and tipped her head in a "follow me" gesture as she opened the door and got out. I climbed out on the other side and followed her lead to the front of the car.

She slipped up onto the hood and I noticed that she was wearing jeans and tennis shoes. Her hair was down, a mass of golden curls across her shoulders. I had an almost uncontrollable urge to plunge both my hands into it and kiss her.

I had only seen her in skirts and heels, except that time that she was washing her car. In her skirts she always looked a little stiff. But not that night. Her jeans were faded and worn, and she moved in them like a second skin. She slid all the way back on the hood and leaned against the windshield, crossing her ankles. She looked so comfortable with herself, and with me. So confident. I think I was already falling in love with her.

I ran my hand up the fender as I moved up to the front of the car, trying not to stare at her. "You know, I could drop a 454 in this baby. She could really scream. Knock out that dent in the door, maybe spray her black . . ."

Miss Claraday shook her head and chuckled. Have you ever heard anyone really chuckle? It's an awesome sound. Deep and rich, like the smell of a forest floor after a cleansing spring rain. I know that sound stopped me in the middle of that thought and I never picked it back up again.

"No, thanks. I don't need her to 'scream.' Come talk to me."

She held out a soda to me. I took it, trying not to show her that I was shaking.

"Thanks."

She took a sip from her own soda and sighed. "So, tell me about Sara, and what you plan to do about this mess."

I turned my back to her and leaned against the grill, looking off toward the old boxcar, trying to play dumb, then glanced back at her. "I don't know what you mean."

She waved a hand, almost like a dismissal, and looked up at the stars. "Don't bullshit me, Bobbie. I'm not here to play games with you. I want to help. I'd have to be blind and deaf as well as stupid not to know what happened. Now, are you going to talk to me or not?"

I slid up on the hood and leaned back on my hands, following her gaze into the blackened sky. "You mean you're not going to tell me how wrong and sinful I am? You really want my side of it?"

She laughed. It was such a sweet, musical sound. I had never thought laughter could lift my spirits so much.

"Bobbie, love is love. I don't care what gender you are. Or what color, race, creed, origin, or anything else. I don't care if she's green and you're blue, it doesn't matter. I care about you girls, and I'm for love." She paused a moment, as if in thought. "Whatever form it takes."

I smiled in spite of myself. "But I don't love her."

"What?" She looked at me, her eyes were wide and unbelieving. "You don't love her?"

I hung my head a little, rubbing an oil stain on my jeans, trying to put it into words. "I love her, she's my friend. I'm just not *in love* with her. We aren't lovers. I mean, I'm . . ." I sighed. How could I make her see? "You wouldn't understand."

"Bobbie, look at me."

I did, I don't think I had a choice.

"I do understand, partly. I understand that you're gay, and

I know what it means to lie and hide your life from the world. I know some things, I understand some of the feelings that you're having. What I don't understand is why you would take a chance like that if you aren't in love with Sara. And how are you not lovers? Help me understand that."

"You don't understand, you couldn't."

"Okay, maybe I don't. So help me."

"It was just sex, Miss Claraday. We aren't lovers, we're friends. We just . . . sometimes I . . . we get lonely. Sometimes we just . . . need."

I was trying not to whine, I'm not sure if I succeeded or not. I was desperate for her to understand. "You don't get it, do you? Don't you ever want contact with another person? Anyone. Just to know that you aren't alone. Don't you need that too?"

She shook her head. "Of course you want contact. But you're still a child. You can wait for sex. It's not going to be gone by the time you're old enough to handle it."

"Handle it?" I leaned up and brushed my hands together. I was getting angry. Maybe not angry, more frustrated. I so desperately wanted her to understand, and she didn't. She was treating me like a child, and I hadn't felt like a child for a long time.

"I think I've been doing just fine *handling* it, thank you. I'm old enough to know exactly what I want, and go after it. I can *handle* myself just fine."

I guess I sounded a little angry, I didn't mean to. Or maybe I did. I'm not sure. I wanted her to understand, but I didn't want her to. I was afraid of what she would think of me if she knew that I was falling in love with her.

She smiled differently then, not the secret smile that I was coming to love, but one that was dry and unfeeling, with no humor in it at all. Wry.

"I have no doubt. I guess I didn't say it very well. I meant that you need to handle it *responsibly.*" She held up a finger to hush me before I could even form an argument. "Before you get angry with me, think about it. You got caught outside, in broad daylight, having sex with someone you don't even love. And you had to know at least some of the consequences of getting caught. That's not responsible. You need to use more discretion."

She looked hard at me. "Unless this 'outing' was what you wanted . . . ?"

"No! This isn't what I wanted at all. Why would I want this?"

I slid off the car and began pacing the length of it. It's a bad habit I have, pacing. But Miss Claraday had me thinking. Really thinking, for the first time in a while. She was right, Sara and I hadn't acted responsibly. It had been a stupid thing to do. And Miss Claraday was waiting for me to admit it, and I didn't want to. I leaned over the hood and looked at her.

"I guess I didn't think about getting caught. I thought we were being careful. We just got carried away." I sighed, frustrated again. "But it was just sex. Nobody understands that. We are not horrible, evil monsters."

"No, you're not."

"We didn't kill anybody, we didn't even hurt anybody. We just had sex, that's all! Don't people want honesty and truth from kids?"

She laughed. Not at me, I don't think, but not with joy either. A dry, humorless sound. "No. People don't want honesty unless it agrees with their beliefs."

"So I'm supposed to lie? That's what we're teaching kids today?" I shook my head. "No wonder the world is so fucked up."

She laughed again, sounding more sincere this time. "Maybe the world is messed up, but you seem to be making it just fine." She looked at me thoughtfully, with half of that secret smile playing about her lips. "You know, I almost asked Sara to come tonight, so I could talk to both of you. I'm glad I didn't."

"Why is that?"

"Because I thought you two were in love. It's bad enough

that one of you knows I was wrong, it would have devastated me if both of you knew." She winked. "Besides, Sara will be all right, I was more worried about you."

I leaned on the hood, striking a pose that I thought looked cool. "So, she's tougher than me."

She shook her head. "No, not tougher. Just . . . *harder*. You might be tough, but your heart isn't really that hard."

I looked at her, her eyes just almost sparkled at me. They were this incredible hazel color, almost gray. I had never noticed that before. And I had never noticed the tenderness in them before, either. I knew for sure, in that moment, that I loved her.

Her eyes caught mine and she frowned. "Is it so horrible to lie? Would that be worse than this?"

"No. Nothing is worse than this. The lying, the hiding, I could have done that. It's just . . . the fear that's so bad."

The little worry furrow between her eyebrows deepened and her look became so intense. "How bad has it been, Bobbie?"

"What?"

"You know. How badly are you being treated?"

I shrugged. I didn't want to tell her. I didn't want her to know how bad it was. I didn't want to admit where my thoughts had been lately, how desperate I was.

"You know, different people, different reactions."

She looked steadily at me, and I knew I couldn't lie to her. I thought those incredible eyes of hers could see beneath my mask, right into my soul. I dropped my head and nodded.

"It's been bad."

"At home?"

I laughed a little at that. "Home is the least of my worries. Not much has changed there, I didn't get along with my parents before, and I still don't."

"And at school? I know it's been bad, I've been in the bathroom. Lovely new writings on the walls in there."

I smiled, maybe a little ironically. "I've read them. The

third stall from the door is the most, um"—I searched around in my head for a nice way to put it—"creative."

She leaned sideways and put her chin in her hand, watching me. "That must hurt."

I went back to pacing, just the length of the front of the car, I didn't want her to be out of my sight. "It only hurts if you care. I don't."

"I think you do." She traced a pattern on the hood with her finger and whispered, "Tell me about it, Bobbie."

I shrugged and kept pacing. "You don't want to hear it."

She stopped tracing and reached across the hood, catching my arm. "I may not want to hear it, but I do want you to talk about it. Keeping it all inside isn't good at all."

I looked at her, looking at me so earnestly. Suddenly, all the anger, all the pain, welled up in me all at once. "You really think you want me to talk, don't you? I don't think you know, I don't think you have any idea how bad it gets."

She let go of my arm and sat up. "So enlighten me."

I took a deep breath and rolled my eyes toward the sky. "I can't. I can tell you, but you still won't know. You can't imagine how it makes me feel. The stares. The catcalls. The constant pushing and shoving in the halls. And I could even deal with all that, but the fights . . ."

I blinked hard, trying not to let the tears leak out, took a deep breath, and blew it out loudly.

"There are fights? At school?"

"They aren't even fights, really. More like beatings."

Her voice was low and stern. "Names."

"I can't, Miss Claraday."

"You can. I want names."

I looked at her, she was really serious. "There's too many of them. And I don't always know who it is. Sometimes they catch me from behind and I never see them."

"It's that bad?"

"That bad and worse. You can't even begin to imagine."

"They have to be stopped. I have to stop them."

I looked at her, so serious, so angry, and I almost laughed. "Stopped? By you? No offense, but you can't stop them."

"What about the other teachers? Do they help at all?"

I shook my head. "They don't see it."

"I'll band them together. We'll watch closer. We'll stop this, we'll protect you."

"You don't understand. Those other teachers, they don't see anything. They don't want to help. Even when they're standing right there, they don't see anything. You're the only person that tried to do anything at all."

"I'll keep doing something. I'll punish those kids, I'll demand that the faculty get involved . . ."

"You can't. They know, and they aren't doing anything. They hate me as much as the other kids do. You can't help either."

She looked offended. "I can try, I can do something."

I shook my head. "Those teachers let this happen, right in front of them, they let it happen. If you try to stand up for me, what happens to you?"

"Damn!" She brought her fist down on the hood of her car. "There must be *something* I can do, some way I can help."

"I think you're doing it."

She smiled a little. "But there must be a solution, a way out of this mess."

I opened my mouth, just about to suggest . . . then closed it and shook my head. "Not until I get outta here."

Her brow furrowed in worry. "Can you make it that long?"

I shrugged. "I guess I'll have to. I don't really have a choice."

"I'm so sorry, Bobbie, I wish . . . I wish I could help you."

"You can't."

"But I can be here for you. Promise me that you'll talk to me when you need to. Promise me that you'll do that, you won't just . . ."

She trailed off. Maybe she did know where my thoughts

had been. Maybe she had seen it in me, the desperation, the hopelessness. She looked at me, an intense, deep look. I got the feeling again that she could see right through me, right into my heart, into my soul.

"Promise me."

I nodded. "I promise."

She sighed. "You must feel so alone."

"Alone." I slid back on the hood and sat next to her, leaning back on the windshield and looking at the stars. "I miss Sara."

"Do you?" She leaned back too, and seemed to draw away from me a little. I figured she was uncomfortable, thinking that I was thinking about sex.

"Yeah, I miss her. I miss my *friend*. That's all. I miss talking to her, spending time with her. Spending time with anyone that doesn't look at me sideways and wonder what I want from her every time I'm near her."

She seemed to relax a little. "I could be your friend, if you'll let me." She reached over and touched my hand. "I could be your friend. I don't wonder."

I sighed and closed my eyes. Her touch was intoxicating. My mind was fighting with itself. Part was so relieved to have someone to listen to me, but at the same time, I wanted so much more from her. And her hand felt so right on mine . . .

"Bobbie!"

"What?" I had been so lost in that soft touch of her hand on mine, I hadn't realized she'd been speaking. My mind was again wandering into places it shouldn't have been. Her touch, just that soft hand lying on top of mine, like a friend. But I wanted it to be so much more. . . .

"I said, I think it's time for you to go home."

I glanced at my watch and realized that it was nearly two in the morning. I hadn't even noticed the time passing.

"I guess I should."

We climbed back into her car and rode in silence until we reached my corner. There was so much more that I wanted to tell her, so much I wanted her to understand, and I couldn't even begin. She pulled over under that broken streetlight and I tried to tell her what it meant to me to be able to talk to her.

"Um, thanks, Miss Claraday. I appreciate you talking to me. You don't know . . ." (God, I always sounded so stupid talking to her!)

She reached out and touched my hand again. "I'm glad you came, Bobbie. I want you to come to me any time you need to, okay? I'll be here. It doesn't even have to be bad stuff, okay? You promise to come to me."

I nodded, not trusting my voice at all.

"Next time, maybe we can talk about happier things. Maybe listen to some music."

She gave my hand one last pat and I climbed out of the car. I turned up the collar of my jacket, tucked my hands deep into the pockets of my jeans, and watched her pull away into the darkness.

The air was chilly that night, but I hardly noticed. I wandered around for a couple more hours, lost in my own thoughts. I was trying to put everything into some order, to wrap my mind around all that had happened. To understand everything I was feeling. I wanted it all to make sense.

Chapter Nine

I didn't make it all make sense that night. I'm not sure it does even now. But I know that Miss Claraday saved my life. And I knew that I loved her, and that I wanted to be closer to her.

I quit thinking about suicide. I really didn't think about much other than Miss Claraday and cars. I was still working, socking away money, and I managed to bring my grades up in school. I didn't have much else to do. Other than daydream.

Miss Claraday picked me up again, a couple of weeks after that first night, after a particularly bad week. If I remember correctly, it was because there was a dance coming up at school, and the kids had become even more cruel than usual. (I didn't go to that dance, I didn't participate in any school activities that year.) I think it was because of that dance that I got in another fight. And I didn't win that one either. It was worse than usual, I hurt after that one almost as much as I had after the first. I'm not sure, but I think they wanted to be sure I wouldn't go to that dance. They concentrated more on my face than usual. And the bruises showed that time.

And that was the week that Sara disappeared.

She just didn't show up to school. I watched for her all week, but she didn't come back. By Friday I was sitting there in lit class, looking at her empty seat. Miss Claraday looked at me and shook her head, just slightly. I don't think anyone else noticed. I looked at her, she looked back. I decided right then to sneak out again that night and hope she was there.

I sneaked through that window and walked down to the corner. She was there, pulled under the broken streetlight, waiting for me. I climbed in and looked at her.

"How'd you know?"

She smiled, that oh-so-slow secret smile, eased the car back onto the road, and turned toward the park. "Same place?"

I nodded. The radio was on this time and I glanced at it.

"Do you mind if I play a tape?"

She waved her hand. "Go ahead."

I pulled *Born To Run* out of my pocket and slid it in. Miss Claraday drove straight out to those old railroad tracks. She crossed them carefully and parked behind that old boxcar beyond the park. We left the tape player on and sat on the hood. She gestured toward the music.

"Tell me about this."

I shrugged my shoulders. "It's our favorite. Mine and Sara's, I mean. Do you know where she is?"

She shook her head. "No. I tried to find out from her file, but it's been sealed. All I know is that her records were sent to some specialty school. And her sister's not talking."

I think the noise I made at that was rude. "That's a first."

"I'm sorry, Bobbie, I wish I had more for you." She touched the fading blackness around my eye from a fight the week before, and the fresh bruise on my cheek from the last fight. "You've had another bad week."

I closed my eyes, even her light touch hurt. "It's been bad. But nothing I can't handle."

"You sure?" She looked so worried.

I nodded. "I'm sure."

She smiled then, that agonizingly slow secret smile that I loved so much. "Then tell me what you like to do when you aren't in school or under a car."

I grinned. "This. I like to do this. Just come out here, watch the stars, talk to a friend."

"Am I your friend?"

I looked at her and smiled. "I think so. Don't you?"

She let out her breath. "Yes. Yes, I do. What else do you like to do?"

"Music."

"Music?"

"I love it. I live by it."

"Ah, the music. Tell me about your music."

"Which music?"

"The kind you like."

"Oh, I like it all. Everything, fifties, sixties, today's stuff. Everything from Hendrix to The Temptations, to Ledbelly. Jazz, rock and roll, all of it."

She raised her eyebrows. "Wow. All of it?"

"Yep!"

"Okay, so start with this one."

It was my turn to smile. "Bruce. I love that man. I mean, I love him. Just listen to this, will you? It's amazing how he can get right into your emotions like that. He writes about what I want."

She raised her knees up and hugged them to her chest. "And what is that?"

I stared off at that old boxcar. I really couldn't see it, it was just another shadow in the darkness, but it didn't matter. I wasn't looking at it anyway. I was looking at the music coming out of the speakers behind me.

"Just a better life. It's like he's struggling with all the same fears and dreams the rest of us have. He just wants to come home from work and have love waiting for him at the end of the day. I understand that need to get out of his present life, to lose himself in something better. I'm like that. I want to get out of here. I want to work hard, love hard." I shrugged. "Besides, nobody sings a great car song like Bruce."

"And I'll bet you know car songs!"

"Every one! I love cars. I love to work on them, and to drive them. The way a good motor purrs, the way a car responds when you handle it right. And I like to fly."

"Fly?"

"Yeah." I was glad it was dark, because I think I blushed a little. "You know, roll down the windows, put out your arms, feel the rush of the wind as it lifts your hair and cools your face. Fly."

She grinned like a little girl. "Fly. I get it." She looked harder at me. "Feel the rush of the wind as it lifts your hair and cools your face." She repeated my words back to me. "I had no idea you were so articulate, Bobbie. So . . . poetic."

"Poetic? Me?" I laughed. "I'm not. I'm not a poet, I don't even like poetry. Bunch of dead guys that wrote stuff I can't understand, what's to like? And I don't even know what articulate means."

She laughed. "You could look it up."

I laughed back at her. "I could, if I wanted to."

"But you don't."

"Nope, not really."

"Are you always this resistant to learning?"

"Are you always a teacher?"

She laughed again. "Touché. I'll tell you what, I won't be your teacher here, but I'd like something from you."

"What's that?" I really didn't have to ask, I'd have given anything, done anything for her.

"I want you to look at poetry again. "I'm not asking for much extra time or effort, you could do it at school. We'll call it extra credit, and we both know you could use that."

I sighed. "You really want me to? I mean, I'll do it, but why?"

She looked up at the sky. There weren't any stars that night, and the clouds covered the sky as far as we could see, making it even darker than usual. "Just give it a try, Bobbie. Look at it in a different light, look at it like . . . a song waiting for the music to be put to it. You might like it."

"Okay, I'll give it a try," I agreed, even though I wasn't interested. Like I said, I'd have jumped through hoops for her, if she'd only asked. "Just don't expect too much, okay?"

"Okay, it's a deal." She took a deep breath. "So tell me more about the music you love so."

"As long as you don't expect me to be too poetic."

She laughed and touched my arm like an old friend. It felt so good to have someone so comfortable around me. Part of me wanted to scream that I loved her, to reach out and kiss her. But part of me didn't. It was a small part that didn't, but it was there. That part of me didn't want to lose that comfort level. That friend.

We talked for hours, about music, cars, me. Okay, mostly I talked. She listened. I don't think anyone had ever listened to me like that before, or seen me like that. The real me, no holding back. No masks.

She didn't make me feel like she was only seeing what she wanted. She didn't see me as a student, or a lesbian, or even as a child. She looked at me like a *person*. And I responded by opening up to her. More than I ever had with anyone before, I think. I had to, I couldn't keep back when she looked at me. Because she *saw* me. Most people looked at me with contempt, or just looked beyond me, through me, as if I weren't even there. But not her. She looked *at* me and really *saw* me. *Me*.

When she dropped me off at the corner that night, she looked at me and smiled. Not that sweet slow secret smile, but one that looked like genuine friendship.

"Let's do this again, Bobbie. Next Friday night. Can you do that?"

"Are you kidding? I could do this every night. This is what I like to do."

"Not every night, I can't stay up this late and make it to school. But Friday's good for me if you're okay with it."

Okay with it. Was she kidding? I would live for it! "Sure, I think I could work it into my busy schedule."

She laughed. "All right then. I'll pick you up."

"Same time, same channel." I grinned and tapped the hood of her car. "I'll be here."

She grinned back and I watched her pull away before I tucked my hands into my pockets and headed home.

I spent all the next week with my nose in poetry books. Had I been left alone to do it, I probably wouldn't have made it past the first poem or so. But I wasn't left alone. Miss Claraday was there. Not constantly, of course, but I could tell she was around, and now and then I caught her watching me. She watched me like she had that first semester that she'd been there, when I thought she was trying to catch me doing something wrong. I realized how wrong I'd been about her.

She had never wanted to catch me doing wrong. She was just interested in me. I found that so hard to believe at first, but it was true. How else could I explain it? She watched me, and she smiled a lot that week.

So I was reading poetry. Like I said, I wouldn't have stuck with it if it wasn't for her. She started me out Monday morning on a book from the library. By Wednesday she was handing me a book of her own. And I read it. I looked at it like songs waiting for music. And I discovered that I liked it. At least some of it. And suddenly, I understood it.

I found so much in those writings, so much emotion, so much beauty. Miss Claraday was right, it was just like reading song lyrics. I even began to enjoy it. I don't think it changed my view of the world, but I think it led me to a better understanding of the world and the people in it. You might say it expanded my interests a bit.

By the time Friday night rolled around, I was so eager to see her again, to tell her about the writings, I almost couldn't make it through the day. I went out earlier than usual that night, but I found her waiting for me. As if she was just as eager to see me, or maybe she just knew I'd be there.

We went directly out to that old boxcar, she didn't even ask. I found that night different from the others. We had something in common now, something we could talk about together. She expanded on the poetry, explaining more to me than I had understood, and I did the same with music. We weren't just there to help me, we were there as friends spending time together. I was more comfortable with her than I had ever been before. And she seemed to feel the same way. She was so relaxed, lounging on the hood of her car, touching my arm, laughing out loud, completely at ease with herself and me.

And we talked. I mean, we had talked the other times, but this felt different. This felt so . . . equal. We weren't trying to fix my life, we were just two people enjoying time together, as equals, as friends. And I loved her all the more for it.

I tried to tell her what it meant to me that night when she dropped me off. She pulled to the curb to let me out and instead I turned to her. "Next Friday?"

She smiled. "Sure, I'd like that. This is fun."

"Is it?"

"Yes. I just wanted you to know that. I've enjoyed this, it's a nice release for me too, you know."

I smiled. "I love you, you know."

The words were out of my mouth before I even realized it. I hadn't meant to say that, I hadn't meant to say anything at all. But I had, and I couldn't change it, I couldn't take it back. She turned away from me, turned her face to the window.

"Oh, Bobbie. Don't. Don't say that."

I realized that I had caused a sudden change and I searched around for a way to fix it. "I have to say it. I mean it."

"No, you don't. You don't even know me."

"Maybe. But it's not infatuation. It's real."

She didn't move, didn't look at me. "You don't know what you're asking."

I leaned toward her, wanting her to understand, not sure if even I did. "I'm not asking anything. I'm just telling you."

"Well, don't. I can't hear that."

"But . . ." I suddenly realized that I couldn't fix the change I had caused. I had ruined the only thing I had to look forward to. I had crossed some sort of line, made her uncomfortable in a way that I hadn't intended. These talks with her were the only thing good in my life, and I had just put an end to them. I had just lost her as a friend.

She kept her face turned away from me. I could see a pale replica of her face staring back at me in the glass of her door. She didn't speak.

I mumbled, "Oh, God, I'm sorry," and got out of the car. As soon as I shut the door, she sped off. I ran my hands through my hair and cried.

That's when I started going back to the bar.

I know how crazy that sounds. I knew exactly what I wanted, and I went to the place I knew she'd never be. What was I thinking? What goes through the mind of a confused seventeen-year-old? I don't know why I did it, but it made perfect sense to me at the time.

I was sneaking out of the house almost every weekend. I'd roll my bike a couple of blocks down the street, jump on, and head for the city, for the bar. I'd get there just after midnight and close the place down. I went both Friday and Saturday nights, every weekend.

There were women there (of course), and I put on my best happy face and had a good time. But I didn't go home with anyone. I didn't sleep with anyone. And I didn't start a relationship. I just went out to drink and dance. And to be around others that didn't think I was sick, other people that accepted me. People who weren't uncomfortable because I was there. People who didn't know what my real life was like.

It was getting pretty routine for me. School during the week, work on cars after school, the bar and the booze every weekend. Routine. Until my world turned upside down again.

It was a typical Saturday night, as typical as it can be for a seventeen-year-old that frequents bars, anyway. I hadn't been there long, but I was already on the dance floor. I danced (I don't remember who with) until I noticed someone sitting at my table. I excused myself to the woman on the dance floor and walked over to the table and the person sitting there. And there she was, like a ghost, like an unbelievable mirage.

Miss Claraday.

I was completely stunned. I couldn't speak. I couldn't think. I just stared at her.

She was wearing a black leather miniskirt and a white blouse that was almost sheer, unbuttoned enough to show cleavage, and tied in a little knot just below her breasts. She had those fantastic legs of hers crossed, clad in black stockings and high heels. Her hair was down, I had never noticed how beautiful it was, falling on her shoulders in thick golden waves, the disco ball reflecting rainbow colors around it.

She was holding a drink in one hand, the other was flat on the table. She looked like a picture of the perfect woman.

She smiled at me, that secret smile of hers rolling so slowly across her face, and pointed toward a chair.

"Sit down, Bobbie, before you fall down. And close your mouth, you're drawing attention."

I closed my mouth (I hadn't even known it was open) and sat down. She was sitting there, right in front of me, and I couldn't believe my eyes.

"Bobbie, stop staring. You act like you've never seen me before."

"I don't think I have. You know where you are?"

"Of course I do. I'm not a fool, Bobbie, nor am I completely naive."

"I'm sorry. I just didn't expect to see you *here*. Looking like *that*."

She laughed, sounding perfectly comfortable. "You make it sound so terrible."

"Oh, no, it's not terrible. You look wonderful. I mean, you always look wonderful, but now, now you look . . . you look . . ." I couldn't even find the words, I just shook my head.

"What are you doing here?"

"I came to see you." She laughed again in the musical way of hers.

"But, why . . . how'd you . . ."

"I came to see you. We are friends, aren't we?"

"Yes, but . . . I thought . . ."

She put up one finger and shook her head. "Forget about that, okay? Never mind. Isn't it enough that I came? Isn't that good enough?"

"I guess so." I nodded. "Okay."

She laughed again. "I was just watching you dance, you're very good. What would it take to get you to dance with me?"

I got up so fast I almost knocked over my chair. I held my hand out to her, she took it, and we walked onto the dance floor.

I don't think my feet hit the floor the whole time we were out there. I *glided*. My mind was so confused, so ecstatic, I couldn't think. I just moved. She felt so good in my arms, her body against me, I thought I'd lose my mind completely. I had never felt so much desire for anyone or anything in my life. It wasn't just want, or need, it was *desire*. Hot and passionate, it was like a flame burning in my heart.

As if that confusion and desire weren't enough, she turned her back to me, stepped back against me. She took my hands in hers, wrapping one of my arms across her shoulder, placing my hand on her breastbone. The other she wrapped around her waist and slid down onto her thigh. I buried my face in her golden curls and smelled her fragrance until my knees almost gave way.

Then she turned back around to face me. She reached up and wrapped her arms around my neck, pulled my hair out of its ponytail, and plunged her hands into it. Then she started grinding her hips. Everyone else in the place was doing disco, we were dirty dancing. (And that was long before that movie came out.)

She moved like a cat, supple and strong, and I matched her perfectly. I don't think I'm that great a dancer, but I just followed her and we were perfect together. We didn't speak, we didn't go back to the table, we never finished our drinks. We *danced*.

The moment froze in my mind. Even today, I can close my eyes and see her, her hair hanging in her face, her lips slightly parted and held close enough to mine that I could feel her breath on my mouth, her hips grinding into mine, sweat beading on her face, her eyes smoldering.

In that moment, for the first time in my life, I had no idea what music was playing. I was so caught up in her that I didn't know anything else. I had no life outside of that moment. No one else, nothing else existed. If anything did exist, it didn't matter. Time had stopped. She caught me in her eyes and I was lost. I was in heaven. That one moment was an eternity.

No, it wasn't. It was about thirty minutes, but it *felt* like an eternity.

Then she broke the spell. She pulled my head down and whispered in my ear.

"Drive me to my hotel."

I didn't say anything. I don't think I could have spoken if I'd tried. I just took her hand in mine and headed for the door. Outside the bar, I asked her where she was parked. She shook her head and whispered "cab" just before she licked my ear.

We climbed onto my bike, she circled her arms around me, and told me which way to go.

I have no idea where that hotel was. I couldn't remember if I tried. All the way there she was driving me crazy. Her breasts were pressed into my back, she wouldn't keep her hands still (not that I tried to make her, believe me, I didn't!). She rubbed them everywhere she could reach, from my neck to my knees. I pulled up to park, and before I could even shut off the motor she was off and kissing me, hard. She tangled my hair around her fingers and pulled me up onto my feet, still kissing me.

She hung on to me walking in the door, I don't think she cared if anyone saw us. She backed me against the wall in the elevator, kissing me hard. As soon as we were in her room, she grabbed me by my jacket, sliding it over my shoulders as she kissed me again.

I had had this fantasy a million times. I was going to make love to her gently. I was going to show her how I felt, show her my passion, my desire. I was going to savor every moment with her, make it last, sweep her off her feet, fulfill her every whim. And I was going to be fantastic.

I didn't do any of that. I started to, I took her face in my hands and looked at her.

"God, I've waited so long—"

She didn't give me a chance to finish. She grabbed my ass in both hands and said, "You have no idea. Now shut up." Then stuck her tongue in my mouth.

She literally *tore* our clothes off, starting with mine. I was completely naked before I could even think about it. She shoved me down on the bed and dropped to her knees. When she buried her face in me, I could have climbed the walls. I think I might have.

And she talked. A lot. She told me how I tasted, how much she liked it. She told me what she wanted, in no uncertain terms. And she didn't use nice Miss Claraday the English teacher words. No, she was saying words that I had never imagined coming out of her mouth. Her language was filthy. I would have been in shock, had I been capable. But I wasn't.

She took me to the point of frenzy, stopped, and stood up. She ripped her own clothes off. Okay, I helped, but she did most of it.

She stood there naked, looking oh so fantastic, with her hair mussed, her makeup smeared, and her cheeks flushed with hunger. Her body was fabulous, even better than I had imagined in my wildest fantasies. I wanted to kiss every inch of her. So I did. I pulled her to me and kissed her. Everywhere.

Oh, the taste of her skin! The bitter sweetness of her sweaty skin on my lips! I didn't think there could be anything better, until I slid *into* her. Every fantasy I'd ever had, every experience, could never have prepared me for that moment. The softness of her, the silkiness . . . it really was more than I could bear. I had to stop, had to pull away. I had to breathe.

But she wouldn't let me. She came right back to me. She was merciless, wild. She was rough and demanding, I wasn't prepared for that. I usually chose to be in control in any sexual situation, but this time I wasn't. She was in complete control. She told me exactly what she wanted, and what she wanted to do. She completely dominated me.

I loved it.

I'd like to say that we made love all night, but as long as I'm being honest, I can't. We didn't make love at all. We just fucked. Like animals. For hours.

I dozed off (or maybe passed out, I'm not sure) sometime around dawn, and woke up a short time later. She was gone.

I searched the room, hoping to find something. A note, maybe. Something to tell me I wasn't crazy, she had really been there. I found my shirt, ripped. I found my jeans, inside out in a pile on the floor, one boot still in them. The bedsheets were strung out all over the room. I picked them up and searched them. But there was nothing left of her. Not a shred of her torn clothing, not even trash in the wastebasket. There was nothing but silence.

I put on the tattered remains of my clothes and went home.

Chapter Ten

So, I was back in school on Monday. I was still a little sore (I told you she was rough), but I felt great. I just knew that she was mine. After all that we had done, and it was, after all, her choice, how could she not be mine? She couldn't, there wasn't any way. I went into her class expecting . . . something. I mean, I didn't expect her to rush into my arms or anything, but I thought she would have some reaction to seeing me. She didn't.

I mean, she didn't react *at all*. There was no note, no embarrassment, nothing. She didn't act any differently than she had on Friday. I sat there through the whole class. But there was nothing. *Nothing.*

I was shocked and almost scared. I began to wonder if I had imagined it all. But no, I was a little sore, and I had a hickey just below the collar of my shirt. Maybe it was someone who looked like her? After all, I was drinking, and we hadn't exactly held a conversation. Maybe it was all a big mistake.

But it had been her. She had called me by name at the bar, and at the hotel. And we had talked, a little. And that smile, that secret little smile . . . *it was her.* She might not remember, but I could never forget. But her lack of reaction, almost lack of recognition . . .

I went through that whole week like that, one minute I

was convinced that I was crazy, my mind was playing some horrible game with me, the next minute I knew I wasn't crazy, but I couldn't explain away her lack of . . . response. By Thursday I was a bundle of frayed nerves. I had to end the turmoil in my mind. I decided that there was only one way to straighten it all out. I had to see her again, away from school.

I turned in my book report on Friday, just like everyone else. But mine had a note inside it that told her to pick me up at the corner. I just hoped she'd find it before that night.

I sneaked out of the house and went down to the corner. She wasn't there.

I waited.

She didn't come.

I went back to my house and got my bike. I rode to her house. The garage door was open, so I knew that she was expecting me. I rode my bike in and she closed the door before I could even shut off the motor. I dismounted and opened my mouth to speak, but she beat me to it.

"I didn't pick you up because this is a really bad idea. And you shouldn't be here, either."

I was so confused, I didn't know whether I should argue with her or leave. Typical of me, I decided to argue. "But you knew I'd come, you were waiting for me."

She sighed. "I knew. But you can't stay, you have to go. There are consequences—"

I interrupted her. "I don't care. What, are they gonna hurt me?"

"Maybe they'll hurt me."

That did hurt. I was putting her in jeopardy. That made me angry, not at her, but she was the only one near enough to lash out at.

"You told me I should come to you whenever I needed someone to talk to. You said you were my friend."

"I know, I know. And I want to be your friend. But I can't. I said all that before . . . before Saturday night."

So I wasn't crazy, she was just *really* good at covering up.

Maybe she was ashamed, or just didn't want to see me again. I had to find out.

I shrugged, acting as if it were no big deal at all, or at least trying to. "What, I can't talk to you because we had sex? That should ruin our friendship?"

"No." She shook her head. "You shouldn't come over here because I want you."

That was an indescribable moment for me. My grin must have looked as if it were splitting my face. All my problems were suddenly gone. She wanted me. She loved me, I just knew she did, and nothing else mattered. I would go to her, and we'd live happily ever after.

"Great! I want you, too!"

She was shaking her head again. "No, Bobbie, it can't be. I can't have you. Don't you see? I'd lose my job, probably never get another one, you'd be kicked out of school, maybe even run out of town. We could be killed! This can't happen."

I ran my hand through my hair, trying to think. "Because we're gay. You said you didn't care about that."

"I don't. It's not because we're gay." She stepped over and took both my hands in hers. "You are my student. My *seventeen-year-old student*. Even if this was a straight relationship, it couldn't be. The school board, your parents, society itself would never let it happen. I shouldn't have let it happen. You're a child."

"I haven't been a child for a long time."

I pulled my hands out of hers and touched her face. I kissed her, very softly. She wrapped her arms around me and kissed back. Then I hugged her tightly to me. Before she could argue with me, I picked her up and carried her into the house. She clung to me like a bride, or maybe a lost, frightened child. I found her bedroom and laid her down gently on the bed. She kissed me again. I stepped back and began undressing. She looked up at me with tears in her lovely eyes.

"Bobbie, we can't do this . . . I—"

"Shhh." I touched her lips. "Don't tell me about what's right or wrong." I kissed her neck. "Just tell me what you want."

I heard her exhale and felt her relax. "You. I want you."

That was all it took. I gave her myself, and all the love I had within me. I finally got to show her how I felt, tenderly, softly, just as I had imagined I would. That was the first (and possibly the *only)* time in my life that I was perfect. Really. Even someone who messes up as much as I have has one chance to do something perfectly, to be perfect. That was mine, and I did it. I made love to her like I had wanted to, softly and passionately. I made sure she was satisfied. I was perfect, I could feel it in her body, in her very breath, and see it in her eyes.

Making love to her was completely different than sex with her had been. She had been so wild that night, rough, demanding. It was wild sex and nothing more. But this was different, as different as night from day. She gave up all control. Every moment of it was sensual, soft. We didn't speak except to whisper our love. Everything was slow, soft, and sweet.

I held her, knowing that I never wanted to let her go. And I felt her warm tears on my shoulder. She sighed as I stroked her hair.

"I could love you, Bobbie. It would be so easy."

"Wonderful. I already love you."

"Oh, don't, you can't. You can't love me. This can't be."

"This already is. You just said that you could love me. I love you. I'll get a job, we'll get a place together, it could work. It *will* work."

She was shaking her head, more tears threatening to come.

I tried to lighten it up a little. "There's only one more thing. Something I have to know."

She looked up at me, her eyes soft and wet.

"What the hell is your name?"

She started laughing, giggling through her tears.

"I know, it sounds crazy, but you never told me. I've

checked your mailbox and the phone book. All I find is A Claraday. Amy? Ann? What's the A for?"

"Agatha."

I blinked. "Agatha? The most beautiful woman I've ever seen, and your name is Agatha? Where did that come from?"

"I'll tell you a story, if you're up to it."

"Up to it? Stop. I'm not a child, don't talk to me like I am. I'm up for anything."

She sat up and searched my face. "No, you're right. You aren't a child, and I shouldn't speak to you like one. You are a woman, no matter what your age says."

Then she told me a story. She told it in third person, as if she were speaking of someone else. I think she had to, to remove herself that much just to get through it.

I watched her as she sat there naked in that bed, naked in every way, physically, emotionally, she was completely exposed to me. She was so open, so raw, so vulnerable. I watched her struggle through that story, searching for the right words. I watched the emotions moving across her face, in her eyes.

I don't think I can do justice to her telling, but I'll try to give it to you the way she gave it to me that night.

Twenty-four years ago there was a middle-aged couple who, after years of trying and praying, finally had a child. They named her Agatha Estell, meaning good, kind star. She was an intelligent, well-behaved child, and they lavished love on her. They gave her everything she could want. They instilled in her all of their moral and ethical beliefs. She was their star. And she was good, and she was kind. Kinder than they would ever know.

She was kind because she loved them, and didn't want to hurt them. You see, from the very beginning of her memories, she knew two things. She knew that she loved children, and that she would never have any of her own. She was different from her parents, different from all the other kids she knew. It came to her before she even started school.

Her mother had a friend. A tall, graceful woman with straight blond hair down to her knees. She was beautiful. This little girl had the biggest crush on that woman. She used to sneak into the parlor when her mother was visiting and just watch the woman.

Then came a string of other crushes. Teachers, friends, the baby-sitter. The little girl never told any of them. She never told her parents, or anyone else. Somehow she knew, even at that age, that no one would understand. That no one else around was like her.

So she spent her childhood hiding. She hid in her schoolwork, becoming the class nerd. She didn't date in school, telling her parents that she wasn't ready, that she wanted to concentrate on her grades. And she did concentrate. She skipped two years, eighth and eleventh grades. When she wasn't in school, she was in church. Her parents thought for a while that she might become a nun.

She started college when she was barely seventeen. Things were different there. She found out that she wasn't alone. There were other people like her. Other women. She found out that she could have relationships with other women, and the sky wouldn't fall, lightning wouldn't strike her down.

So that's what she did. She had these relationships in secret. She never told anyone. She never told her parents. She knew that it would hurt them, and she loved them too much to do that.

By the time college was over, the other girls that she had known were ready to live their lives openly, or were getting married, claiming that it had just been a phase. Or that it never happened at all. She knew that it wasn't a phase for her, but she also knew that she could never be open.

So she did what she had always done. She went on. Alone. Hiding. She became a teacher, thinking she could spend her life with her other love, children. She took several substitute jobs, before finally landing a permanent position. She thought she had her life under control. Then she met this girl.

But this girl was her student.

She was confused at first. She liked women, but she suddenly found this strong attraction for this girl. She was confused, why would she be attracted to a child? She looked over records, checking to see if this girl had failed and was really older than her classmates. But she hadn't. And that made her a child.

Oh, how that girl tugged on her heart the first time she saw her! She knew that this was the one, the great love of her life. She got to know this girl, and found that she wasn't a child at all, but a young woman, with all the emotions and complications of a woman.

But legally she was a child, and her student. No one would ever permit this relationship. Here was a grown woman, madly in love with her student, still legally a child. They wouldn't see in her what she saw. They would never be able to see that she was emotionally and mentally older, and physically! So much older than her years. But they would never be able to see that.

So if she made her feelings known, she would lose her job at best. At worst, she'd end up in jail. That wasn't a chance she was willing to take.

When the young woman, the student, became an outcast, this woman decided to try to become her friend. She thought that if she was close to her without crossing that line that society had drawn, she might be able to satiate some of her desire. But she was wrong. The closer she got to her, the stronger her desire became. The more she wanted to love her like a woman.

She didn't think the young woman would love her back. She was safe as long as they were only friends. She would be as close as she could, and just leave it at that. But when the young woman confessed her love, the woman didn't know what to do. She wanted to hold her and kiss her, tell her she loved her back. Instead, she refused to talk to her. She drove away and cried.

And her desire grew even more, knowing that she was loved back. She fought it, but finally gave in. She knew the young woman was sneaking out late at night, sneaking into bars. She followed her three times before she got the nerve to follow her inside. But she did get the nerve. She went inside and found that young woman one night. She found her and took advantage of her. She took her and satiated her physical desire, with no thought to the consequences.

She was so ashamed of that. Not that she had been with the young woman, just that she had taken advantage of her. But being with her was also the best moment of her life.

And that's where it has to end. She can't see the young woman anymore, because she's not sure she can without letting the world know how she feels. The more she's around her, the harder it becomes. She can't do it anymore. She was born to be a teacher, not anyone's lover. Only a teacher. And that's just what she will be. That's all she can be.

She will teach, and she will go on, with a memory and a broken heart. And she will hide, because that's what she does best.

Agatha looked at me when she finished her story, her life and emotions exposed to me, the tears no longer only threatening, but flowing freely down her cheeks. "I've wronged you, Bobbie. And I'm so sorry."

I wiped the tears from her face, feeling my own in my eyes. "But you didn't force me to do anything I didn't want to do. You aren't Maggie May. You didn't seduce me into anything I didn't walk into with open eyes. I wanted this. I wanted you. I've wanted you since the first time I saw you. I still do. No wrong was done."

She closed her eyes. "Wreck your bed, and in the morning kick you in the head. Maybe I am Maggie May."

"Maybe you are. And I love you."

She opened her eyes and smiled through her tears. "But it doesn't change the fact that I can't spend my life with you, as much as I might want to. I can't give up teaching, it means too much to me. And I can't tell my parents, it would crush them. This is who I am, who I was meant to be. I can't change it."

"But you don't have to change anything. We don't have to tell your parents, we don't have to tell anyone." I knew I was pleading, I probably sounded pathetic, but I couldn't help myself.

She was shaking her head, with such sadness in her eyes. "We would be found out. Do you really think I could see you every day and pretend that I didn't love you? Do you know how hard it is just to get through one class with you?"

"Yes, I do know. I have to do it too. I know that if I look at you the wrong way people will start treating you the way they treat me. I couldn't stand that."

"Nor could I. I'm not as strong as you. Or Sara. I couldn't bear your burden. I can't take the abuse that you take. I'm afraid of it. I've been hiding far too long."

I held her tightly to me, not wanting to let her go, trying to think of a way we could be together, not wanting to admit that I couldn't. I held her and cried, feeling her hot tears on my chest, trying to find a way to make it all right. She was the one for me, I knew that with all my heart. She was my soul mate, I could feel it. But I couldn't change the world, I couldn't change her mind. Maybe, if I hadn't ever been caught . . . but I couldn't go back in time. I couldn't stop the wheels that were in motion in both our lives.

It was almost five in the morning when she pushed herself away from me.

"You need to go."

"No, Agatha, I want to stay with you. Just a few more minutes . . ."

She got up and handed me my clothes. "It's time for you to go home."

There was no point in arguing. What could I say? I couldn't force her. I had her heart, but I couldn't share in her life.

I looked back once, as I rolled my bike out of her garage. She covered her face with her hands and didn't watch me leave. She didn't even wave.

That was the fourth Great Revelation in my life. There is no Happily Ever After. Even things that are meant to be are sometimes impossible. It didn't matter that I knew where I was supposed to be in my life, I couldn't get there. Just because I'd found my soul mate didn't mean I could have her.

Chapter Eleven

That was the last time I saw Agatha Claraday away from school. I went down to the corner a few times, and waited. She never came. I didn't really expect her, she had told me it couldn't happen. But I went, and I waited.

When she didn't come, I went by her house. It was always closed up tight, all the lights out. I'd sit on the corner under that big tree, where I'd first watched her wash her car, and watch that darkened house. I thought about going up and knocking, but I never did. Why? I couldn't get out of my head the way she had said that she couldn't take being treated the way I was. I couldn't be responsible for putting her through the hell that I was living.

Her class each day was torture, and a blessing. I lived to see her every day, yet some little part of me died each time I walked into that room, knowing I could never be to her what I was meant to be.

While it was harder to go each day, school did get a little easier for me. The physical attacks slowed, then stopped. I'm not sure why, maybe they just got bored with me. Even the verbal harassment dwindled. It never went away entirely, but it fell to a tolerable point.

No one there ever wanted to be my friend, but after they quit trying to beat me up, a couple of the guys even talked to me a little. They wanted to know what girls did together. I think they just wanted titillation, but I took it as an opportunity to educate them. Perhaps that wasn't the best approach, but it's the one I took. At least, until one of the guys asked if he could watch. Then I quit trying to educate them. I just ignored them, and eventually they went away.

So school was going by pretty quickly. It was the last part of my senior year. I still couldn't find out what had happened to Sara. The only one that really knew was her sister, and she wasn't telling anyone. Besides, I couldn't have talked to her alone anyway. The faculty made sure I was never alone with a girl. Ever. Not even for a minute. What did they think I was going to do?

Anyway, I worked harder than I ever had, and brought my grades up even more. I quit sneaking out of the house, quit going to the bars. I just threw myself into my schoolwork. By graduation, "Bat out of Hell" battled the Bee Gees on the radio, Elvis was dead, and I had earned a scholarship redeemable at nearly any trade or business school. I didn't participate in any school activities at all. I was too busy, and I'm sure I wasn't really wanted. There was the prom, I didn't go. And the senior trip. Again, I didn't go. But I'm getting a little ahead of myself.

On my eighteenth birthday I ungrounded myself. It wasn't a huge scene or anything, I just told Mom I was going and she couldn't stop me. I expected a fight about it, but she didn't put up much of one. I never knew if she lightened up on me because she wanted me to stay, or if it was because she wanted me to find someplace else to go. Either way, I went.

I started going back up to the city. Not to the bars this time, but out to look for work. I went to every shop and garage in the city, putting in applications, talking to managers and owners. I was laughed at a lot. I was told to go out and find a pretty dress and a nice boy. I was told that girls didn't have the capability to understand engines. It was so incredibly frustrating.

So many times I just wanted to give up, but I didn't. I just imagined that it was the same in every city, and it was either that or living somewhere just like that little town I was in. The thought of being stuck in a place like that for my whole life kept me struggling. And it finally paid off.

It really was funny when it finally happened. I was at a little station, putting gas in my bike. All of the mechanics were gathered around this big Cadillac, and there was a very angry-looking gentleman watching them. I heard them talking, trying to figure out what was wrong with the car. I listened a minute, then stepped up and told them what it was. They ignored me. I glanced up at the angry man, obviously the owner of the Caddy, and shrugged. I turned to leave and he called me back.

"Hey, you. Come here."

I walked over to him.

"You think you know what's wrong with it?"

I nodded.

"You ever work on cars?"

I laughed. "Since I could walk."

He looked at me kind of funny. "Can you fix it?"

I shrugged. "I think so."

"So what is it?"

"Timing."

He shook his head. "They set it already. You're wrong."

"They set it by the book?"

"Yes."

"That's the problem. You've got air and all the gadgets in there. And the book for that year's useless. You have to set it higher. Not much, most of these guys probably couldn't tell the difference."

"How do you know that?"

I shrugged. "I helped restore a line of these babies once. This guy had one for every year. I remember what a pain in the ass it was to figure out. You can't use the light on this one, you have to set it by the sound of the motor, by the feel of her. She's touchy."

"And you think you can do that?"

"Yeah."

"Well, go to it. You can't fuck it up any worse than these numb-nuts have already."

I turned to look at the car and those guys all stepped back. I think they figured I was going to screw up and they didn't want to be involved. Well, I didn't screw up. I fixed the problem very quickly, stepped back, and looked at the man.

"You're all done, sir. You shouldn't have any more problems, but if I were you, I'd get your fuel filter replaced sometime soon. I give it another thousand miles before it clogs your line."

The man looked at me and pointed toward the mechanics. "They told me it was okay."

"Oh, it is." I shrugged. "For now. But I'm telling you, another thousand."

He stepped closer and leaned down for a better look. "How can you tell?"

I pulled a rag out of my back pocket and started cleaning it off for a better view. "See this mark right here . . . ?"

I told the man when to get his filter changed, and he thanked me and asked me what I was doing there. I told him I was looking for work. He laughed.

"And they wouldn't hire you?"

"Nope. Turned me down just last week."

That man picked up a phone and made a call. Then he handed me a fifty, got in his car, and drove away. I paid for my gas and was about to leave when another man pulled in and stopped me. He turned out to be the owner of that station. He introduced himself to me and told me that the man in the Cadillac had called him. He asked me a few questions about cars and motors, what was compatible, that sort of thing. I answered them. And I was hired as a mechanic.

I worked evenings and weekends until school was out. I hoarded every dollar I made until I had enough to rent a little apartment.

I rented that place just before summer. Every time I went into work, I took as much as I could carry on my bike and stashed it in my new apartment. It was kind of weird, I found out then that almost everything I owned belonged in a garage, not a house. Really, it was all motor parts and tools. On the last day of school, I packed up the rest of my stuff (which turned out to be one bag of clothes) and turned to my mother.

"Well, I guess that's it."

She nodded and refused to look at me.

"Mom, I really think this is best for both of us. I've already got a job, I need to be closer to it."

"I'm not arguing that. I just hope you can still find yourself a nice boy."

I rolled my eyes. "I won't. I'm gay, Mom. This is who I am. Why can't you just accept that?"

"Because it's wrong. I didn't raise you that way."

I shook my head. Why wouldn't she just accept it? Why couldn't she love me anyway? I was moving out of her house, out on my own for the first time in my life. Did she know that it was a little scary? Did she care? That's all I wanted, for her to care.

"Mom, this is a big thing to me. I'm proud of myself, getting out on my own. I wish you were. I wish Dad was here to see this."

"Why? He ran away from his responsibilities to his country, what makes you think he would own up to his responsibility to you? He did nothing but brainwash you. And left me to deal with the consequences. I'll tell you who you should thank. Dan. He stepped in and provided for you when your father wouldn't. He's the one you should be thinking about."

I shook my head and sighed. I just didn't feel like getting into this argument with her again. "I left my number in your address book."

She turned away from me. "You call and let me know when you've come to your senses."

I walked out her door and climbed on my bike. I found that I was shaking a little when I started it up. I was all alone now, there was no one to turn to, no one to check up on me. I closed my eyes and took a deep breath, then realized that I was okay. And not just okay, I was *free*. I rolled my bike out of that driveway and pointed it toward the city, toward my new life. My *freedom*. I grinned, gave it some gas, and screamed out of that little town like that infamous Meatloaf tune. And I never looked back.

I worked through the summer at that shop, and got a lot of business. I heard people talking about me sometimes, usually something like "Have you been over to Johnson's garage? He's got a girl over there. . . ." I guess I became kind of a novelty. That was all right with me, I didn't mind. They found out when they came that I knew what I was doing. No one ever tried to get to know me, or tried to get personal, but they weren't mean to me. And I didn't want to be personal anyway.

That fall, I used my scholarship at a trade school, for mechanics, of course. I was the only female in that class. Most people looked at me sideways, and I ignored them. I kept to myself and let them think whatever they wanted. I didn't care.

I didn't make any friends. I told myself I didn't need to. I told myself that I didn't want friends. Everyone in the country was disco dancing in the spotlight, but I found the "Darkness on the Edge of Town," and I hid in the safe anonymity of it. I was the *Stranger in Town,* and nobody tried to change that. I didn't either. I closed myself off from the world. I worked, I went to school, and I went home. I didn't associate with anyone. I was alone.

I felt like I had lost everything. My father, my only real friend, the love of my life, they were all gone. Everything I loved. Even my music was going out of style. Disco and punk were taking over the airwaves, and I still felt like a "Lonesome Loser." That was exactly it. I was lonesome, I had lost everything I cared about. I didn't have anyone to turn to, no one that loved me, no one that I loved. I wanted my father. I needed him. I was still angry, but now that I wasn't with Mom either, suddenly I wanted a parent. Or maybe just someone older that would tell me that I was doing the right thing. Someone to be proud of me for making it on my own. And I missed Sara. I didn't have one single friend. No one to talk to, laugh with, cry with, no one to share my freedom. We had planned to leave that place together, but I was alone. I woke up night after night from dreams of Agatha. Woke up with tears in my eyes and pain in my heart. I would think of her and my arms would literally ache to hold her. And the rest of my body . . . well, let's just say that I needed her the most. But I didn't have her. I didn't have anyone. I could hear people all around me, but I felt like I couldn't touch them. I couldn't be a part of them. Like someone in a bubble, I was surrounded by the world, yet I was completely isolated. Alone. The only thing I had left was work.

Like I said, I was kind of a novelty at work at first. Then people came and found out that I was good. They were amazed that a girl knew what she was doing. I even started to get some loyal customers, people who actually asked for me to work on things for them. That was pretty great. I was doing all right.

I spent almost a year like that. School, work, nothing else. I didn't go out, I didn't make any friends. I didn't even go to the bar. I had a phone, and the only calls I ever got were from the shop. I didn't have one single visitor. But I was on my own, making my own way. And that was good. I told myself that it was good. I told myself I was fine. I told myself that I wasn't lonely. I told myself I was happy.

And I tried to be.

It was just after my nineteenth birthday that my life turned upside down again. (Did I mention that that happened a lot?)

I was at home studying, because I didn't do anything else, when someone knocked on my door. I was already surprised, because no one had ever been to my apartment. Not even the landlord, I paid my rent on time and didn't ask for anything. And I was even more surprised when I opened the door and saw Sara standing there.

I think I held myself together despite my shock. I ignored all the questions and emotions flooding my mind, and hugged her.

I invited Sara in and offered her a soda, taking one for myself and sitting across the room from her.

"So, how'd you find me? I know my mother didn't tell you, she's still freaked out."

"No, all she'd tell me was that you moved up to the city. She wouldn't even open the door more than a crack to talk to me." She shook her head. "It's crazy, what people think about us."

"Yeah." I watched her. I couldn't see any bruises, but she was moving a little stiffly.

"So I hunted you down. I hit the gas stations and garages, figuring I'd find you at one of them. And they pointed me in the right direction."

I sighed and took a drink of my soda. What was work going to do after they found a girl looking for me? What would they think? And how would they react to it? Suddenly, I didn't care. What could they do that hadn't already been done to me? I looked at Sara. She looked tired. "So, how've you been?"

"Not so good, Bobbie. I need help."

That was the first thing that night that didn't surprise me. Why else would someone step out of your past? "That's why you're here."

She nodded. "I didn't know who else to turn to. I don't know anyone else. And I don't know if you're still mad at me."

That surprised me too. "Mad at you? I never was. I just couldn't get near you. Who told you I was mad?"

"Nobody." She shrugged. "I just assumed, you know, after all the shit . . ."

"That wasn't your fault, Sara. None of it was. You caught just as much shit off that as I did. I didn't blame you. I don't. Your mom, your sister, maybe, but never you."

"Well, I just . . ."

"No." I tried to sound as firm as I could, without coming off as bossy. "Forget it, okay? It's all water under the bridge. Ancient history. Okay?"

She nodded. "Okay."

"Good, then that's settled. Now, tell me what you need."

Sara looked relieved. "Well, I know it's kind of awkward, but my mom kicked me out of the house. I don't know where else to go. It wouldn't be for very long, and I could pay rent. Not much, I never could make the kind of money you could, but I could pay some."

"Hey, okay." I shrugged. "You can stay, it's not a problem. I'm paying the same amount whether you're here or not. Why'd your mom kick you out?"

"It's a long story."

I shrugged again and held out my arms to show her all the excitement in my life. "I got time."

She sighed. "Well, I guess you can imagine that it got pretty bad after we . . . you know, got caught, or whatever."

She looked embarrassed, I nodded. "Yeah, I'll bet it was bad for both of us."

"I'm sorry, I didn't know. . . ."

"It's okay, things got better for me. Tell me about you."

"Well . . . I guess my mom went nuts."

I nodded. "Just a little. What about your dad?"

She shrugged. "He beat the hell out of me for a while."

"Oh, God." She had never before admitted to me that her father was abusive. I had wondered, even suspected, but I hadn't ever asked, and she hadn't volunteered the information. I felt bad for her. "I'm sorry, Sara, I—"

"Don't be. If it wasn't over you, he'd have found some other reason. He always did." She laughed, just a little. "It's funny, you know. You had a great dad, and couldn't keep him. I had a shitty one, and couldn't get rid of him."

I started to offer sympathy again, but she just waved me off.

"Eventually, Dad realized that he couldn't beat me straight. Then it got worse. A lot worse. My mom went nuts."

I nodded my head and she looked at me and shook hers, widening her eyes. "No, I mean it. Really nuts. She got on some crusade to save my soul. We were in church every time the doors were open, I think. She crammed so much God down my throat . . . I hate religion. I mean, it's *not* like I don't believe in God, I do. I just don't think I'm going to hell for being gay. She thinks so, but I don't believe it. I can't."

I nodded, knowing exactly how she felt. Sara sighed.

"Then she started on the men. It wasn't too bad at first, she was just introducing me to a lot of guys and stuff, trying to get me interested. Then she started setting me up with them. I figured I'd go out with one or two, a couple of times, and she'd drop it. No such luck. She just pushed harder. She started talking to them before the dates, practically giving them her permission to fuck me. She even took me to the doctor and put me on birth control. God, can you believe that? She put me on the pill and gave anything with a dick her consent. I guess my consent didn't mean much to her." She looked at her hands. "Or to most of them."

That frightened me. The thought of Sara . . .

"Did they hurt you?" I couldn't imagine what she'd been through. I wanted to hold her, comfort her in some way.

She held her head up and looked at me. I could see the Sara I knew in her eyes. Whatever hell she had gone through hadn't broken her spirit. I was glad to see that.

"They couldn't hurt me. Not enough to matter anyway. Not where it counted."

I nodded. "And then you disappeared. Where'd you go?"

She blinked slowly and took a deep breath. "I was sent away. They called it a 'residential facility.'" She rolled her eyes. "Better known as a nuthatch. They psychoanalyze every breath you take and monitor your every move, even in the bathroom." She rubbed her face with her hands, looking more tired than I thought anyone could look.

"If you're not crazy when you go in, you will be by the time you get out." She took a deep breath. "Anyway, it all blew up yesterday when Mom found out that I wasn't taking my pills. We got in a huge fight and I told her a few other things. Like the fact that I wasn't 'repenting my sins' in confession, and my conversations with my therapist revolved more around how she was driving me nuts than my changing my sexuality. She kicked me out. Told me she never wanted to see me again and I had ten minutes to get out before she called the police."

"So you left."

"I grabbed my stuff and split."

"But where'd you go? Last night?"

"I slept in my car. Out by the park." She looked at me almost apologetically. "The title's in my name, so she couldn't take that away. But I guess it's really yours, too."

I waved my hand at her. "It's yours, I've got no use for it."

She nodded and smiled just a little. "This morning I went to your mom's place to find out where you were. I spent the rest of the day finding you."

"Damn, I'm sorry, Sara. I thought I had it bad."

"How'd you handle it?"

"Well, my mom didn't force me to date. Or go to church. She just grounded me. And Dan, my stepfather, ignored the fact that I was alive. That wasn't much different, really. He didn't pay much attention to me before. So I pretty much threw myself into school. I spent a lot of time studying and working on cars to save enough money to move the hell out of there. I had to sneak out after they were in bed to have any fun at all."

Sara laughed. "And who were you having fun with?"

I smiled. "You know, people."

"Women?"

"Yes! Surely you don't expect me to go straight just because we got into trouble, do you?"

"No. But who were you going out with?"

"Now, now. I can't kiss and tell."

"Kiss and tell my ass! Come on, anybody I know?"

We were both laughing then. It felt like all the time apart just melted away. All the bad things that had happened just seemed to dim a little. We laughed like we had in that cool water, what was it, two years ago? Everything had changed in that time, except us. She was my friend, still.

"Maybe."

"Really? Someone I know?"

"Most of the girls I went out with were from up here. Girls I met at the bar."

"There's a bar?"

"A little joint downtown. I've been going there forever."

"Really? A place we can go?"

I suddenly realized that Sara hadn't ever been to a gay bar. And for some reason I had never told her about going. I guess after Jennifer, I just didn't want to go. And by the time I did, Sara was gone. I grinned.

"Wall-to-wall lesbians, baby! We fit in perfectly."

"You got an ID?"

"Yes, I just haven't used it in a really long time."

"Could you get me one?"

I shook my head. "The guy that helped me isn't in the business anymore. But I could take you with me. You just couldn't get caught drinking, we'd both be thrown out."

"I understand. I wouldn't want to do anything to get you in trouble."

We looked at each other and burst out laughing. We laughed until we cried, like neither had in a long time.

When she regained control, Sara wiped the tears from her eyes and sobered.

"Sorry. I didn't mean for that to be a joke."

"It was good though." I giggled.

"It was. But we got off the subject. Who?"

"All right, all right, but I'm only telling you because we might see her at the bar and I don't want you to freak out. Then again, I haven't seen her around . . ."

"Oh, just give it up already!"

Maybe it was a bragging point on my part, maybe I was just talking openly to someone, I don't know. But I gave it up.

"Miss Claraday."

Sara's mouth fell open. "No!"

"Yes."

"Really?"

"Uh-huh." I raised both hands "Honest."

"No way. She's not gay. Miss Claraday, no." She looked at me. "She's gay?"

"Oh, honey! You don't even know!"

"Did you . . . no! You didn't!"

I grinned. "I did!"

"No way!"

She was so incredulous, I had to laugh.

"Oh, my God, this is so weird! I can't believe you did Miss Claraday! I remember you had such a crush on her. Wasn't it weird? I mean, she was your *teacher*. I can't imagine fucking someone who used to be my teacher."

"Not used to be. I was still in school."

"No! This is too much! God, I couldn't have. I'd feel like I was being graded. What did you call her? How long did it go on?"

"Graded?"

"You know."

I laughed. "I'd have made an A."

"You lying sack of shit. You aren't that good."

"Maybe not to you, but you aren't my type."

"That's right, you like older women."

"They'll surprise you, maybe you should try it. Everyone should have a Maggie May."

She shook her head. "I can't imagine calling out 'Miss Claraday' in bed."

I laughed. "Like I would. Her name is Agatha."

Sara tipped her head. "So, how long did that go on?"

I shrugged. "It only happened twice. Once at her house, once she found me at the bar."

"You picked your teacher up in a bar?"

"No, she picked me up."

"This is too crazy."

I shrugged again.

"Okay, give it up, was she any good?"

"Sara!" I was trying to sound shocked. I guess I wasn't very convincing because she just laughed.

"Come on, Bobbie. It's not like I'm asking for details. Unless, of course, you'd tell me?"

"Not a chance."

"But was she any good?"

I wanted to cry with the memory of her, my Maggie May. Her sweetness, her wild side, her softness. But I smiled instead. "Fantastic!"

Sara raised her eyebrows. "Really? I'd never have thought it."

"It's true. She was incredible."

"Just not good enough to stay with, huh?"

"I would have. I would have stayed with her forever, she just didn't give me the chance."

We were quiet for a moment. Then she said softly, "Agatha. I never knew her name. She's gone, you know."

I felt a sudden stab of pain in my heart and tried to hide it. "No, I didn't know."

Sara nodded. "My sister's still in school. Miss Claraday left before school started last year. She got another job somewhere, I think. I don't know where, I don't think anyone does."

I didn't know whether to cry because she was gone, or be happy that she got out of there, that place that hated our kind so much. I glanced at my watch.

"Hey, it's getting late, it's almost one. I'd love for you to stay here, as long as you need. It's not fancy, but the couch is comfortable. Can I help you bring your stuff in?"

"No, I'll just get my bag tonight and worry about the rest in the morning."

Sara went out to her car while I found a couple of extra blankets and a pillow. She came back in with a gym bag.

"That's all you've got?"

"Well, I have another bag of clothes in the car, and some personal stuff. That's it."

"Geeze. I'm off tomorrow, we'll see what you need and try to find it for you. And it's Friday, so we'll go out. It'll be fun."

"Oh, Bobbie, I really appreciate this. I really wasn't sure, but I didn't know where else to go. . . ."

I hugged her. "Not a problem. I want you here. Now let me show you where everything is."

I showed her around the apartment (which took all of a minute or so) and said good night. She hugged me again and I went to bed.

I lay awake a long time that night. I hadn't thought I would ever see Sara again, and here she was. I hadn't thought I would ever be talking about Agatha again. I wondered where she was, what she was doing, if she was happy. I remembered her tears on my skin, and felt my own wet my face.

It was late when I pushed my thoughts to the back of my mind, and finally found sleep. And I dreamed.

I dreamed of golden curls in the sun, a perfect profile on the hood of a car in the starlight. I dreamed of a secret smile that lit up a pair of soft hazel eyes, and a touch that could reach into my heart.

Chapter Twelve

I woke up late Friday morning, the sun was coming through the window in warm rays and streaming across my bed. I looked at the clock, it was after ten. I hadn't slept that late in a long time. The memory of my dreams lingered, and I lay there a few minutes, trying not to cry.

Then I heard Sara rattling around in the kitchen. So I rolled out of bed and went out there. She greeted me with a grin and a plate.

"Good morning. You're just in time for breakfast. You don't keep a lot of food around, but I managed to rustle up a little something."

She handed me the plate, on it was a warm biscuit and a steaming omelet. It smelled delicious. We sat down and started eating.

"Where'd you get the biscuits?" I knew I didn't have any in my house, I didn't have much food at all. I didn't cook much.

Sara laughed. "I made them. I can cook, you know."

"Well, I knew you could cook over a campfire, but that wasn't anything like this. This is great. Why didn't you ever tell me you could do this?" And it was great. She was a fantastic cook.

"Thanks. I never told you? I guess it just never came up.

We weren't in the house enough to think about cooking there. Besides, Dad hated it when I made messes in the kitchen."

I smiled, remembering our long hours out camping, or in the car, just being outside. Even if the reasons behind it weren't good, the memories of that time were. "No, I guess we weren't. But this is really good."

She shrugged. "Easy stuff. I love to cook, always have. I could be happy cooking forever."

"So do it."

She shook her head. "Those fancy schools cost a fortune. Besides, they only teach you the expensive gourmet stuff, not what you need in real life."

"But you don't need to go to school. You could go to work in a small restaurant, you know, a meat and potatoes kind of place, and work your way up. It takes longer that way, but . . ." I shrugged, shoveling more omelet into my mouth.

She sighed. "I don't know, maybe. I'm not trained for anything else. Not like you. I guess I could put in some applications and see what happens."

I nodded. "Monday. Today." I pushed back my then empty plate. "We need to figure out what you need. Go get your stuff."

I cleaned up our plates (she had already taken care of everything else) while she went and got the rest of her stuff out of the car. We went through her things and found that she had most everything that she'd need.

She was a little short on clothes, especially jeans, and had only one pair of shoes. Well, they weren't really shoes, either. They were black work boots. Like the ones I wore at the shop.

"Geeze, Sara, you don't own any other shoes?"

"No. I don't need anything else."

I shook my head. "Are you a dyke or what?"

"Hey, I like my boots."

"Me too, honey, but you have to have something else."

"Why?"

"Well . . ." I held up those boots. "Can you dance in these?"

"I could try."

I looked at her.

"Like you were any better off when you moved here."

Actually, I wasn't. I was probably worse. I hadn't owned any clothes that weren't stained with grease or oil. But I didn't want to tell her that. "You should take a look in my closet. All the latest fashions for the self-respecting lesbian."

"Okay, okay, you win. I'll buy a pair of shoes. Happy?"

"What about jeans?"

"God, you're gonna break me!"

"And a decent shirt, unless you want to borrow one of mine. You're going out with me tonight, you need to look good. You wouldn't want to ruin my reputation now, would you?"

"Reputation! Like you've got one! And even if you did, it wouldn't be the first time I fucked it up."

"No shit. See what you do to me?"

We were laughing again. And again, I had that sensation, like the night before, of time melting away. We were back under that shade tree, lying in that cool water, being friends. Being comfortable with another human being. That was when I realized that I'd been lying to myself. I hadn't been happy the past year. Living alone, never having any kind of human touch. I hadn't been happy, I'd been lonely.

Sara and I spent the afternoon shopping. I never did get her to buy much, but I bought a few things for her. I loved it.

We went out to an early dinner at a small lounge that catered to "alternative lifestyles." Sara had never seen such a place before, much less been in one. I had only been there once, but I wasn't going to tell her that. Just like the first few months I knew her, I found myself taking on the role of teacher. I wanted her to know what I knew about the gay community, I wanted her to find the joy I had denied myself for the past year. I took her everywhere I could think of, showing her that we weren't the only gay people around. I wanted her to be comfortable. I wanted to make her happy.

Sara was delighted with almost everything I showed her that day, and I was so enjoying her happiness. I hadn't thought before about that lack of companionship. That incredible loneliness that I had convinced myself that I didn't feel. And how it felt to get a friend back. Just to have someone I could be myself around, someone comfortable. Sara and I had been through a lot together, and it felt so good to me to be around someone that knew where I was coming from.

I looked at her across the table from me at dinner. Her eyes were bright, she was smiling, my heart felt as if it were being squeezed inside my chest. I wanted to keep her around so badly, I was willing to do almost anything. I needed someone. I made her a proposition.

"Sara, I want you to stay with me."

"Bobbie, I am staying with you."

"No, I mean kind of permanently. You know, after you get a job and get on your feet, we can find a bigger apartment. You know, like a two bedroom."

"Well, I think I'd like that."

"It'll be a lot easier to share expenses."

She nodded. "But I don't think you realize what you're getting into. You've been out on your own for a while, but this is the first time for me. There's a million things I want to do, a million places I want to go."

"I know, and I want to do all that, too. I've been working and going to school, I spend most nights studying. I need a life."

"But I'm probably gonna go nuts for a while." She waved her hands to take in the whole place around us. "You know, on all of this. I want it, I want to be involved."

I should have thought about that. It should have been a red flag waving in my face. But it wasn't. I wanted her around. I wanted a life. I wanted a friend. I didn't care about the price.

"I know. Maybe I need to go a little nuts for a while. Maybe I need to get involved, get a life. Maybe I need a friend."

Sara reached over and squeezed my hand. "I need a friend, too. And I think you're the prefect one."

And so it was decided. Sara wasn't just staying at my place, now it was *ours*. I'd still be paying the bills for a while, but that was all right with me. I was happy about it.

We went to the bar that night. Not the one that I'd been to before, it was gone, but we found another. It wasn't too hard, once you knew what to look for, even back then.

Yes, we went out. I'd forgotten how much fun Sara and I always had together. We did nearly everything that night. We flirted with all the women. We drank. We danced. We laughed. We laughed a lot. We danced a lot. I drank a lot.

It had been so long since I had had any fun at all, and I guess I took it too far. It wasn't the first time I'd been drunk. Or the last, I'm afraid. But I was a little drunk that night.

Okay, maybe a lot drunk.

Sara had to drive me home. And help me up the stairs. And into bed.

She crawled into my bed beside me.

"Do you mind if I sleep here?"

"Sara . . ." I was ready to protest. We had nearly ruined our friendship once before. I didn't want to do it again, no matter how lonely I was. But she stopped that protest before it got started.

"I'm not talking about sex, Bobbie." She sat up and swung her feet over the side of her bed, her back to me. "God, I'm not asking anything from you. I just want to be close again. I've been lonely, too, you know. I just wanted to know you're there."

I realized that I hadn't thought of her loneliness. I had

been so caught up in mine that I hadn't thought that she might be feeling the same way. After all, she hadn't had much of a life either. And I knew she hadn't made any friends in that backward little town she had left the day before. She started to stand, I pulled her back into bed and hugged her tight.

"I'm sorry, Sara. Don't go. I want you here. I want to feel close too."

She curled up beside me and went to sleep. I think I was awake for a long time that night, watching her sleep beside me. And my drunken mind actually worked, a little. As she slept there, I had my fifth Great Revelation. True comfort is found in a friend, not a lover.

We had been wrong in high school. We didn't need sex for comfort. Comfort is just there, in a true friend's company.

I think the loneliness of not having a lover is bearable as long as you have a friend. But the loneliness of not having a friend weighs down on your heart like lead.

Chapter Thirteen

You would expect that revelation to help me get my life together. Looking back now, I would expect that, too. But it didn't. It didn't seem to do much for me at all. In fact, that's when things really started getting crazy.

Not right away, of course, but very soon after. Right away things started to look like they were getting better.

Sara went out that first Monday she lived with me and got a job cooking at this little grill downtown. Not a glamorous job, but a job that she liked.

I was paying all the bills then. And I think that really kept me on track for a while. It was about two months or so before we moved, and Sara and I both worked hard. I had school and work, and she had her job at that little grill. And she was good at it, maybe as good at it as I was at my job.

And I was good. I made more than enough money to support both of us. And I bought things too. Things for Sara, mostly. I wanted to buy her things. I wanted to make her happy. And I think I did for a while. Then her job took off, in a big way.

It was just a little grill, but within a month the place had tripled its business. I told you she was a really good cook, didn't I? I guess even I didn't realize how good she was.

But she didn't stay at that little grill very long. As soon as she had a little experience, she went out and found a bigger and better place. She didn't stay there long, either. She really didn't stay anywhere very long. She kept getting better offers. Before long, she was choosing where she would work. And determining, even demanding, things like shifts and salary.

She was doing very well. I was too.

I finished school, and that gave me a substantial raise. Then I left that little shop for a bigger garage. I guess I thought I would be a nobody there, just another blue jumpsuit working on cars. I was wrong.

My reputation preceded me. I wasn't just another blue jumpsuit at all, I was back to being a novelty. The girl that knew cars. When the novelty began to wear off, word of mouth took its place. Customers followed me from the old shop to the new place. And others started requesting me specifically to work on their cars. What an ego boost! That was good, but the commission was even better.

With both of us making more money, Sara and I could afford a bigger apartment. We found one across town, a two bedroom, and moved. She took over half the bills, and that left quite a bit of money to play with. That's when the partying started.

At first we convinced each other that we deserved a night out. And we might even have been right. After all, we had worked hard, we had earned it. We deserved a little playtime.

And playtime was all it was at first. We went out, we had a few drinks. We found a couple of nice girls and brought them home. Stephanie and Carol. I saw Stephanie, Sara was dating Carol. They both ended up being very short-lived relationships. They weren't bad, just short. You know, you meet someone, go out, take them home. Everything's new and fresh and fun. But it wears quickly. You find that you really don't have much in common, or that someone thinks something else looks better. Either way, the relationship just sort of dissolves, and you find yourself back where you started. So what do you do? You go back out and find someone else.

Then that night out that Sara and I deserved became more

frequent. We were going out every Saturday night. Then it became a weekend out. Every weekend. And then the weekends began to stretch. They went from two days to three, sometimes four.

And we were drinking. A lot. Much more than anyone should. And then the women started.

All the women . . . it was like a constant parade through our place. With the sheer numbers of women that came in and out of that apartment, the super must have thought we were running a brothel. I'd like to say that they were all there with Sara, or even skip this part altogether, but honesty won't allow that.

There's an old joke that goes something like: What does a lesbian bring on a second date? A U-Haul. Well, Sara and I didn't run into that for very long. Those short-term relationships went out the window by the time the night out became a weekend. We usually didn't have second dates after that. We . . . "played the field."

That's the nicest way I can think of to put it anyway. We brought home different women every weekend, sometimes every night.

I don't remember all of their names, I don't think I even knew all their names then. I don't know how many there were. Not a clue. That became a bragging point for Sara and me, that we didn't know how many. That we fell into the "too many to count" category.

We were players. "Studs." We were at the bar all the time, and always available. But our hearts were untouchable. We were those mysterious women in the corner that all the ladies wanted to see, wanted to tame. We were hot. But we were so *cold*.

By that I mean that we never felt anything for any of those women. Our hearts were cold, our actions were cold. We didn't fall in love, we didn't even really care much. I don't think we were ever really mean, but we were unfeeling. *Cold*. I don't know if that makes sense to you, but that's the only way I know to put it.

But we were hot items, and we thought we were pretty cool. We thought we were in control.

Now that I look back on it, we weren't in control at all. Our lives were running away with us, and we couldn't even catch up. We were going as fast as we could, and life was passing us by. Real life. The stuff that matters. And the saddest part was that we didn't even know it. God, we were stupid.

Yeah, we did some pretty wild stuff back then, none of which I'm proud of now. And very little of which I'm going to put down on paper. It might incriminate me.

I'll just say that we did nearly everything your parents tell you not to do. All the stupid stuff no one should ever do. And we did it often. The drinking, the drugs. Do I have to mention that? Not horrible amounts, we never became addicts or anything. Just enough to muddle our brains, make us stupid. And the women.

I'm sorry most about the women now. I wish I could erase that whole thing, that whole time in my life. You see, there were a lot of women. We weren't very picky, and, I'm afraid, we weren't always very nice. Like I said, we were players. We got what we wanted, and got the hell out. We didn't call them the next day. We didn't always acknowledge them the next time we saw them. And that's not nice. It's even mean.

And we were never careful. We never thought about safe sex, or psycho ex-girlfriends, or any of that other stuff out there that can kill you. Looking back on it now, I wonder how we even survived.

I don't know how long that insanity lasted. Too long, I think. Disco died, old-time rock and roll made a brief showing. The decade changed, the Reagan years began. John Lennon was murdered. The big-hair bands came in.

Then one night, back when Springsteen had a *River*, and Seger was running "Against the Wind," I woke up. I woke up in the bar.

I don't mean I was passed out or anything, I just suddenly came to my senses.

It was around ten-thirty on a Thursday night. Sara and I had both missed work that day, too hungover from the night before to make it. So we went back to the bar that evening (now *that* makes perfect sense, right?). We were sitting there, drinking, and watching this woman. She was small, with light brown hair and a nice figure. We had been discussing how to get her in bed (and laying bets on it, I'm sure), but we weren't talking then. We were just watching her. She had a way of moving that caught your eye, and kept it. She had an appeal that neither of us could name, but we both saw it.

That woman suddenly turned around and locked eyes with me. The shock nearly made me choke on my beer. I had been sitting there watching her like fresh meat, and she wasn't at all. She was Jennifer.

That's when it hit me. The sixth Great Revelation. I really didn't like myself. I had become something that I despised. And what I was was no one's fault but mine. I hadn't been able to handle a relationship with Jennifer because I couldn't face her past. And now I was worse than she'd been back then. I couldn't respect anyone else until I respected myself. And I didn't.

I was stuck in this rut, going nowhere. Because I was out of control. I had to take control of my own life, no one could do it for me. I had been wrong all that time, I wasn't in control, I wasn't going anywhere. I could see no future for myself.

It hit me just like that. All at once. *I have to make a change.* And I suddenly felt sick.

I looked at Sara. My friend. I wanted to show her that we needed to do . . . something. I didn't know what.

"Hey, Sara, what the hell are we doing?"

She looked at me as if I had just grown an extra head. "Bobbie, you are freakin' me out. I don't know what you're talking about."

I tipped my beer toward Jennifer. "Her. I'm talking about her."

Sara shook her head. "I'm not following you."

My foggy mind was beginning to feel clear. "Look at us, Sara. We're sitting here, in a bar, in the middle of the week, trying to find a girl we haven't fucked yet."

She shrugged. "So? Is that a problem?"

I turned around and put my elbows on the bar, resting my chin in my hands. "I think it's just become one."

She shook her head. "What the hell are you talking about?"

"That girl we were watching. That's Jennifer."

"So you know her." She shrugged. "So what?"

"I don't just know her. God, don't you remember? Jennifer was my first. I couldn't handle how much she had slept around before me. I thought she was a slut."

Sara shrugged again. "Maybe she was."

"You still don't get it!" I realized that I had doubled my fist and brought it down hard on the bar in frustration. I un-clenched it and laid my hand flat on the bar, taking a deep breath and forcing myself to calm down.

"I, *we* have become exactly what I couldn't stand in her. I couldn't face the fact that she'd slept around so much. Now I'm just what she was then. Maybe worse." I shook my head. "I gotta get out of here. Come on, let's go home."

Sara shook her head and held her hands up. "No. I don't want to go home."

"Come on, Sara."

"No. I'm not running out the door just because you got a weird case of the guilts, or whatever. You wanna go, go. But leave me out of it."

I looked at her for a moment. I wanted her to go with me. I wanted to grab her shoulders and shake her. I had just had a Revelation, made a life discovery. I wanted her to see it. But I couldn't show it to her. I think that's when I realized that each person has to make their own discoveries, learn their own set of lessons, find their own truth. My lessons weren't the same as Sara's, or anyone else's. She had her own to learn. I couldn't make her see mine and expect her to understand.

I gave my friend the best smile I could, turned my back to her, and headed for the door. Before I reached it, someone touched my shoulder. I turned around, hoping Sara had followed me, and found myself face-to-face with Jennifer.

"Are you leaving without saying hello?" She sounded smug, and a little hurt.

"Jennifer, I'm sorry. I . . ." I trailed off, not knowing what to say.

"It's okay, Bobbie. I understand."

She turned away from me and started to walk off. I reached out and caught her arm.

"I don't think you do understand. You want to go get some coffee?"

She smiled at me. "Sure."

We went to a little coffee shop down the street. We sat down, ordered; then she looked at me.

"So, I understand you've found some, uh, experience."

That cut really deep. But I figured I deserved it. I hung my head, ashamed of looking down on her back then, before I had walked in her shoes. Ashamed of walking in those shoes now. And thankful that she had put it so delicately, even though I didn't deserve it.

"I guess I have."

She took a deep breath. "That'll come back to haunt you someday, you know."

"I think it just did." I sighed and rubbed my face. "God, Jennifer, I'm sorry. I'm sorry for the way I was back then, and for the way I've been since. I was young, and stupid, and . . ."

She laughed. "And now, suddenly, you're old and wise?"

"No. No, I'm far from wise. But I just realized that, and maybe that's the first step to becoming."

She paused, waiting for me to finish. When I didn't, she asked, "Becoming wise or old?"

I grinned. "Either way, I'm getting there. You might say I'm a work in progress."

"I like that. A work in progress." She smiled and raised her cup to me. "Aren't we all!"

I touched my cup to hers. "Maybe we are. But I'll get there, one Revelation at a time."

She sipped her coffee and smiled again. "Oh, yes, your Great Revelations. I'd almost forgotten. Still keeping track, huh? So, what are you up to?"

"Mmmm. I just had my sixth." I raised my cup to her again. "Thanks to you."

"Sure. Glad I could help."

We talked for hours, Jennifer and I. Hours. We must have had six cups of coffee that night. And that was okay, I probably needed it to sober up. And once I did, I felt like my head was clear for the first time in a long time. We talked about so many things, relived old times, caught up on the new. I guess I just had to walk in her shoes awhile to find that she really was a good person, after all. And I was finally on my way to becoming one.

Chapter Fourteen

Becoming what I thought of as a good person didn't happen overnight, but it did start then. I settled down a lot. I didn't completely stop going out, but I did stop sleeping around. And I cut my going out down to a minimum. Most of those nights out were spent actually *talking* to women. Mostly women that I had slept with.

I felt this overwhelming need to apologize to many of those that I had treated badly. I say badly, I guess I just didn't treat them at all. And I felt bad about that. So I spent quite a bit of time apologizing to them, talking to them.

Some of them took that apology well, accepted it gracefully, and moved on. Others thought I was trying to sleep with them again. And a few decided I'd gone crazy. I didn't care. I was making conscious decisions again.

Conscious decisions. Thinking them through. Not decisions based on my sex drive, or with a fuzzy head. I was clean and sober for the first time in probably months.

I threw myself back into my work. I quit calling in, and started picking up extra hours. When that didn't fill up my time, I took on a few private jobs on the side.

Nothing illegal, just more mechanic work. People came to me and asked me to fix things for them. Like the local dirt track racer that didn't want to be affiliated with the garage. And there was a little older lady in the apartment down the hall. She had an ancient Ford that probably wasn't worth the money it would take to fix it, and she couldn't afford it anyway. I kept it running enough to get her around town, and tried not to take any money for it.

I worked all the time, partly to fill up my time, partly because I was ready to make some real money. I wanted to sock it away until I could make something of my life, something I could be proud of. And, maybe someday, something someone else could be proud of as well. And I worked to stay out of the apartment.

Sara and I were drifting apart. It's not that we didn't get along, we were just growing in different directions. I know, that's such an overused term, it sounds like a cop-out. But it isn't, it was true. We got along just fine. We were just becoming different people.

Okay, we had a few disagreements. But that was because I had my eyes opened, and my mind cleared, and it frustrated me to think that she was still blinded. I wanted her to see that she was wasting her life. And she wanted me to stop sounding like her mother.

And Sara was beginning to settle down, too. In her own way. With a girl named Annie. I remember the night she came in and told me. She came into my room in the middle of the night, and crawled into bed beside me. She did that sometimes, when she was feeling down, or just wanted to talk. She crawled into my bed and I waited, staring up at the darkness where the ceiling should have been.

Finally, she sighed. "Are you awake?"

"I'm awake. What's on your mind?"

"Bobbie, I think I found her."

I raised my eyebrows in the darkness. "Found her?"

"The one."

"The one." I repeated her words, waiting for them to sink in.

"Yes. She's incredible. She's sweet, and fun, and . . . she's everything. I think I love her."

Why did I suddenly feel like a mother letting go of her

child? I shouldn't have felt that way. Sara was an adult, she had every right to her own happiness, and her own mistakes. And I was happy for her. But I still felt a little sad. Like I was letting go of something precious and rare. I smiled, trying to sound cheerful.

"When do I get to meet her?"

"Tomorrow, if you like. I've invited her back."

"Great." I rolled over and hugged my friend, knowing that that was the last time we would lie there and talk like that. I knew it, and I couldn't change it. I wasn't sure I wanted to.

"I'm happy for you, Sara. Really happy for you."

"I'm happy too. But I'm worried about you."

"Don't worry about me. I'm gonna be fine."

"But you don't have anyone. We've always done things together, you know."

I smiled. "I know. But it's okay. Really. I'm not ready to settle down, you are. I'm happy for you."

She slept there beside me that night. And I knew it was the last time she ever would.

The next day I met Annie. She was lovely, I could see right away why Sara was attracted to her. Tall, slim, blond, she could have been a living Barbie doll. Party Barbie, always ready for a good time. Not that I didn't like her, I did. She seemed like someone who was great to be around, a lot of fun. And that's exactly where Sara was in her life. They fit each other. I wasn't sure that Annie was the one for Sara, but I did like her and I was happy for my friend. Happy that she had found someone that made her happy.

When Annie moved in, I moved out.

I found this little one-room flat at the top of a building down by the river. Well, I say one room, but it did have a separate bathroom, just a sink and a toilet in the corner, with walls and a door separating it from the rest of the apartment. The tub didn't fit in that little bathroom, it sat outside it. One of those great big claw-foot tubs that held, like, tons of water. Other than that, the place was completely bare.

You know those creaky old freight elevators with the metal accordion doors? I had one of those, going straight up to my flat. I used to walk my bike right into it and take it into the apartment with me. I loved it.

It was the first time in my life I had chosen my own place to live just because I liked it. When I lived with my parents I never had a choice, and when I first moved out on my own I just took the first place I found. Even when Sara and I moved into the apartment together, I didn't care what it was like, I let her pick it out. But this time I moved there because I liked it, it felt like a home to me. I know, you're thinking that a one-room flat, not in the best part of town, couldn't possibly feel like home. But it did to me. Maybe because it was the first place that was ever *mine*.

The apartment was no penthouse, but it was open and airy, with wood floors and huge windows. There was a row of support columns running up the center of the whole thing, the entire length, halfway between the windows and the back wall. And other than the ones around the little bathroom and the outside ones, there wasn't a wall to be found. I could have roller-skated in there. I loved all that open space. I always liked space anyway, I liked the outdoors. And without many walls, I didn't have to decorate much. I've never been very good at that sort of thing anyway (again, I feel your shock, you'd have pegged me as a real interior decorator, wouldn't you?). Matching colors and patterns is a concept I just don't get. My idea of fine art is car posters, maybe a special part or two. Oh, and that Snap-On Tools calendar. A staple for all mechanics who like women. I think there's a law somewhere that says we have to own one. Anyway, lots of windows, not too much decorating, it was perfect for me.

I went out and bought furniture. Wow, that was so cool. To buy things that I liked, not something to suit someone else. I found that I really liked wood. Dark wood. And simple pieces, with clean lines. I had never owned furniture before. It felt like such a grown-up thing to do, buying furniture, dishes, things for the apartment. And all of it was simple.

Some might call it plain, but to me it was simple. Simple, easy, clean. I made that place feel like a home. And it was my home. I finally had one.

And I had access to the roof. The elevator stopped at my apartment, but if you had a key you could take it one floor farther up. When you opened the door, you stepped right out into the open air.

I loved being on the roof. The wind was always blowing there, even on the hottest days. When it was warm I took car parts up there to work on them in the sunlight, with the breeze on my face. I remembered Agatha repeating my words. *Feel the rush of the wind as it lifts your hair and cools your face.* I could hear her voice in my mind, repeating those words as I lifted my arms and turned my face to the wind, thinking of her. Was that same breeze lifting her hair, cooling her face?

Yes, the roof was great during the day. But the nights! Oh, the nights I spent on that roof. I'd sit up there in the darkness above the city lights, and breathe in the air. The city smelled different at night, colder somehow.

The whole roof was mine. On one corner of the building, you could stand up there and watch the city lights, the cars traveling the streets, listen to the sounds, so distant and small, as if they were part of another world. But the opposite corner overlooked the river. The Missouri River, in all its muddy glory.

It was on that corner overlooking the river that I'd stand and lean over the safety ledge at the edge of the building at night. I loved being there. The sounds were nonexistent, and the smells that came from the docks and the river were faint, damp, and earthy. I'd stand there in the wind, looking out over the river at night, so much rolling darkness. And I would think. Think about my Agatha. My Maggie May.

I wondered about her. Where she was, how she was, if she ever thought of me. Was she lonely, like me? Was she wrecking someone else's bed? Was she happy?

I thought sometimes about driving. Getting on my bike

and riding back to that little town, back behind the park, out to those old railroad tracks. Riding back in time. But more often I'd just remember.

Remember everything about her. Every word she had ever said. Remember her eyes, her laugh. Her face, her voice, her touch. The way she smelled. The taste of her skin. That oh-so-agonizingly-slow-but-God-I-want-it-to-last-forever smile. That secret smile easing across her beautiful face and lighting up her eyes.

I understood then that every other woman had been an attempt to . . . forget her. Or maybe duplicate her. Every one. From the one-night stands to the short-lived relationships. Every one had been compared to her, and that wasn't fair to them. No one could compete with perfection. And perfection was easily attained in a memory.

I liked living there, in that place that was my own. It was so different than the first time I'd lived alone. The first time I'd shut myself off from the world, and I'd been consumed by loneliness. This time I wasn't. I learned how to be alone without being lonely. I found out that I had to enjoy my own company to do that. Not that I wasn't lonely, I was. I just wasn't consumed by it any longer. I could spend time alone without feeling uncomfortable with myself. It's hard to explain.

Maybe it sounds vain to you, but I liked myself. Always. Well, except for that time when I realized what I'd become, but I fixed that, and I could like me once more. I had my faults, yes, maybe more than most. But I could see the me behind that. I had always known that, even though I had done some bad things, I wasn't a bad person. Not that I thought I was better than anyone else, just that I never went through the self-hatred that so many people seem to go through. I knew I was all right with me, and I was all right with God. I had never even considered that I wasn't. I don't even think I knew that other people didn't feel that way until I met Angela.

*   *   *

I met Angela at work. She came in with a car problem (what else?) and I worked on it for her. It was actually a fuel problem, and I worked on it, but I didn't fix it.

Angela was a tiny girl, with short black curly hair, and big brown eyes. There was something about her that drew me, intrigued me. Have you ever met someone and just knew that you had to get to know them better? Like something was pushing you together, like fate, or destiny, or whatever. Angela was like that to me. She was so timid, like she was afraid of the world and everything in it. She seemed so fragile, so vulnerable.

I knew she didn't have the money to fix her car the way it should have been fixed (it's amazing, what you can tell about people by working on their cars), so I did a quick-fix job on it, just to get her where she needed to go, and told her to come back after closing time.

I guess I need to explain what work was like for me. I went in, I did my job, I went home. I worked with a garage full of men. Not that I didn't like some of them, they were pretty good guys, for the most part. A couple of them tried to be friendly with me. I don't mean flirty, I mean friendly. Like treating me like one of them. They'd ask now and again if I wanted to go out for a beer with the rest of them after closing, or come to the annual picnic lunch they put on each summer. I always turned them down, but they didn't give up. They never asked why I wouldn't go, and they never asked what I did away from the shop. I came in early sometimes, and stayed late. They never asked why, just accepted that I was a hard worker and left it at that. So I had some freedom there, with no questions asked. When I stayed over that night that I'd asked Angela to come back, no one looked at me twice.

We closed at nine, and I sat in that empty garage, waiting for Angela, and wondering why. I was drawn to her, but it wasn't like an attraction. I mean, she was attractive, but that wasn't what was pulling me toward her. I somehow knew that she needed help, and I thought I could give it to her. I don't know why I thought that, I just did.

I waited until ten that night, and she hadn't come. So I gave up. I was just locking the door when she pulled up. She rolled the window down partway when I walked over to her car.

"I didn't think you were coming."

She eyed me suspiciously. "I'm not sure I am. Exactly what do you intend to do?"

I closed my eyes, wondering why she was so afraid. Then I remembered how wary I was of Eric's kindness. I sighed.

"I just want to fix your car for you. You don't trust me, I understand that." I held up my hands. "You don't have to accept if you don't want to. I just wanted to help."

"Why?" She was so distrustful!

I shrugged. What could I say? That I wanted to help and I didn't know why? That I was drawn to her in some unexplainable way? "Honestly, I don't know."

She looked at me for a full minute before she nodded. "Okay."

I opened the garage and she pulled her car in. It was an old Volkswagen Beetle. I went around to the back and opened up the engine compartment. She got out and came around to watch. I held out the cordless phone to her. She looked at it as if it might bite her.

"What's this for?"

I smiled. "You look like I make you nervous. I thought you might feel better if you had access to call the police."

She took the phone and held it, looking relieved.

I started working on her car and we chatted a little. About the weather, the latest natural disaster on the news. The safe small-talk of strangers. When I couldn't think of anything else to say, I pointed to a little boom box in the bay.

"Wanna turn that on?"

"Okay." She pushed the power and got static. "What station?"

"Any, I don't care. Find something you like."

She turned the dial past several stations and landed on one playing Bruce Springsteen. I nodded my approval.

"That works for me."

"You like Bruce?"

I smiled, thinking of Sara. "Love him. Is there anyone who doesn't?"

Angela grinned and pulled a tape case out of her car. She held it open toward me. "Pick one."

I looked inside the case and laughed. She had everything he had ever put out, lined up neatly in chronological order. I picked one out and she popped it in the boom box.

We started talking about Bruce, and moved on to other music. We found that we had similar tastes. With something in common, our chat became easier. She seemed to become interested in what I was doing. I explained everything to her, and she handed me tools. Well, I had to describe them to her, but she caught on pretty quickly.

When I finished with her fuel lines I had her start it up for me. I noticed a flash in her taillights.

"You have problems with your lights?"

She shrugged. "Sometimes the dash lights go out."

I went around and lifted the hood. Glancing inside, I whistled. Angela came around behind me and leaned in. "What's wrong?"

"Your wiring system is a mess. Have you been having problems with anything other than the lights?"

She sighed. "Everything pretty much works. I have to turn off the radio to use the wipers, or I blow a fuse. But it's all right."

I shook my head. "I'd like to hit the guy that sold you this car."

She suddenly looked alarmed. "How bad is it?"

"I can't tell until I get in there for a better look. I think you have a lot of wires that don't go anywhere, and some that aren't properly grounded. I'd have to trace each wire to find out."

"You can do that?"

I glanced at my watch. It was almost midnight. "Piece of cake. But I don't think I can do it all tonight. And if I start, you can't drive it until I'm done."

She shook her head. "I have to have it tomorrow." She held out her hand. "Thanks for everything. What do I owe you?"

I smiled and shook her hand, noticing that she had put the phone down. I was glad that she was finally at ease. "Nothing."

"But I have to pay you! This is your job, you can't do it for free!"

I shrugged again. "I didn't use any new parts, and the job's not done. I'd like to fix this wiring for you. When can you come back?"

She took her hand from mine and eyed me, the suspicion back. "Are you trying to pick me up? 'Cause I get the feeling—"

I laughed, interrupting her. "No, I'm not. I just want to help."

And that was true. Picking her up was the furthest thing from my mind.

She eyed me again. "You're not trying to pick me up?"

I laughed again. "No."

"Then why are you being so nice to me?"

I sighed, thinking of Eric again. "Look, I don't want anything from you. Someone helped me out once, and it made a difference in my life. I just wanted to, I don't know, give back a little."

"I'm a charity case?"

"No, not charity. Simple kindness. Doesn't anyone do that anymore? Look, you can pay for anything that needs to be bought. But my time is my own, to give as freely as I wish. Okay?"

She looked at me a moment, then nodded. "Okay. But at least let me buy you a drink."

That surprised me. I didn't think she was old enough to drink, I thought she was even younger than me. I looked at her.

"Now, *you're* not trying to pick *me* up, are you?"

Her eyes widened with shock. I laughed. "Just kidding. I'll let you buy me a beer next time, okay? I'll order some new wire and some connectors, I think I can salvage the harness itself, that'll save some money. When can you come back?"

We made plans for her to come back to the shop after the parts were in. She thanked me again before she left, and promised not to be nervous next time.

I thought about Angela and her car a lot in the next few days. I don't know how to explain it, the feeling of being drawn to her. It wasn't that searing loneliness of needing a friend, or a physical attraction. I was just compelled to help her.

Now, when I look back on it, I think it was a higher force pushing us together. Fate, or destiny, or God, I don't know. But considering how much knowing her influenced decisions that I've since made in my life, perhaps she was the one helping me.

Angela showed up right after closing time, just as we'd planned. Right away, she put on some music, and I got to work. I had been right, her wiring was a mess. There were wires *everywhere* under there, running from this to that, ending at nothing. It was like untangling a bowl of dried spaghetti.

Angela chattered constantly as I worked, talking about a friend of hers. I wasn't really paying attention to her, or I would have caught it sooner. But I was completely in the hood, my head ducked down near the dash, and her chatter was muffled. And I was concentrating, so my attention wasn't really on her anyway. I was tracing a wire tangled through a large mass of more wires, when I suddenly realized I couldn't hear her anymore. I called out to her, but didn't get an answer. So I tucked my wire cutters in my back pocket and crawled out.

She was standing with her back against the car door, quietly crying. I was really concerned then, and tried to remember exactly what she had said last. I couldn't.

"Angela? What is it? What's wrong?"

"I can't." She whispered the words, sounding hopeless.

"Can't what?" I was wracking my brain trying to remember even the last subject she had been talking about.

"Be this person everyone expects me to be."

I reached out and put my hand on her shoulder. "Don't be what everyone else expects. Be yourself."

"That's just it, I *can't*." She wiped her eyes. "I love her. I know I'm going to hell for it, but I can't stop."

I was more than a little confused, but I put my arms around her and tried to comfort her. She almost collapsed against me, crying like I have rarely seen anyone cry. Sobs wracked her tiny body, I could almost see her heart pouring out with her tears.

I held her, letting her cry until she was finished.

She got herself under control and looked at me, her eyes swollen, red, and full of pain. "I'm sorry, Bobbie. I just don't have anyone else to talk to, and you've been so nice to me, and so easy to talk to . . . I thought you might understand . . . I don't mean to lay this on you."

I pushed her away a little, so I could look at her, and held her shoulders. "Hey, it's okay. But I don't understand. Explain it to me."

"Oh, God, I just . . . I just love her, and I know it's wrong. I'm gonna go to hell for it. I know I am, but I can't stop."

She started crying again. I didn't understand, but I tried. I did my best to comfort her.

She cried and talked to me for a couple of hours that night. Her thoughts and her words were broken, but I finally got the gist of it. She had been raised in a strict Catholic family. She had been taught all her life that homosexuality was a sin.

And she had fallen in love with a woman. She told me about trying to deny her feelings, fearing for her immortal soul. And how she couldn't.

Oh, she was so torn up inside, in so much pain that it hurt just to look at her. I tried, I tried everything I could think of to make her feel better. I'm no religious expert, nor do I claim to know the Bible forward and backward. But I just can't believe that a God that created love could damn a person forever for loving. I just don't see it. Nor do I see God making a mistake. He made Angela exactly like He wanted her, why would He send her to hell for being what He created? I told her these thoughts, but I don't think I was much help to her.

Angela did finally calm down enough that we could finish the wiring in her car. We were there nearly all night. Before she left I gave her my phone number and made her promise to call me, but I wasn't sure she would.

I went home that night feeling helpless. I stayed up for several more hours, trying to understand her feelings. I wanted to help her, I wanted to make a difference. Maybe I eventually did make a difference, I don't know. I hope so. But I never did understand.

Chapter Fifteen

Angela did call me, much to my surprise. We met again, at a little bar (not the same one, this one was a calm little place without a dance floor that she knew about) for drinks. And she *was* old enough to drink, she was in her last year of college. Nursing school, actually. Can you believe that? Someone so torn up about their own life, learning to help others.

We talked a lot. And drank a little. Not like I used to drink, we just sat and sipped maybe two drinks. I really was over that whole drinking to get drunk thing that I'd done the year before, thank God. Anyway, we talked. About nearly everything. Well, she did most of the talking, I listened. I learned to listen really well.

My first impression of Angela had been right. She was timid and fragile. She was afraid of so much. She was completely hidden from the world, so afraid of what people would do and say if she told them that she was gay. She couldn't even *say* the word *lesbian*.

She was amazed by me. Me, of all people. Me, the person who cut herself off from the world so she wouldn't have to face it. How could anyone think I was amazing?

Angela did. She said she couldn't believe that I was in a job where people would think I was gay. That I didn't date guys to cover, that I didn't care what people thought or did. She thought I was so brave. She was wrong.

I wasn't brave at all. My closet was different than hers, but it was still a closet. I didn't talk about my personal life anywhere other than the bar, with other gay people. And that wasn't brave, they all already knew. Hell, I didn't *have* a personal life to talk about. I wasn't afraid, I had just stopped myself from feeling, from caring. And that was a cage for me, just like her closet was for her.

We talked a lot that night, and many times after that. She quit coming to the garage to get her car worked on. She started coming to my apartment. I worked on her car a lot, more than I should have. What she really needed was a new car. But I kept it running, and she kept coming back. She usually came alone, but once in a while she brought her girlfriend, Cindy.

I had thought Angela was fragile and afraid, until I met Cindy. Cindy was so much worse. I don't mean she was bad, just that she made Angela look strong.

Cindy was fastidiously neat, and always polite. She was pretty, but in a way different than anyone else I knew. Her hair was the most awesome red, but it was lank and lifeless. Her delicate features were hardened by a constant frown. She just always seemed so unhappy. Dark. Not really unhappy, just dark, like she had spent her whole life fighting, and now she was wary of everything. She was kind and sweet, but in a distant way, like she always had something else on her mind. She was too thin, looking malnourished, frail, and delicate. And her eyes were . . . haunted. I don't know how else to describe them, sunken and dark, always darting around as if something were after her. As if she were hunted. Fearful. *Haunted.*

Yes, Angela was torn up inside, but Cindy was tormented. I talked to her too, trying to understand. I had never felt what they felt. I had never gone through the doubts, the spiritual questioning. Until I met them, I didn't know that not everyone accepted themselves like I had. I had realized that I was gay and just accepted it. I never questioned why, I just knew that I was the way I was created. I knew I could never do anything about it. It was just a part of me, like the color of my eyes. I didn't choose it, it chose me. I never thought about hating it.

Oh, I understood hatred, I'd faced that. But it was hard for me to grasp the idea of *self*-hatred. To hate yourself, to believe that God hates you, for being what you are. How horrible that situation must be. You don't need anyone else to hate and torment you when you feel that. You do it to yourself.

And as I listened to them, I realized that they might not be the only ones that felt that way.

I don't know what I was doing, but I think I was trying to save those girls. I knew that their torment wasn't the same as what I'd been through, but hell is still hell, right? I thought that somewhere I had something inside myself that could help them. I didn't know what or where, but I knew it had to be there, or we wouldn't have been pushed together. Even if it was just listening to them, I had to be able to do something. So I tried.

And I failed.

When I look back now, I think I should have seen the signs. I think I was so wrapped up in trying so hard to fix it that I missed the biggest problem. The signs were there, I should have seen them.

Don't get me wrong, I'm not blaming myself. I probably couldn't have stopped it. I just *wish* I could have. I wish I'd paid more attention to it, to *them,* instead of just their words. Maybe I could have seen it. After all, at one time I hadn't been so far from where Cindy was then.

No, I had never gone through the self-loathing, but I knew the desperation, the feelings of hopelessness. And the fear. I don't think there was much difference between where Cindy was then and where I had been a few years before.

But, just like everyone learns their own life lessons, everyone carries their own burdens, and fights their own demons. As much as I wanted to, as much as I tried, I couldn't bear the burden for Cindy, or walk her road for her. I could try to support her, but I couldn't help her fight her demons. And she lost the battle.

She committed suicide a few months after I met her.

That shook me to my very soul. Nothing in my life had ever prepared me for anything like that. I knew pain, I knew loneliness, and I knew loss. But I wasn't at all familiar with death. Much less sudden and violent death. I didn't know what to do.

I think I kept myself together by trying to hold Angela together. She was devastated. I think anyone would have been. What do you say to someone in that situation? *I* don't know. I don't think I said much at all. I let her cry. When she cursed God and swore at the world, I let her. I held her. When she was hysterical and needed to be restrained, I held her tighter. When her pain and fury drove her to the brink, and she had to scream and storm, I let her bring it to me. I let her cry, and I cried with her.

She talked a few times about following Cindy. About how she had to be with her, she couldn't live without her. How she couldn't let her go through hell alone. I stayed with her on those nights, staying up and watching her long after she'd cried herself to sleep. I watched her and wondered if I could stop her.

I couldn't save Cindy, but I'd like to say that I saved Angela. I'd like to say that. I'd like to be the hero here. But I'm not. I wasn't the only one who did everything I could for her. She had more friends than she thought, and we all did what we could to help her through. We stayed with her in shifts those first few weeks, not wanting her to be alone. Some of the ladies from her school came through for her. Even when they didn't understand her life, they understood the pain of losing one that you love. And one of the guys, I can't remember his name now, took her to church. I know, that sounds crazy, but it turned out to be just what she needed. This guy found a Metropolitan Community Church. They accepted Angela for who she was, and helped her accept herself.

It took a really long time, but she finally pulled herself together. I was always proud of her for that. I think maybe I was wrong about her. She wasn't as afraid and fragile as I'd first thought. Coming out of that situation alive, coming out *whole,* that took real courage, real strength.

Somewhere in there, during Angela's torture, I made the decision to come out. I mean, I had never really lied about who I was, but there were other things I did. I stayed out of all personal conversations. When the guys at work started talking about what they were going to do in the evening, I avoided them. I refused to comment when asked if I had anyone special, or asked if I would like to go out. (Yes, even I got asked out once or twice!) It had never been a big deal to me, I just chose my own closet.

But Cindy and Angela made me think. I began thinking about other people. Did some of them feel the same hopelessness that Cindy had? Did they go through the same self-hatred that Angela had? How many faced the brutality that Sara and I had faced in school? How many young people had followed Cindy's path to destruction, just because they couldn't imagine going through life gay? And how many just needed to know that they weren't the only one out there to make a difference? Would knowing a gay person change their lives? Would it have changed mine?

I didn't know the answer to any of those questions, and I still don't know them all now. But I did know that I could never find the answers if I didn't come out to the world.

So I did.

I didn't do it in a huge way. I mean, I didn't shout from the rooftops, or call the six o'clock news or anything. It was very small.

At first, I just quit avoiding those conversations at work. When the guys talked about maybe going out for a beer after work, I joined the conversations. I even joined them for a beer one night. When they asked if I had anyone, I told them I didn't but I wasn't going to stop looking. And finally, someone got up the courage to ask.

It was at work, and I can't remember his name. He was a young guy, younger than me, with a shock of red hair and a neck to match. I never did like him. He asked me out once, and I turned him down. It wasn't long before he started dating some waitress from one of the fast food joints down the street. It was well known around the garage that he treated her badly, and that she had cheated on him. But somehow they had managed to stay together.

So one day his girlfriend was there to pick him up after work. She had obviously been working herself, and looked tired. But she stood there patiently, off to one side, waiting, while he told some long joke to a group of four of five guys gathered around him. I said hello to her and listened to the joke. It was something crude and male oriented, but I found it funny at the time. I laughed.

He looked over at me. "What are you, a dyke?"

I looked back at him and smiled as sweetly as I could. "I really prefer the word lesbian, if you don't mind. Dyke is so crude, don't you think?"

The guys all guffawed at that, and he turned red enough to match his hair. "You stay away from my girlfriend. I better not catch you talking to her again."

That was too much. I mean, I'd just said hello to her. What, he thought I'd steal her away from him and recruit her to the other side by just saying hello? I found him ignorant and cruel, and I got angry.

"Buddy, if I was the least bit interested in her, she wouldn't be *your* girlfriend, she'd be *mine.*"

Oh, he was mad then. His red face turned purple. Really, purple. I thought he was going to explode. And maybe I shouldn't have prodded him, but I was just tired. Tired of the hiding, tired of the jokes, tired of people's ignorance. Tired. Or maybe it was a flashback to my stupid youth, I don't know. But I prodded harder. I grinned at his anger.

"And I'd have kept her satisfied enough to stay home."

That's when he blew. He yelled, "You bitch!" and lunged at me. But the other guys stepped between us, and a couple of them grabbed ahold of him.

"Let me go, I'm gonna kill that bitch!"

One of the guys holding him shook his head. "No, you're not. You're not touching her. You walked right into that, and you deserved it."

He glared at them before turning around and stomping off to his car. I heard him mumble something like "fucking dyke," but I didn't pursue it any further. I turned around and resettled my hat on my head. I was shaking. I had just come out in front of what? Five of my coworkers.

One of the guys reached out and clapped my back. "That was a good one, Bobbie. A real good one!"

I squared my shoulders and turned to face them. "Sorry if I offended anyone. I didn't mean to."

One of them laughed. "Naw, he deserved it."

Another guy looked at me. "You're really a . . ." He stopped there. I don't know if he was searching for the right word, or if he just wasn't ready to say it. I raised my eyebrows and helped him out.

"Lesbian? Yes, I am. Does that matter?"

He shook his head. "Nope, I figured as much anyway."

Another shook his head. "I didn't. I didn't know. You never told me."

"You never asked."

They looked at each other kind of funny, and that was the end of it.

By the next day everyone knew. Just like high school, the word spread before I even got to work. I guess it wasn't a big shock to most of them. They had suspected or even assumed that I was gay, so they didn't really react much at all. A few of the guys that didn't know me as well saw how the others accepted me, and I guess they didn't think much of it either.

Oh, there were some that made a few comments, even avoided me, but it didn't really matter to me. What mattered was that I was finally living honestly, and I think a lot of people respected me for that.

So my coming out that night started out as such a small thing. But it grew. I discovered that I had a say in the world. I had a voice. And sometimes people listened to it. A lot of people. They asked questions, I answered them as honestly as I could. Most of them just needed to talk to someone who was "different" to realize that they aren't so very different after all.

And it got bigger. I found organizations, started participating in rallies. We had them back then, you know, they just weren't anywhere near what they are these days. Back then, we were mostly underground, at least in the part of the country that I lived. I mean, there were quite a few gays living in the Westport area, and most straight people avoided Memorial Park at night. They called it Queer Hill. They said it with contempt, but they avoided it. And that made it ours. Our space, at least after dark. And the dark was our time to be out and bold.

Like I said, it wasn't anything like what people do today, but we had our moments. We didn't have any public figures to stand with us, but a few supported us from the background. We'd gather up in force, march around with signs, demand equal rights. And almost every time there were more than a dozen of us in one place, the news cameras would show up. It wasn't real news then, just human interest tagged on at the end of the broadcast. But it was there.

And it kept growing. I never intended to become political, but somewhere along the way it just happened. I found myself speaking publicly. I'm not sure how it happened. One minute I was calmly explaining to someone that I just wanted to live without fear, the next minute I had a microphone in front of me. And I don't think I'm a great speaker at all, but people were paying attention. So I got louder. And louder. And somewhere along the line I lost my focus. I didn't lose my voice, but I lost my listeners.

You see, when I started out I was fighting for equal rights for everyone. Then it became very personal to me. I lost sight of that equality-for-everyone goal. I began to fight for myself, my community, my people.

Then I found myself one day, standing behind a podium in front of a bunch of people that had been beside me all the way. And I was yelling about lesbian rights.

And as I yelled, I saw people turning away. People that had been marching beside me, carrying signs, suddenly weren't interested anymore. And I realized that I was fighting a lost cause.

Then it hit me. The seventh Great Revelation in my life. Fighting for anything alone won't get you anywhere. There aren't enough people who care about lesbian rights alone to make a difference. And those that had been standing beside me didn't care about just my rights. They had their own fights, too. If I wanted their support, I had to support them. I have to fight for everyone's rights, or I can't expect anyone to fight for mine.

That was a huge eye opener for me. I know, I should have seen it sooner, but I hadn't thought about it. I was so wrapped up in my cause, and yelling about it, to notice anyone else's. And how could I expect them to help me if I didn't help them? It was so simple. And suddenly it made perfect sense.

I changed my tune, I stopped yelling "lesbian" and started yelling "everyone." And I didn't just talk about it. I began to do everything I could to achieve equal rights for everyone. All women. All minorities. *Everyone.* What a concept.

And some of those people that had turned away began to turn back.

*   *   *

And that's how knowing Angela changed my life. Without even knowing it, she showed me that I needed to come out. Not only for myself, but for all those who couldn't. And it all snowballed from there.

Angela. It took her nearly a year before she recovered from the loss of Cindy and accepted herself as a worthwhile person. Like I said, I didn't save her, I wasn't a hero. But I'd like to think that I had a little to do with her recovery. She turned out just fine, though, whether I had anything to do with it or not. She found love again, eventually. That was really cool. She and I were out having a drink one night, after yet another long day working on her car, when Sara came into the bar. I introduced them, and they became fast friends. It was years later that they got together, but they eventually did, and still are today.

But now I'm getting ahead of myself.

I was young, healthy, living out loud. I was seven lessons into knowing everything I needed to know in my life. I liked my apartment, I liked my job, I liked myself. I felt like I was the kind of person I should be. I was doing something with my life, I was proud of who I'd become. I was alone, but I wasn't lonely. I had friends, I had things that I believed in. Oh, there was something missing, I wasn't complete. But I was doing well.

Things were going along according to my plans, well, my revised plans anyway, until I was twenty-two. That's when my world turned upside down once again.

Chapter Sixteeen

Well, this was a long time ago, and a lot of things were changing. Not as much as they have since, but they were. It was becoming easier to live openly. Not as easy as it was a decade later, and not as easy as it is today (and it's still not as easy as it should be), but better than it had been when I was outed nearly a decade before. The world was finally catching up to me. Or at least it was beginning to.

Like I said, I was twenty-two, living the kind of life that I wanted, and becoming the kind of person I wanted to be. It was spring, the country was living on the brand-new Reaganomics system. Seger was running "Against the Wind," Springsteen's "Hungry Heart" began to "Fade Away," and the Stones were *Sucking up the Seventies*. I was working. Working at the shop, and working on living life the way I wanted to, the way I thought I should.

And I was hard at it one beautiful morning, a Friday, one of those days when the temperature is just right, the sky is blue, and the world looks good. One of those days that make you think that anything can be possible. That's when my little world rocked on its axis once again.

It was a busy morning already, all the bays were full, cars on every lift, when Mr. Davis came into the garage and told me his oil light was on.

By that time in my career I usually didn't crawl around

under cars anymore. That's what the lifts are for. But that morning the lifts were all occupied, and Mr. Davis was a special customer. He was a sweet older man, and he'd been bringing his ancient Buick to me for years. He had switched to that garage because of me. He swore I was the only one who could make his car run. He was the high school principal, and a quick glance at my watch told me that he'd be in a hurry. A quick check of his oil told me he was really low, and a glance behind his car told me why. There was a trail from under that old car leading back the way he had come, as far as I could see. So I grabbed a creeper and rolled under his car.

I found the problem quickly enough (leaking oil isn't hard to spot), the drain plug wasn't in all the way. I tightened it up, but I could feel it slipping and I knew it was beginning to strip. I was tightening it up enough to hold him over and thinking about how much oil I needed to replace when I heard a voice call out to him. My hands froze on the wrench I was using and that voice echoed in my head.

"Mr. Davis, is everything all right? Do you need a ride?"

"Oh, Agatha. Yes, everything is fine, or at least it will be. I just have an oil leak, but Bobbie's going to fix me right up."

My heart jumped into my throat, and for a moment I couldn't breathe. I knew that voice. I'd heard it every day for so long, and I still heard it in my dreams. There was only one Agatha in the world who had a voice like that.

I swallowed that lump in my throat that felt like my heart, took a deep breath, and rolled out from under the car. As I stood up, Mr. Davis stepped aside and I saw her.

The years hadn't changed her at all. She stood there in her heels and tweed skirt, her golden hair put up in a neat bun. She was just as beautiful as that first time I'd seen her, so many years ago, standing in that ditch with my hand in hers.

I looked into her eyes and I swear, as stupid and corny as it might sound, I could almost see the sparks fly.

Mr. Davis was still speaking. ". . . can tell you, Agatha, this is the place to bring your car. That Bobbie can work wonders. She's kept my old rust bucket on the road way beyond its years."

Agatha raised one eyebrow as she looked me up and down. I felt my breath quicken, I knew what she was seeing. The grease-stained blue jumpsuit, the work boots, the bandanna tied over my hair. Did she see other things there as well? The maturity in my face? Could she see the lessons I'd learned, the way they'd changed me? Or the increased muscle mass beneath that jumpsuit? The pounding of my heart? She never showed any recognition, never even paused.

"Has she now? Well, I'll have to remember that. You never know when I'll need some work done." She offered her hand to me and I wiped mine on a shop towel before I shook it, closing my eyes and trying to control the shiver caused by her touch.

"How late are you open?"

I cleared my throat, feeling like I needed to swallow my heart again, and turned around to pour oil into the car. "We're open till nine, no appointment needed. I'd be happy to help you out any way I can."

She nodded once. "I'll keep you in mind then. Mr. Davis, if you're all right here, I'd better be going."

He smiled at her the way a father smiles at his favorite child. "Yes, of course, I'll just be a few moments late."

"I'll be sure to tell them." She turned to me. "Bobbie, it was nice seeing you."

She graced me with one of her smiles, slowly turning up one corner of her mouth, spreading across her face, and lighting up her eyes before reaching the other corner of her mouth and pulling it up. That secret smile I had seen in my dreams, had longed to see in the light of day. Then she turned and walked deliberately to her car.

Mr. Davis watched me watch her with a strange smile on his lips. "How are we coming along, Bobbie?"

I jumped just a little, and hurried to pour the oil in his car. "Just fine, sir. I'm almost done here."

He leaned in close and clapped me on the back as he watched me. "I tell you, Bobbie, that woman is about as good with students as you are with cars. I wish we had ten more just like her."

I coughed. "Yes, sir, I'm sure you do." I tried to sound noncommittal as I put to oil cap back on. "I'm all done here. You're due in for a full oil change, but that plug is just about stripped out. We don't carry any that old here, but I'll order you one."

I closed the hood and rapped it once with my knuckles. "Just take it easy on her until we get her all fixed up. I should be able to get that plug in for you by Monday, if you want to swing by after school."

"That'll be fine, thank you." He reached for his wallet. "What do I owe you for today?"

I shook my head. I just wanted him to leave. "You're in a hurry, I'll just write a ticket and keep it open. We'll take care of it Monday."

"Are you sure? I can . . ."

Just go! I wanted to scream at him. I opened his car door and motioned him inside. "You're going to be late, Mr. Davis. Any problems over the weekend and you can have the garage call me at home."

He climbed into his car and thanked me again before he left. I wanted to slam the door and run, but I forced my face into something like a smile, shut the door calmly, and waved him out of the drive.

I went out back and found one of the guys smoking. I bummed a cigarette from him. He handed it to me, lit it, and grinned.

"I didn't know you smoked."

"I don't."

"Unless you see a ghost."

My eyes widened, I must have looked comical. "What?"

"You look like you just seen a ghost, pal."

I breathed in the smoke. I hadn't smoked in years. It tasted awful and made me cough. "I think I did."

"Anybody famous?"

I shook my head. "Just my Maggie May."

He raised his eyebrows. "Maggie May?"

I waved my hand at him, blowing smoke. "It's a long, complicated story."

He nodded and offered me another cigarette. I waved him off and he stood to go back to work. "Hey, Bobbie?"

"Yeah?"

"Tell me that story sometime, okay? I'd like to hear it."

I smiled at him as he walked away. *I don't think I can ever tell that one.* I tossed away the cigarette, unfinished. I had hoped it would calm my shaking a little. It didn't.

I don't know how I made it through that day. I half expected Agatha Claraday to walk in any minute. I was afraid she would. I was afraid she wouldn't. I knew she wouldn't. But I was afraid anyway. I was a bundle of raw nerves.

And it only got worse in the afternoon. When the buses started going by, I knew school was out. My shaking returned. I couldn't keep my hands on the tools, or my mind on the job. I dropped things, I turned bolts the wrong way. I just kept waiting, and shaking. Two hours before quitting time the boss told me I was useless and sent me home.

I didn't stay home any longer than it took me to shower and get dressed. I went out for a drink.

I didn't go to the dance club, I went to the little bar that Angela and I had spent so many quiet evenings in. They call it a "neighborhood bar." It didn't have a dance floor, the jukebox wasn't turned up very loud, and there weren't many people going there anymore.

I went there for the peace and quiet. No one gets wild there, no one's there to pick anyone up. And there wasn't anyone that I knew, no one that would ask any questions. There was hardly anyone there at all. It was just a little bar with a jukebox and a couple of pool tables. Just right to have a beer and calm my nerves.

I was standing at the jukebox, thumbing through the songs without really even looking at them. An arm reached around me, set a beer in front of me on the song list, and pushed a button.

I turned around and there she was, standing so close that I could smell her light perfume, holding a beer of her own. Agatha. My Maggie May.

She blinked slowly and smiled. "You're a tough woman to find."

I tried to keep the tremble out of my voice. "Not if I know someone's looking. How'd you manage?"

"I started at the garage. I thought you'd be there until closing, but you weren't. They sent me to a place across town. You weren't there, either, but Sara was. She called your house. When you didn't answer, she sent me here." She stepped back from me, making it a little easier for me to breathe. "Can we talk?"

"Sure." I smiled at her, sort of. I tried anyway. "Step into my office."

I pointed at a little corner table and we sat down. She put her head in her hands. I barely heard her whisper, "I don't know where to start."

I reached over and touched her wrist, she dropped her hands and looked at me. I smiled. "How about with hello?" I gazed into her hazel eyes, half covered with blond curls. "You haven't changed at all. You're beautiful."

She blushed slightly. "And you look great. You've built up a bit. And your hair's longer."

I shrugged. "I guess. You look exactly the same. Beautiful as ever."

She blushed again. "But I'm not the same."

"No?"

"No." She shook her head. "How have you been?"

I shrugged. "Okay, I guess. I love my job, I've got an apartment I like . . . you know. I do all right." I sighed. "I think about you a lot."

"Oh, Bobbie, I think about you a lot, too. All the time." She looked up at me. "Are you seeing anyone?"

"Not really." I picked up my beer and started to drink.

"Would you like to?"

I almost choked on my beer. "What?" I couldn't believe what I thought I'd just heard. I looked at her.

She ducked her head. "I'd understand if you didn't want to . . ." She looked back up at me again, her eyes looked so frightened, half hidden beneath her hair. "But I'd love to go out with you."

I was stunned. I mean *stunned*. For a moment I couldn't think. I couldn't even feel my mouth to speak. I was right back in that bar years ago, seeing her there and not believing it. Here was the one woman I would have done anything for, the one I could never have. And I thought I'd heard . . . Was I dreaming? I blinked, hard.

"Bobbie?" She looked worriedly at me. "Bobbie?"

I shook my head. "I'm sorry." My brain felt cluttered and jumbled with confusion. I shook my head again, trying to clear it. "I thought I just heard you ask me out."

She nodded. "I did. But I understand if you don't want—"

"No!" I interrupted. "No. I mean yes. I want to. I want . . . I just . . . I'm a little surprised. Shocked." I shook my head, trying to rattle my brain back to working order.

"You said—"

She held up her hand. "I know what I said. I was wrong. I'm ready now, if you'll still have me."

"Have you? My God, why wouldn't I?"

"You've changed, Bobbie. And I have too. I'm finally ready for you, but have you grown past me?"

I looked at her, still as incredible as the first time I'd seen her. I did want her, I'd never stopped. But now I had a past that I wasn't proud of, I was even ashamed of. Would she still want me if she knew?

I took a deep breath. I wanted her, but I wanted her with-out surprises, without . . . I don't know. I guess I just didn't want her to go into anything blind, and be knocked over later. I let that breath out slowly and looked her in the eye.

"I haven't grown past you. But there are other things . . ."

"I know. There are a lot of things that are different. That's okay."

I wasn't so sure it was okay. "Do you know that I'm out now? Really out?"

She nodded. "I know. Is there somewhere quiet we can go? Just to talk?"

"Sure." I smiled. "Anywhere you want."

She giggled.

"What?"

"Do you realize that this is the second time I've followed you to a bar with the full intention of taking you home?"

I grinned back at her. "But this time, Maggie May, I don't have to go back to school."

We did go somewhere quiet. We went to my apartment. I opened the door and she stepped inside.

"Oh, wow. I love this, Bobbie. It's beautiful."

I turned around and closed the door, proud of my home, but embarrassed that she liked it so much. "Aw, I don't know about beautiful. But it's home."

She looked around, running her hands across the dark wooden furniture, walking over to the tub. There was a small, freestanding cabinet that I had put next to it. She touched the items there, picked one up, and looked at me, one eyebrow raised.

"Scented oils? Bubble bath?"

I blushed darker and shrugged. "I like a nice hot bubble bath."

She smiled. "I never knew that. And it's so out of character for you. I'd have guessed you to be the hot, quick shower type, not the long, soaking bath type."

I shrugged again. "I would have agreed with you a year or

so ago. But I've discovered a few things about myself since then."

"Like that you enjoy baths?"

"Like that." I followed her to the windows.

She looked out and sighed. "What a view."

"I've got a better one. Follow me."

I took her into the elevator and closed the accordion door, leaving the wooden one open. As it moved up to the roof, the breeze began to blow in, bringing the city smells with it. I opened the door for her and followed her out.

She inhaled deeply, and seemed to lift somehow. "Oh."

"Is something wrong? Do you want to go back down?"

She turned to me and smiled. "No. It's incredible here. This is yours?"

"Yes. I come up here a lot. I like it here."

I led her to the edge of the building and showed her the city laid out before and below us. Then I went to the other corner. She followed me to that edge, on the river side, and leaned over, breathing the cool spring air in deeply.

"This is beautiful, Bobbie."

I brushed the hair out of my face. "It is."

"You spend a lot of time up here."

It was a statement, not a question, but I answered it anyway.

"Yes, I do. A lot of nights. I love it up here. It's cool, the wind blows almost all the time."

She smiled. "Does it lift your hair and cool your face?"

I smiled back at her. "Yes, it does. And it helps me think."

"What do you think of, up here all alone?"

"I think of you."

"Me." She smiled.

"Yes. You know, wondering where you are, what you're doing, if you're happy. Remembering."

"Remembering?"

I wanted so badly to take her in my arms, kiss her. "Every moment, every look, every touch."

"Any regrets?"

"About you?"

She nodded.

I shook my head. "Only that I couldn't hold on tighter."

She reached over and touched my hand. "You can hold me tight now."

And I wanted to, more than anything. But could I, really? "Agatha, I'm not sure I can. A lot has happened. A lot has changed. I've changed."

"I expected that. I didn't expect to find you the same. And I expect that I've done some changing, too. Bobbie, I'm not asking for an immediate lifelong commitment. I just want a chance."

I touched her soft face. I wanted to give us that chance. But I couldn't, not without being completely honest. "I'm not sure you do. Come sit down with me."

She followed me to the lawn chairs I had set up there, and sat down. And I began to talk.

I told her nearly everything that night. I told her that I was active in equal rights, including gay rights. I explained that I was involved on every level, I was vocal, I was even seen on the news once. I wanted to be sure she knew how out I was, how visible I was as a lesbian. I didn't want her to be shocked when she was accused of being one just for being seen with me. Anyone seen with me would eventually be outed, like it or not.

She nodded. "I'm not sure I'm ready to shout to the world, but I'm ready to stop hiding."

"Are you sure?" I shook my head. "Make no mistakes, Agatha, you have to be sure. Once you're out, there's no going back. It can get pretty ruthless out there. I don't want you to get hurt."

She laughed quietly. "Bobbie, for someone so young, how'd you get to be so old? So wise?"

I shrugged. "I don't know. Just lived a lot, I guess."

"I think you really have. So, if I'm ready for this, will you go out with me?"

I smiled. "I'd love to, but there's one more thing."

"Yes?"

"I didn't wait for you, Agatha."

"I didn't expect you to. I told you not to."

"I know. I just want you to know that there have been others. A lot of others."

She looked at me expectantly. I rubbed my face and plowed on. "There was a period of time . . . when I was . . ." I shook my head. "I don't know, I was looking for something, I guess. I looked really hard. In a lot of places. With a lot of women. A *lot*."

"A lot? What does that mean?"

"It means a lot. Look, I'm not proud of it, I just want to be honest with you. I didn't wait for you. I did anything and everything I wanted. *Anyone*." I shook my head. "I wish I could go back and change it now, but I can't."

She nodded. "I understand. I expected you to live your life. I'm surprised you don't have someone now."

I sighed. "Not for a long time."

She ducked her head again and refused to meet my eyes. "Did you love anyone?"

"Once."

"What happened?"

I reached over and lifted her face. Tears were threatening to spill from her eyes and she looked frightened.

"You tell me, Maggie. It was you. Still is."

She smiled through those threatening tears. "I'm still your Maggie May?"

"It's a compliment, you know. Does it bother you?"

"No. It's just . . . I don't always feel like the older woman around you."

"You shouldn't. I've grown enough to realize that age, like so many other things, is relative."

She raised her eyebrows and smiled that slow, secret smile. "Like so many other things."

I smiled back at her and we sat there gazing at each other for a long couple of minutes. Then I sighed.

"So, I've told you all the complications. Do you still want to go out with me?"

"Yes."

"Then yes." I reached out and took her hand. "You once said that we could never be, and you could never be out. What changed?"

She dropped her face into her other hand. "Where do I start?"

I smiled at an old memory. "I'm up for a story, if you are."

She laughed softly. "Yes, I'm up for it. But where do I start?"

"At the beginning?"

"I'm not sure where that is."

"How about the last time I saw you?"

"I could try that." She took a deep breath.

The last time I saw you (she said) was at your graduation. I remember telling you that it was so hard to see you in class every day. Well, not seeing you was worse. I felt alone and . . . lost.

At the beginning of the summer I went to see my parents. They tried really hard to cheer me up, and I tried to be cheerful for them. I guess I didn't do a very good job. My mother started asking about men again, and I just couldn't take it anymore. I felt like she was putting me in a trap, and I couldn't get out. I just couldn't listen to her any longer.

So I decided to leave. My father begged me to stay, telling me that Mom was just worried, she just wanted to see me happy. I wanted to tell him that I couldn't be happy, but I couldn't do that, either. But, oh, I wanted to. Had it been the other way around, my mother instead, maybe. But I wasn't as close to my father as I was with my mother. I wasn't comfortable talking to him about any relationship, much less you. I wanted to tell him, I wanted to tell Mom, but I couldn't. And I couldn't stay without doing it. So I left.

I went home, and you were gone. I threw myself into my work, hiding within it, just like I've always done. Lesson plans, studying up on everything I was going to teach, I even took a few summer correspondence courses. I did everything I could to keep my mind occupied.

And just before school started my mother died.

I went back to my father's house to help him make funeral arrangements, help him get through, get back on his feet. I wasn't planning to stay any longer than that, but he kept asking me to.

So I turned in my resignation and found some substitute work closer to him. I thought he was asking me to stay because he needed my help. Now I don't think he needed my help at all, I think he wanted to help me.

I ended up spending almost a year with him. Summer came again, and with it my thoughts turned to moving on. Even though Dad was there, and our relationship was growing, I needed to move on, I needed to . . . be free. Well, I guess Dad noticed my restlessness, because he suddenly decided to have a talk with me.

I was cleaning the kitchen, thinking about you, thinking about going somewhere, anywhere. I didn't know where, I just wanted to go. Just get in the car and drive until I ran out of road. Fly. Dad came in and sat at the table, and just watched me for the longest time. Finally, he caught my arm and asked me to sit down with him.

I sat and looked at him. He looked so old to me, so haggard and worn. He tried to smile, but all I really noticed was how badly he was shaking. It was a long time before he spoke, and when he did, his words shocked me.

"Who is she?"

"What?" I honestly didn't know what he was talking about at first. When it dawned on me, I thought I could cover it up with my initial surprise.

He shook his head, seeing right through me. "Agatha, don't you think it's time you start telling me the truth? Come now, I'm not such an old fool that I can't see my own daughter's unhappiness. You left this house last time because your mother was pushing you to find a man."

"Dad—" I wanted to stop him, I wanted to get up and walk out, or scream, or anything, just put an end to this conversation before it went any further.

"Just hush." He held up his finger. "It's hard enough for me to get through this without you interrupting." He sighed so deeply, like he was gathering his courage.

"Your mother pushed. She didn't mean to upset you, but she did. You and I both know why you haven't found a man. I think your mother knew it too, she just couldn't face it. She died never knowing the real you. Don't make me do the same thing."

He leaned forward and took both my hands in his, looking at me earnestly.

"I love you. I want to be included in your life. You're all I have in this world. If we can't be honest with each other, what kind of relationship do we have?"

I shook my head, wanting to say no, wanting him to take it all back. But I was crying and couldn't even speak.

Dad got a little teary eyed. "You're my *child,* Agatha. I'd do anything, I'd go through anything, to see you happy. But you haven't been happy in a long while. I didn't have the strength to bring it up when you were here last, but now I have to. Because I can't stand to see you this way. Will you tell me?"

I still couldn't speak, I just shook my head.

"Then I'll tell you. I think you've found someone, someone you're unhappy without. And I think you've not told me because it's not a man. Who is she?"

That's when I really fell apart. All the tears, all the words, came out in one big flood. I told him everything. I told him that I was gay. I told him that I had always known, and that I had never planned to tell him. I told him how I hadn't told him and Mom because I didn't want to hurt them.

My father held me while I cried, just like he had when I skinned my knee as a little girl. He stroked my hair and told me everything would be all right again. He held me until I cried myself out, and told me that he loved me. There I was, delivering what I thought was the worst possible news to him, and *he* was comforting *me*.

Then he held me away from him and asked again. "Who is she?"

I shook my head and wiped my eyes. "Someone I can't have."

"I don't believe there's anyone who wouldn't be honored to have a woman like you. If you love her like this, she must care about you."

"She does, or at least she did."

"Then why can't you be with her?"

"She was my student."

"Your student. You didn't pressure her?"

"No, of course not! I would never do that! She was already out to the world, I wasn't even the first woman . . ."

I stopped, realizing again that I was talking to my *father,* I couldn't say that to him.

He closed his eyes. "Your student." He took a deep breath and let it out slowly, thinking. "Is she still?"

"No."

"Is she of age?"

"Yes."

"And she loves you?"

"She did. I don't know how she feels now."

"Then it shouldn't be a problem. If she is of age, and she loves you, I don't see what difference it would make how you met."

"I don't even know where she is. I told her that it could never be. A teacher and her former student? Society would never accept us."

"Society may never accept you anyway. But who has to know that she was your student? I believe that there is someone out there for every person in this world. I don't pretend to know why for you that someone is a girl, but if that's the case, then so be it. And to hell with what people will think. Society isn't always right. You have done exactly what society expected of you all your life. You can't spend the rest of it miserable because you are afraid of what people will think. You're stronger than that."

"I don't think I am, Dad. I saw the way she was treated, and I don't think I'm strong enough to face that."

"You're as strong as you need to be. I taught you that God never throws you anything you can't handle. You just need to decide if it's worth the pain." He paused and looked away from me. "You'd be surprised what you can live with . . . or without."

I realized then just how much he missed Mom. And for the first time, he and I knew the same pain, the same loneliness. His love was gone forever, and I didn't know where mine was.

Then he turned back to me and said something I'll never forget.

"You go find her, Agatha. If she is truly the one, you find her and tell her. Then you bring her to me. I want to meet the person that stole my little girl's heart."

After that conversation with my father, I drifted around for a while, going from school to school, taking jobs wherever I could find them. There were a few full-time offers, but I turned them down. Then this position came open and I took it almost without thinking. It somehow just felt right.

This is my second year here. I like the school, I like the people I work with. I like it here. But I've never gotten you off my mind. I was thinking about moving on, trying someplace new. In fact, I had just talked to Mr. Davis earlier this week about this being my last year.

Then I saw you.

I think that's why I came here, and why I stayed. I think we are meant to be together, Bobbie. I don't know why, or how, but I think this is what's supposed to be.

I again watched her struggle through her story, wanting to hold her when the tears ran down her face, wanting to stop her and tell her it was all right when she choked up. Then she said those last words.

I looked at her. "I think you're right. Fate, destiny, God, I don't know, but I believe that."

"Yes, I believe."

I had always felt that she was the one for me, now I knew that she felt it too. I wanted to take her in my arms and never let her go.

Chapter Seventeen

Well, I guess Agatha marched right into Mr. Davis's office Monday morning and told him that she would probably not leave at the end of that year.

He asked me about it when he came in for his oil change that afternoon. He watched me fix that old Buick of his, followed my into the office to pay, and stopped there. He looked at me.

"Bobbie," he said, "Agatha Claraday came into my office today."

"Yes, sir?" I was trying not to show him anything. I didn't know what she had told him.

"Yes, she did. She marched right in there and told me that her plans had changed and she'd be staying on with us because she found what she was looking for."

"Well, I guess that's good, right? You said you liked the way she teaches."

"Yes, yes, I did. But she's been looking for something, and she's finally found it. You wouldn't know what that was, would you?"

I shrugged.

"It wouldn't be you, now, would it?"

"Sir?"

"She told me this morning that she was gay. And I know she was ready to leave until she saw you the other day. I saw the way you two looked at each other. Now she's staying. Are you what she was looking for?"

I stood there, not sure what to say to him. "Well, I did know her several years ago. I . . ."

He reached out and offered me his hand. "If you're the reason she's staying here, you have my blessing. I wish you the best."

I grinned at him and shook his hand.

And he shook my hand every time he saw me after that.

Agatha and I took our relationship slowly that first few months. We spent a lot of time together. We went for long drives, and long walks. We sat up on my roof night after night, and we talked. We talked about everything, our hopes and dreams, our thoughts on everything from politics to bubble gum.

The more I talked to her, the more I realized that she was right all those years ago. I didn't know her at all. I mean, I knew her, but I didn't know the real her, the deeper part that takes time to get to know. And as I came to know her, I was more and more amazed at what a wonderful person she was. I found that I loved her more each day.

So that's what we spent that time doing, getting to know each other. And I found out that I had been wrong about her. That first time I had seen her in the bar, I thought she was the picture of the perfect woman. I discovered that she wasn't a picture, she was perfect, at least for me. She became my best friend, my confidante, my partner in everything. And only after all of that, did she become my lover.

And then we couldn't be apart anymore. She moved in with me.

I'm not sure why we chose my apartment instead of hers. Her place was in a better part of town, but mine seemed more like home. Of course it did to me, but Agatha liked it better, too. And it seemed more private. I think we wanted that privacy as much as anything else, to be able to be to-

gether without other people around for a while. Not to separate ourselves, not at all. Just to be . . . us.

Well, I guess the rumor that she was gay had been floating
around the school for a while, we didn't realize it. When she
moved in with me it confirmed that rumor, at least as far as
the school was concerned. She started getting some flak from
it at work. Not much at first, and she was somewhat prepared. I mean, we knew it would happen eventually. But the
first time something was said in front of her, she came home
crying.

Mr. Davis showed up on our doorstep the next evening.
He sat and had a long talk with us about how bad he thought
it was going to get, and about how he was going to stand behind us. And he did. But he was right, it did get worse.

It got a lot worse, for her anyway. There were letters of
complaint sent to the school board, even a nasty editorial in
the local paper that talked about how "those people" shouldn't
be in a position to influence kids. Mr. Davis was true to his
word, and stood up for her, writing letters to the editor about
how teachers should be judged on their teaching skills instead of who they choose to live with. I loved him for that.

And the students didn't seem to care at all. At least most of
them. Agatha was a great teacher. She was fair. She was fun.
I think that's all most of those kids cared about. There were
some that were cruel, but not too many, and they didn't take
it very far. Mr. Davis and the rest of the staff made sure of
that. Well, *most* of the staff.

It got so bad that a group of parents decided to petition
the school board to fire her. They all signed their paper, and
showed up at the next school board meeting. That's when the
greatest thing happened. The students, some of them the children of the people trying to get her fired, grouped together
with some parents that supported her and some of the faculty, and showed up at the same meeting to counter.

You should have seen them! They were all filing in to support her, to fight for her job. Man, it was like an old western showdown. Mr. Davis was with them, and so many of the other teachers. There must have been seventy of them in all. All those people came, willing to stand up for her, even against their own parents and coworkers. They loved her that much. I was so proud of them, and of her.

And she kept her job.

There were other consequences to her coming out. Or being outed, I guess that's closer to it. Most of them have been small things, some big. Mostly bad.

I repainted her car a few times. And patched a lot of tires, replaced the headlights a couple of times. I even replaced the windshield once. She put up with some graffiti on the bathroom walls, but the verbal comments were kept to a minimum. And there was never any kind of physical attack on her at all. Mr. Davis made sure of that.

But there were a few good things that came out of it all. A harassment policy was implemented, and I think that helped a lot of people, students and teachers alike. And students began to come out to Agatha. Slowly at first, but the group grew. It seemed like there were more all the time.

There is now a support group at that school for gay and bisexual kids. Agatha started it (well, I helped, but she did all the hard stuff) after I told her about Cindy, and those kids started coming out to her. Getting that going was a hard fight, and she was persecuted for it. Horribly.

It took almost two years to get it going, but Agatha stuck with it, through the ridicule and threats, jumping through all the hoops that could possibly be thrown at her. And it's been worth it. I think there is more tolerance at that school than there is in most of this country. I still volunteer there at the support group whenever I can, but that isn't much these days.

But I see the way it's changed things. There are kids out today, *out by choice.* And they aren't being treated the way Sara and I were. I'm sure that they still have problems, you can see on the news every day where someone is beaten or killed. But I think that we have done something to help. Just a little something. I like that feeling.

It was sometime around the time that the support group was finally being implemented that I had my eighth Great Revelation. You can't argue people into accepting your beliefs. Yelling will never make someone listen better. Yelling just adds to the noise and confusion. You can get your point across better if you whisper. You can't shout to the world that your way works, they'll never understand or accept it. No, you have to show them that it works, show them that you are good people, and eventually you will be accepted. You don't have to be a hurricane, just a drop of water in the storm. Eventually other drops will come together and form a driving force.

At least, that's the way it worked for us.

My Maggie May did take me to meet her father. Howard. A very distinguished-looking man, with iron gray hair and a broad, strong face. He met me at the door with a firm handshake and a speech. A very well practiced speech about how he didn't understand but accepted her life, including me. And how he didn't ever want me to act any differently around him than I would any other time. If I held her hand at home, I should do it at his house. He was so nervous, and so sweet at the same time, I couldn't help but love him right away.

Howard may very well be the kindest man I've ever known. It wasn't long before he became the father figure that I had lost so long ago. Not that he was anything like my father, just that I came to love him so easily. As soon as everything settled down at the school and we knew we were there to stay, he moved up here to be closer to us.

I eventually bought my own shop. Just a small place, but big enough for me, and business has stayed steady, there's really more than I can keep up with. Howard used to stop in now and then, just to putter around with me. I guess he missed working. He hardly ever comes now, but we're all getting older, right?

I guess it was around the time that the Eagles disbanded, Rick Springfield was on top of the world, and Mellencamp was still a Cougar, Maggie and I bought a house. A cute little three bedroom with a fenced backyard, just down the street from Dad's apartment. We loved it there, it was just so much a *home*.

We got a dog.

Perfection, right?

I guess this is the part where you expect me to say we lived happily ever after.

Not quite.

I didn't think it would be tough for us. After all, we were in love. She was the love of my life. She was my confidante, my best friend. Love can conquer all. But that doesn't mean you always agree. Love conquers, but it doesn't stop you from arguing.

My Maggie May is the perfect woman, but she has a strong will. She is strong and independent, I think that makes her sexy. I love that about her. But I have one of those strong wills, too. And that independence. And that sometimes makes us butt heads.

Don't get me wrong, I'm not saying that we weren't meant to be together, that we aren't soul mates. We just didn't have that sticky sweet, always perfect life. You know, you see it all the time on the movies, in the personas that Hollywood depicts, even off screen. We never had that. I don't think anyone does, not really, anyway. No matter what they show the world. So, it was never perfect. We didn't always agree, but we learned to compromise. And what we had was good.

I thought I had everything I could ever want. I had my soul mate, the love of my life, the one I thought I could never have. I had a job that I loved, enough money to be comfortable. Not rich, but secure. I had a father when I thought that I had lost my only one. I had a good home, and a spoiled rotten dog to greet me when I came back to it. I should have been fulfilled. And I almost was.

Almost, but not quite.

Neither was Maggie.

We talked about it a lot, that unfulfilled part of us. The two of us were good, we were great. We were happy. But we wanted more. We deserved more. We decided that we *needed* more.

Does that make us greedy? I don't know, but we both felt it. We thought about (and talked about) all the possible consequences before we added another person to our lives. We were prepared. Or so we thought.

Now there's Stella.

I was not prepared. How could I have been? I was never prepared to love Stella as much as I do. I mean, I knew I would love her, but I never knew how she would complete us. I didn't know I needed anyone as much as I needed my Maggie. But I was wrong. Stella taught me that, and so much more.

Chapter Eighteen

I didn't give birth to Stella, but she is my daughter. And Agatha's. Having her was a decision we made together. And it was a tough one.

You have to understand, everything was different then. Now, gay couples are having children all the time. Okay, maybe not all the time, but often enough, comparatively. But this . . . this was a long time ago.

Like I said, Reagan was in the White House, there was still a cold war. Prince was looking forward to "1999," and girls just wanted to have fun. AIDS was just catching public notice, and nearly everyone was in the closet.

I had never heard of same-sex parenting. I'm sure it existed, I'm sure we weren't the first, but it felt like it. We had to climb almost every obstacle imaginable.

And climb we did.

We climbed and climbed. We jumped through so many hoops. We climbed all the obstacles. We tried. We screamed, we cried.

We tried all the regular routes people take to get a child. The adoption agencies wouldn't even talk to us. A couple of lesbians? No way.

So Agatha tried to adopt without me. Why her, and not me? Let's face it, back then, if either of us looked good on paper, it was the teacher, not the mechanic. But it didn't work. She still couldn't adopt. Not as a single woman. They wanted same-race heterosexual couples only. No exceptions, no deviations. She couldn't even foster, much less adopt. Women's liberation be damned. It didn't do a thing for us in that department.

So we explored other avenues. We had heard that almost anyone could adopt children from third world countries. So we tried that route. We found agencies that dealt with overseas adoption, we went to them. We pleaded our case.

We had heard wrong. Not even those agencies would let us have a child. It amazed me. There were children who needed homes, and we offered one. But it wasn't good enough. Somehow, someone decided a child was better living in poverty, or starving to death, than being raised in a loving home by two lesbians. Or even a single parent. It made no sense to me.

So we thought about artificial insemination. Nasty little phrase, isn't it? I shiver at the sound. But that was okay, as long as we could get a child. So we hunted up clinics across the United States. And Agatha went without me, we figured that she'd have better chances as a single woman.

So she went alone. A single woman from Missouri looking for sperm. It was absolutely unheard of. And impossible.

We were at the end of our rope. We began to talk about the possibility of simply picking up some guy in a bar somewhere . . .

And that was not only an option that didn't appeal to us, it was downright ugly. Not that neither of us had ever been with a stranger. Agatha had done that once or twice in college. And me . . . well, I was trying to forget that time of my life. But just to pick up someone at that point in our relationship, in our lives, we hated even the thought.

I understand that there are people who have "open" relationships. And that works for them. But it just, it just wasn't us. There was just something between us, an intimacy, I guess, that neither of us wanted to share. Maybe it was self-ishness, I don't know, but it was there.

Anyway, picking up a stranger in a bar was the last thing we wanted to do. And we thought our options were down to that. A stranger, or someone we knew. And I couldn't bring myself even to think of anyone we knew. I mean, how could I look at that man, knowing he had shared the most intimate, the most sacred moments with us, *with her,* and not hate him for it?

And God only knew how many times it would take. We might have to keep seeing him. I couldn't do that. I couldn't even think about it.

So we were back to the stranger.

The stranger. Our last option. We decided it had to be done together. She was going to carry the child, but we had to do it together. Why her? Well, obviously it was easier to be pregnant at her job than it was at mine. And frankly, I didn't want to. Not that I wouldn't have, if she hadn't wanted to, I would have. But she wanted it. And after all, she had a natural break in her career, I didn't.

So, we decided it would be her, but we had to do it together. I couldn't walk away knowing I was leaving her alone with a stranger. And I couldn't stand the thought of being there with them. But, oh, we both wanted a child so much. What else could we do? It had to be done together. So we had to find someone willing to do that.

It sounds so easy, doesn't it? Two women, looking for a man willing to take them both to bed. Every man's fantasy, right? Should have been easy enough.

It wasn't.

We began to look for our stranger. We went out, went to bars. Where else do you pick up a man? It was strange to me, I hadn't been in a straight bar since . . . since before I could legally go into them. I felt completely out of place. Completely alone.

But we searched. We searched for weeks. Agatha could easily pick up a man, but they balked when they realized I'd be joining in. And the ones that approached us were . . . not what we wanted. To say the least.

Actually, we couldn't seem to find what we wanted at all. I don't think we ever would have. I'm not sure either of us really wanted to. But we did want a child, so we tried.

I remember the last night we searched. I actually was alone. Agatha was across the bar, talking to a man. She was glancing my way and smiling, somewhat bravely. I was trying to smile back at her, but I couldn't. The man she was talking to reached out and touched her arm, and I dropped my head to the table. I couldn't see the possibilities in that man, only the flaws. Only the way he reached out and touched Agatha. My Agatha. My Maggie May. I wanted to kill him.

I raised my head off the table and rubbed my face, trying to get the image of him reaching for her out of my mind. And a man sat down across the table from me, in her chair.

"Bobbie?"

I looked at him a moment, his long hair, his tall, thin frame, his baby face. Then it struck me.

"Eric!"

He grinned. "I thought that was you! What the hell are you doing here?"

I sighed. "It's such a long, long story. I'm looking for a man."

His jaw dropped and he stared at me. "You're *what?*"

I shook my head. "I know, I know." I shrugged. "What can I say?"

"But . . . but you're not . . . you're not . . ." He stared at me.

I realized how I sounded to him and almost laughed. "Oh, no. No, no, no. Of course not." I pointed toward Agatha. "There's my lady. We're looking for a man together."

He shook his head.

I leaned in and sighed. "We don't want a man. We're trying to have a baby. We can't adopt, we can't find a sperm bank that'll do it. We only need a man for, you know."

He looked Agatha and the man over. "So this is the guy you're going to . . . get?"

I rolled my eyes, thinking about that image that wouldn't

leave my head. "I don't know. We haven't found anyone else yet."

"What about me?"

I smiled, but it felt sad on my face. "No, Eric. I know I'm gonna hate whoever it is, and I don't want to hate you."

He looked completely confused. "Hate him? Why?"

"For touching her." I clenched my fists. "I could never share her with anyone and not hate them for it. Even if it means getting the child we so desperately want."

It all became clear to Eric and he suddenly looked as shocked as when I told him I was looking for a man. "Oh, my God, you're gonna have her sleep with him?"

I nodded.

"And that's what you want?"

"No!" I rubbed my face again. "No, that's not what we want. But we don't have any other choice. We want a child."

Eric threw up his hands in exasperation. "But you don't have to sleep with him! You just need his . . . you know."

"And he's just gonna hand it over."

"Why not? I would!"

I stopped. Stopped thinking, stopped breathing, stopped everything. And I just stared at Eric.

"Are you serious?"

He grinned. I think I once described Eric as a pure sweet soul. That was the most accurate description I've ever given anything.

"What's your lady's name?"

"Agatha."

He got up and walked over to her. I'm not sure, but I think he called her by name and told the guy she was talking to to get away from his girl. She looked at him kind of funny, then looked my way. I grinned at her, and she let Eric lead her back to our table. She sat down and raised her eyebrows at me.

"Agatha, this is my friend Eric. I think he has a solution to our problem."

Eric grinned at her. "You two live here in town?"

She eyed him and nodded.

"Cool, let's get out of here then."

We went home that night, with Eric right behind us. Agatha looked at me as we drove, glancing in the rearview mirror from time to time. I waited for her to say what was on her mind. She finally sighed.

"Are you sure, Bobbie? Are you sure he's the one?"

I smiled. "I'm sure."

"But you said no one that you knew—"

I held up my hand. "I said I didn't want anyone I knew touching you. Eric won't."

She stared at me in silence for a moment. "Really? He'll just . . . just . . ."

"Yes." I nodded. "I think he will."

I was pulling into the driveway when I told her that. She leaned over and hugged me, I think she was crying.

We sat down with Eric and talked. And talked. And talked some more. We looked at every angle, every possibility. We made agreements. We discussed every possible complication we could think of. We analyzed every angle. And we talked some more. I think we talked it to death.

Then Eric began to give us the gift that we needed. The most precious gift, the gift of life and love.

And it worked.

Not the first time, but it eventually did. We were going to go through a doctor, but we couldn't find one that would do what we wanted. I don't know why not. What's strange about a woman walking into the doctor's office with a cup of sperm, asking for it to be inserted? I didn't see anything wrong with that, but the doctors we talked to had a problem with it.

So we did it on our own. It wasn't too bad, a little trial and error, but we got the hang of it. And my Maggie May became pregnant.

Then Eric disappeared. And that was part of our agreement. His name was not put on the birth certificate, and he was not to be involved in the child's life. She was to be ours, Agatha's and mine.

Not that Eric wouldn't have been a good parent, just that we all agreed that this was the way we wanted it. And he had never wanted kids. But we did, and he simply gave what he could to us, and walked away, never asking anything in return.

I love him so much for that.

Chapter Nineteen

So Stella is our daughter. I expected to love her, how could I not? How could I not love the child of one I love so much? And a gift given without reservations, without expectations. I expected to love her the moment I saw her. I was wrong. I loved her from the moment of conception.

The first time I felt her move inside Agatha, I cried with joy. Really. I didn't know that was possible until that moment.

I think I drove Agatha crazy while she was pregnant. You know those obnoxious people that can't keep their hands off a pregnant woman's belly? I was one of those. I couldn't help myself. I was fascinated with the whole process. The thought of bringing life into the world . . . it's just incredible.

I had always heard about the "glow" that expecting mothers get, but I had never really seen it. Not like I saw it in my Maggie. I had thought that she was the most beautiful woman in the world before, but she just got more beautiful. Looking at her, seeing how much our child was growing within her, took my breath away.

I doted on her constantly, massaging her back, rubbing her feet, running out at all hours to get whatever she was craving that night. I hung around her constantly, wouldn't let her do anything strenuous, wouldn't even let her reach up to the top cabinets in the kitchen.

I talked to her belly, read to it, played it music through the headphones. I was always touching her, just to feel a kick. She'd get so mad at me, there were times she had to run me out of the house just to get some peace.

The guys at work teased me a lot about how I was so whipped. They were wrong. I wasn't whipped. I just worshipped the ground she walked on. What's wrong with that?

And I was there, in the delivery room. It really is incredible, the miracle of childbirth. The whole process, from conception, all the way through. People might tell you that babies are ugly when they come out, all messy and gross, but they are wrong. That baby was the most beautiful thing in the world. Next to her mother.

And Maggie *was* beautiful, her hair plastered to her face, covered in sweat, exhausted from bringing forth life. When you watch someone go through that, it's incredible. But when you see them go through it with *your* child . . . when you lay eyes on that child created out of pure love . . . there are no words.

It's funny, how history repeats itself. We realized as we waited for the birth of our child, that we were doing almost the same thing that Agatha's parents had done. They had worked so hard, prayed so hard, to have a child. Then we had done much the same thing. We knew how they felt by the time it was over.

We named her after her mother. There was no way I was going to curse her with the same name as me. Barbara Ann. (That song's playing in your head again, isn't it?) No way I was going to do that to my daughter. So she became Estell, after her mother. But the first time her grandfather saw her he called her Stella. And she is. She's my star. She has her mother's golden hair, and such bright blue eyes. She has become my world.

It seems so strange to me, that I could love this much. I didn't think I could love Agatha any more than I already did.

But when she gave me our child, I found de
her that reached so much further than I had in
didn't think I could love anyone as much as I
do. Watching Stella grow, being a part of her l
the greatest miracle for me.

That's my ninth Great Revelation. The heart can hold this much love and joy, more than I ever thought possible. And even when it feels so full of love that it'll explode any minute, it can hold more.

Happily Ever After now? I believe there is such a thing, but it's not what you hear about in fairy tales. It's not that easy. I think every family, every relationship, has its ups and downs. No matter how in love you are, it's still work. It's not always easy. Even with this much love, it hasn't been easy for us. There are hard times, no one gets along perfectly all the time. It's still work.

I think Happily Ever After means that you enjoy the work you put into your relationships. That at the end of the day you go to bed believing that it was all worth it.

So, there is Stella.

Stella has always been such a serious child. She never was one to cry much, and she's always been such a *thinker*. I used to catch her sometimes even as young as two, sitting and looking over something, figuring it out. *Thinking.*

I guess she was three when I decided to change my life a little. Don't get me wrong, I loved my life, but Stella made me realize that I needed to try to include my parents in it. I know, you're thinking that I'm just a glutton for punishment. But I was someone's child, and I couldn't look at my daughter without thinking that somehow, they might want to know that I was all right.

I remember that year. It's funny, my life seems to be divided by Stella. The things that happened since her birth always seem to be right there, within my grasp. But the memories of everyng before her got buried. And I began to forget them, right up until they exploded back into my life with that CD. But I'm getting ahead of myself again. I'll get to that.

Anyway, Stella was three that year. Tracy Chapman had a "Fast Car," Guns And Roses was on the radio with "Sweet Child o' Mine," and Stella had this little electronic memory game that her grandfather had bought for her. You know, one of those things that light up and play musical notes in a pattern, and you're supposed to be able to copy the pattern. Howard came over to see her, and she immediately ran to her room and brought back that game.

"Grandpa, it's broken. Can you fix it?"

He smiled down at her and touched her hair. "No, lovey, I can't. But I bet your mom can."

Stella brought her game to me. I found a loose wire and repaired it. She looked up at me with such wonder when the lights came on.

"Mom, can you fix everything?"

"Not everything. But lots of stuff."

She looked at me thoughtfully. "How do you know how?"

I smiled down at my daughter. She was always so curious. She had her mother's mind, and my questioning. "My father taught me to fix things, when I wasn't much bigger than you are now."

"Huh-uh. You can't fix things when you're little."

"Uh-huh. Even as little as you. I wouldn't tell you a lie." (Boy, did I ever regret those words, look where they got me!)

She turned back to Howard. "Did you really, Grandpa?"

He reached out and lifted her onto his lap. "Not me, sweetheart. Her father. I'm Mama's dad."

She looked at him, absorbing what he'd said, then turned back to me. "Where's your dad, Mom?"

"He's . . ." I thought for a moment, unsure what to say. Where was he? Could I tell her I didn't know? Should I tell her he was taken to prison and I hadn't seen or heard of him since? Was that good for a kid to know? "He's been gone for a long time."

"Oh." She turned back to Howard. "Grandpa, will you play with me?"

Howard played the memory game with her until she tired of it and ran off into the other room. Then he turned to me.

"Where is your father, Bobbie?"

"I'm not sure, Howard. Last I knew, he was taken by the MPs for being AWOL. That was a long time ago."

"How long?"

I shook my head. "I was around fourteen or so."

Howard became thoughtful. I smiled at the way he furrowed his brow when he was thinking hard. It was the same way Agatha did, and Stella too. Now I knew where that came from.

"Tell me what you know about him. What branch of the military? Do you know his rank? What company he was in? His full name, maybe a birth date?"

I thought as hard as I could, and told him what I knew, which wasn't much. I knew his name and birthday, but not the year. And I knew he was a mechanic in the navy, but I couldn't remember the company or rank. I realized that I didn't know that much about either of my parents. And I decided to try to change that.

But Howard had his own ideas. I didn't find out about them until much later.

So I decided that I didn't know enough about my parents, and I thought I would like a relationship with them. After all, I was a parent myself now, I understood that you love your child no matter what. How could you not? I decided to start with my mother. After all, I knew where she was. Even if she had told me not to come back, that was a long time ago. Maybe she had changed her mind. Besides, she was a grandmother now. That *had* to change her feelings.

So I called my mother. I sat there, gripping the phone, sweating, until she picked up the other end.

"Hello?"

It was her. I knew it would be. She said she was through

moving, and the one thing she didn't do was lie. And I knew that voice. It was her. I opened my mouth, but nothing came out.

"Hello?"

I cleared my throat. "Hello, Mom? It's Bobbie."

She was silent for what seemed like the longest time. Then I heard her sigh. "Barbara Ann, is that you?"

She always called me that. I hated it. But I was trying, and I let it go. "Yes, Mom, it's me."

"What do you want?"

"Nothing, Mom. Just to see how you are."

"I'm fine." She sounded unhappy and bitter. Exactly as I remembered.

"And I wanted you to know you have a granddaughter."

That perked her up. I had hoped it would. "You have a child? Are you married?"

"Yes, the most amazing little girl you've ever seen. I'd like you to meet her. You'd love her, Mom, you really would."

I could almost hear her purse her lips. "And your husband?"

"No husband, Mom. I have a wonderful family, though, and I'm happy."

"Family? You can't have a family without a husband."

"But I do, Mom. A wonderful lady, and the most precious daughter."

"A woman? And the child is hers?"

I took a deep breath, controlling my anger. Speaking to my mother had always made me angry. I guess because she was so set in her views, and I thought they were wrong. And it angered me even more that she immediately assumed that I didn't give birth to my child. Right or not, her assumption made me so angry I had to clench my teeth for a minute. Then I spoke as calmly as I could.

"She's *ours*. Yes, I have a wonderful woman who gave me a daughter. Our daughter."

"That's sick. I can't believe you would ever bring a child

into that perverse . . . life. You need help, Barbara. And don't call me again until you get it."

"But, Mom, she's your granddaughter."

"I would have to have a daughter first. I don't."

And with that she hung up. I sat there and stared at the phone in my hand. I couldn't believe it. I couldn't imagine being so bigoted that you didn't even want to meet your only grandchild. How could that be? How could anyone be so . . . cold? That anyone could hate their own child, for any reason, was beyond my grasp.

I sat there and thought for a while. And it hurt. Not so much for me, Mom and I had never had a great relationship, so I didn't feel like I was losing anything. But I hurt for Stella. I had never had grandparents, but Howard had shown me that they could be so good in a child's life. I wanted Stella to have as much goodness and love as possible. And my mother had flat refused to give anything. I could have hated her in that moment. But that wouldn't have done any good to anyone. I knew the destructiveness of hatred. Hadn't I fought it most of my life? I refused to let any more into my life. I dialed the number again.

The answering machine picked up, Dan's voice telling me that they weren't home. I waited for the beep.

"Mom, if you ever change your mind, I live in Kansas City, and my number will always be in the book, in my name. *Bobbie*. And I wish . . . I wish things were different between us."

I hung up the phone and cried.

That night, I sat by Stella's bed for the longest time, watching her sleep. Maggie came quietly into the room and sat beside me. And I vowed that I would never disown Stella. That no matter what she did, no matter who or what she turned out to be, I would still love her. And I would do my best to understand her. And if I never understood, I would accept her for who she was anyway. Always. I made those vows to my precious sleeping girl, to her mother, to myself, to God.

Chapter Twenty

So my plan was to find my parents and at least try to establish some sort of relationship with them. Like I said, I was a parent now, and I couldn't imagine that any parent wouldn't want to have a relationship with their child, no matter what. And I so wanted Stella to know them. Especially my father. I wanted her to know him, to see where I had come from, to know where she came from. And I missed him. Finally, I was ready to admit to myself how much I missed him. And I did. I missed looking up into his eyes, always loving and knowing, always reassuring. I missed hearing his voice, strong and soft as he sang along with the radio. There were so many things I didn't know. Where had he grown up? What were his parents like? Where had he learned about cars? I wanted to know everything.

But I had contacted my mother first. I wanted Dad more, but I knew where she was, and I didn't even know where to start looking for him. I was going to find him after I talked to her. Surely she could help me find him.

But after trying to talk to my mother, I realized that it had been a dream. She wouldn't even talk to me, much less help me. So I decided against trying to find Dad. It just didn't seem worth it to me. Okay, maybe it was worth it, but I was afraid. I was so afraid that he would reject me too. And, in doing so, reject Stella. I didn't think I could handle that from him.

What I didn't know was that Howard had already found him.

I guess after he found out all he could from me, he went to his golf buddies and got some help. One of them was an old military man, another was a retired investigator. He somehow took what little information I had been able to provide, and he found him. And he went to meet him in person. He kept it all completely hidden from me. I didn't know until one Mother's Day, when Rod Stewart was on a "Downtown Train," and Aerosmith was making a comeback. Stella was five, she started school that year. And my world turned upside down and shook until I thought everything was going to come loose.

Howard was visiting, he spends a lot of time with us, especially since Stella was born. Anyway, he was visiting. The phone rang and he answered it. Then he handed it to me. It wasn't unusual, so I thought nothing of it.

"Hello, this is Bobbie."

"Hi, Bobbie McGee. Happy Mother's Day."

I froze at the sound of my father's voice. Suddenly, I was a little girl. I stood there with vague, disjointed images floating in my mind. I could see my father, smiling down at me with pride, grease on his jeans, white T-shirt dirty and stained, a big grin on his face. I could see him, his big rough hands so gently guiding my small, unskilled ones as he taught me to feel the imperfections in the bodywork on an old brown truck, his voice low in my ear, telling me how to fix them. I saw his head hanging as his hands were cuffed behind his back, and his eyes almost pleading with me through the rear window of the green military jeep as he was taken away. These images and more floated over and through each other in my mind, jumbling my thoughts and closing my throat. I couldn't speak, and if I could, I didn't know what to say.

So, as I found out later, Howard had tracked down my father. I know his golf buddies helped him out, but I'm not sure of all the details. I never asked. It just didn't seem important. But he did find him, in a prison in Kansas of all places. You know, in the movies they always send the AWOL guys to prison in Leavenworth. I didn't realize that was accurate until Howard told me that's where he found my father. So, he found him, then drove over there and stood face-to-face with him. And they had a conversation that went something like this.

"My name is Howard. You don't know me, but I know your daughter."

"You don't know my daughter."

"Oh, but I do. I know she hates to be called anything but Bobbie, she never turns off the radio, and she's the best damn mechanic I've ever seen. And that's all thanks to you."

I can almost see those two standing there, eyeing each other, each thinking he's protecting me from the other.

Dad looked at Howard. "What do you want?"

"I want you to contact her. She misses you."

"Look, buddy, whoever you are, what's between me and my daughter is none of your business."

"Oh, but it is. You see, she's the mother of our grand-daughter."

"Bobbie's got a kid?"

"Yes, she does." He pulled out a picture of Stella. "She's beautiful, isn't she?"

"She doesn't look like Bobbie."

"No, no, not much. She looks more like my side of the family. Bobbie looks like you, though. Same brown eyes."

"She always did take after me." He stared at the picture.

"You can keep that, if you want."

Dad nodded. "And she's married to your son?"

"Not exactly. Why don't we sit down?"

They sat down at the visitor's table and Howard leaned close so Dad could hear him. "Our kids aren't married, but they live together. They're very happy. And Stella . . . that's the child, she's perfect. Well adjusted, smart, stable. Perfect."

"Where is this going, Howard? What are you trying to tell me?"

"Bobbie is in love and happy. And I think she'd like to include you in her life."

"You think?"

"I *know*. But she's afraid you won't want to be in her life. She doesn't know I'm here. She doesn't even know I found you. I wanted to see how you'd react before I told her. If she knew that I found you and you didn't want to see her, it would break her heart."

"Of course I want to see her."

"Her mother didn't. She won't even talk to her."

"They never had a good relationship, Bobbie was too much like me."

"It's even worse now."

Dad shook his head. "I don't know why."

"Because Bobbie doesn't live with my son, she lives with my daughter."

Dad sat there staring at Howard for a minute. "What are you telling me, Howard?"

"Your daughter, *our daughters* are gay."

"Gay."

"Yes. And Bobbie's afraid you won't want to see her."

My father sat there for a long time, just taking in that news. Then he looked up at Howard. "I guess I'm not really surprised." He laughed. "And I'll just bet her mother blames me. She always bitched that I treated Bobbie like a boy. Maybe this is my fault."

Howard shook his head. "I don't think so. I treated Agatha like a girl, and she's gay. I don't think you or I had anything to do with it."

"No?"

"No, I don't."

Dad nodded. "But they're happy, our girls?"

"Yes." Howard pulled out another picture and handed it to my father. This one had all three of us in it. "Very happy."

Dad studied that picture, touched the paper. "They look happy. God, my little girl's all grown up."

Howard laughed. "I know, it amazes me too, when I look at Agatha. Where did all the time go?"

Dad looked around him, taking in his prison. "Mine was wasted here. I'll never get back what I lost, the time with her. She may never forgive me."

"I think you're wrong. She doesn't blame you. She was going to find you, but after her mother refused to talk to her, she gave up. She was afraid you might do the same thing."

"I wouldn't. Would you tell her that I wouldn't?"

"You tell her. She needs to hear it from you. To hear from you at all would mean so much to her."

"I don't want her to see me like this. See me here."

Howard shook his head. "It doesn't matter where, or how. What's important is to establish contact. And I don't think she will, as much as she wants it. You'll have to do it."

Dad took a deep breath. "Okay, Howard. Tell me how to get my daughter back."

I guess they talked a lot more than that, several times on the phone, and Howard went to see him again before he called me. But I didn't know anything about it. Howard kept it quiet, he didn't even tell Agatha. I didn't find all this out until later.

All I knew then was that a ghost was on the phone, calling me Bobbie McGee.

So there I was, gripping that phone with everything I had, unable to speak. Barely able to breathe.

"Bobbie?"

I cleared my throat, swallowing hard. For just a split second I convinced myself that this wasn't real. Just long enough to get out one word. "Yes."

"Bobbie, it's me, it's Dad."

"I know." And I did know. But it felt unreal, like a dream where everything moves slowly and you're almost numb.

We were silent for a minute. My mind started racing, there were so many things I wanted to tell him, so many things I wanted to ask, I didn't know where to start. I couldn't find my voice to try.

I had never heard my father cry, but he sounded like he was near tears.

"Maybe I shouldn't have called . . ."

I was suddenly overwhelmed with the fear that he would hang up. He would hang up, I would lose that thread of contact, and never be able to find it again. That fear gripped my heart and squeezed hard, making my eyes sting, making me find my voice.

"No, no, I'm glad you did. I just don't know what to say."

"I know. Are you okay?"

"Yes, I'm okay. Are you?"

"Well, I'm okay now that I know you are. I know about Agatha, Stella. Are you happy, Bobbie, really happy?"

I looked up, trying to keep the tears from falling, trying to keep them from choking me. Happy? Stella flashed through my mind, and my Maggie May. And my father's voice was in my head. Happy? I was overwhelmed. "Yes, Dad, I am. I really am."

Agatha suddenly looked at me, then Howard. She stepped over beside me and touched my shoulder. My father's voice sounded in my ear.

"That's all I need to know. I'll be all right now."

"Will you, Dad?" How could just that make him all right? Didn't he want anything else? Just that wasn't enough for me. I wanted more. I wanted him back.

"Yes, honey, I will. I've got to go, okay? My phone time is up."

That sudden fear returned. It lanced through me, sharp and sudden, unforgiving, unrelenting. It loomed hugely in my mind, almost tangible. I was about to lose him again. I couldn't let that happen. "But I'm not ready! There's so much to tell you, so much to ask you! So much to say . . . I'm sorry, Dad, I'm so sorry. I didn't know . . ."

"No, you don't have to be sorry. It's not your fault. You didn't know, you couldn't have. It's my fault."

That fear stayed with me, hung over me, choked me. "But, I don't even know where you are, how do I reach you again? How—"

"I have to go now." He sounded stern, like he had when I was small and he had to get his point across. He had never raised his voice or hand to me, but I knew that stern voice meant business.

"You can talk to Howard, he can explain it to you. And I'll call again, once a week if you want. I want to be in your life, if you'll have me."

Have him? That was the only thing that could make my life more nearly complete than it was now. That fear squeezing my heart suddenly eased up, making my heart feel as if it were swelling inside my chest, only to squeeze again. It was almost too much to bear. I wanted to tell him that, to somehow make him know how important he was to me. But I couldn't put it into words. I could only get out a simple "Of course I'll have you, Dad. I want you in my life."

"Then I'll be there. I gotta go. I love you, Bobbie McGee."

He hung up before I could even respond. (Actually, I think the phone there automatically cut off because his time was up.) I stood there holding that phone with tears in my eyes until Agatha reached over and took it from me, hanging it back up.

She hugged me tightly. "Are you all right?"

"Sure." I tried to shrug it off, tried to ignore that tightening and swelling in my heart, tried to gain control of my emotions. They were flailing everywhere, I couldn't get a grip on them at all. But I tried.

She stepped back and looked up into my eyes. She's always been so concerned about me. "That was your dad?"

I nodded, not trusting myself to speak.

"Are you sure you're okay?"

I swallowed hard again. Okay? No, I wasn't okay. I had just hung up the phone with my father. My father, the hero of my childhood, the deserter of my teenage years, the man I loved more than any other. I was elated. I had *talked* to him!

He wanted to be a part of my life again. He knew about Agatha, and Stella, and it didn't matter to him. He loved me anyway. Just like I thought he would, just like I was afraid he wouldn't. Why had I ever doubted him?

But then, why not? I didn't really know him after all, did I? I only had memories, long shelved, like photo albums with a coating of thick dust. Did anyone ever really know what was in those? How accurate were those old memories? The fear returned, not as intense, but it returned just the same. What if those old memories I was dusting off weren't the real picture? Had I built him up too much in my mind? I didn't know. Was I okay? The joy, the fear, the confusion, was I okay underneath all that?

I tried to smile at her. "I think so."

But I was crying.

Chapter Twenty-one

So that was one more shock in my life. One more time that my whole world was turned upside down. And shaken to its roots.

There were more phone calls from my father, many more. He called once a week, just like he'd said he would. I began to get to know the man behind my memory's image. And I found that he was much different from that image.

You see, I had perfect memories of my father. All the way up to him being taken from my life. And I was over the feeling of betrayal about that. Yes, he made a mistake, yes, he was wrong. But by that time, I just felt the loss of time, I no longer blamed him. So he was perfect in my mind's eye. At least in my mind, he was ten feet tall and bulletproof. He was some kind of superman, some sort of hero. He had been my idol, someone that was perfect, he could do no wrong in my eyes. But that was only an image, a fading, fuzzy memory seen through the eyes of a naive child.

I began to find that he was human, and just as prone to make mistakes as anyone else. Like going AWOL from the navy. That mistake cost both of us. Cost us a lot of misunderstanding, and about eighteen years.

But I also found that, mistakes and all, he was still a good man. He had so much love inside him, ready to give to almost anyone, if they'd only take it. He was intelligent and thoughtful. All those times that he was silent when I was small, I'd thought he was withdrawn. But I was wrong. His mind was constantly working, turning over possibilities. *Thinking.*

His sense of humor was great, if a little quirky. And he still had that love of music that he had passed to me. And I still loved him.

I asked him once why. Why he ran, why he didn't just serve out the rest of his contract or whatever it is in the military, and be done with it. He got very quiet.

"I'm sorry, Dad. I didn't mean to upset you. I just wanted to know."

"No, Bobbie McGee, you didn't upset me. I was just thinking." He sighed. "I was already in the navy when I met your mother, you know."

"No, I didn't know."

"Well, I was. She thought she was going to be married to a career military man. An officer, maybe. Someone that would look dashing in a uniform. Then she realized that it wasn't so great."

"Why not?" I laughed a little. "Didn't you look dashing enough?"

He laughed too. "I guess I did, she married me. Then she found the downside. See, I was a mechanic, but they found out that I could work on anything. Jeeps, boats, planes, anything. And they started shipping me off a lot. They had me going everywhere. She didn't care much for living on the base alone."

"So you did it for her."

"Nope." He laughed again. I noticed the more we talked, the more he laughed. Like his heavy load was lifting, life was becoming lighter. Or at least his spirits. "No, I didn't. I think we got along better when I was gone so much. I didn't mind a bit."

"Then why?"

"Because you came along. I could stand to be away from your mother; in fact, I think I kind of liked it. But I took one look at you. You were so perfect. The best thing I was ever able to do. Just one peek, and I knew I could never stand to leave you."

I glanced down at my Stella, napping on the couch. What would I do to stay close to her? What would I have done? I didn't think I'd have made the same choice, but what did I know? I hadn't ever been there. I smiled a little at her. "I think I understand."

I went to see him once, after about a year of phone calls and letters. All of us went. We made the trip in the car, it was just a few hours' drive. I remember that drive because Freddie Mercury had just died, Bonnie Raitt gave everyone "Something to Talk About," and I was so nervous. I think that was the only time in my life that I was actually too shaky to drive.

It was strange and uncomfortable to me, to walk into that prison, knowing that he had been there, all alone, for so long. I was nervous enough seeing him after all those years, and to see him there made it worse. I can only imagine how Maggie felt, going there to meet him for the first time.

They took us to a room, and we waited there until the big steel door opened and he stepped in. He stood there, I could see him wanting to hug me, but holding back, waiting to see my reaction first.

Seeing my father for the first time as an adult was a staggering experience. I almost had to take a step back. I guess I hadn't been prepared for the changes in him. He had seen pictures of me, but I hadn't seen any of him. I knew that he would be older, but I was shocked to see how those years showed. He had lines on his face that hadn't been there before. And his eyes were . . . somehow older. I don't know how else to describe them, just older. As if he'd seen a hundred years in the time that we'd been apart.

He was thinner, and his hair was graying. He wasn't as tall as I had remembered. That could have been the fact that I'd grown, and he hadn't. Or maybe it was that his image in my mind had grown with me over the years, so I expected him still to tower over me. I don't know. But he seemed so much smaller to me. So much weaker.

And yet, a tiny part of me saw him as I had seen him last, towering over me with all the height and strength in the world, standing with grease on his hands, wrench stuffed in the back pocket of his jeans, smiling in the afternoon sun. Smiling at me.

I stepped over and hugged him, and I didn't let go for a long time.

That was such a great visit. Even in that cold place, we were finally together again, and that's all that mattered. I hadn't realized how much I'd missed Dad until I spent that hour with him. I saw the way he and Howard shook hands, firmly, smiling like old friends. And the way he instantly fell for Stella. I could see it in his eyes when he watched her, drawing pictures for him, chatting about all the things that are important to a six-year-old. He looked at her with the same wonder Howard did. And she returned that favor, taking to him so quickly, she could have been me at that age.

And Agatha. Dad took one look at her and turned on more charm than I had ever seen in my life. He talked to her as if she was the most important person in the world. He got her to talk to him, in such a short time, as if she'd been a part of the family all her life. He'd tell her to keep me in line, then turn and drop a conspiring wink at me. He had her giggling along with Stella in no time. It was as if we'd all been together forever.

We kept in contact by phone and letter until grunge rock became popular and Meatloaf made a comeback. That was the year Stella turned eight. And my father came home. Came home just long enough to leave me again.

I say he came home. He really went to Howard's. But he spent most of his time (like Howard did) at our house.

Howard managed to keep Dad's homecoming a surprise

too. He simply called one day and invited himself and a friend over to dinner. When he showed up at our door, his friend was Dad.

I think that was one of the best days of my life. Sitting there at the table, like the family we were, with Dad and Howard, watching Stella vying for attention from both grandfathers, holding my Maggie's hand. I felt as if I were just *glowing* with happiness.

Dad gave me that night. A gift from him. One night of bliss before he dropped the bomb on me.

Yes, Dad gave me that one night. And, because ignorance sometimes really is bliss, he gave me the gift of ignorance for that one night, before he turned my world over and changed my life.

He came by the shop the next day, near closing time. I was working on a '65 Rally Sport Camaro for one of the local collectors. Beautiful machine, that one. Yellow. Dad whistled when he saw it.

"Wow, she's beautiful. Did you do the bodywork on her?"

I grinned at him. "Last year. Fully restored, from top to bottom. But the guy gave her to his kid, who blew the motor trying to drag-race a Porsche down Main." I patted the fender. "So I've got her back for a little while. This is the second motor I've dropped in her in as many years." I shook my head. "Some people need to learn their limits."

Dad leaned under the hood. "Almost finished?"

"She's almost ready to go home. Wanna hear her run?"

He grinned. "I'd love to!"

I slid into the driver's seat and turned the key. That engine fired up beautifully. I revved it a little, got out, and stood beside my father as he watched those horses run. I suddenly felt like a little girl again, standing there waiting for his approval. He closed his eyes and took a deep breath.

"I missed that. The sound of the motor after I'd finished a good job. Watching it go down the road. The freedom of it."

I stood there in silence. What could I say? I would have missed it just as much. Dad reached out and clapped me on the back.

"I knew you could do it, Bobbie McGee, I knew you could. I knew it back when you were two. You're better at this than your old man."

I clapped him right back. "You couldn't have known it then, Dad."

"Oh, yes, I could! I'm telling you, at *two*. You were fitting small parts together, even back then, you tore up your mother's kitchen appliances, just to see how they worked." He laughed. "Used to drive her crazy!"

"I don't remember that."

"But I do. I remember that by the time you were four you could put together a carburetor. I always had trouble with those, but you took to it like a duck to water. I knew you'd be better than me someday."

"I don't know about better. Maybe almost as good."

He turned to me, suddenly very serious. "No, Bobbie, you're better. You've done everything I wanted to do. You have everything I ever wanted. The shop, the family, the skill in the job. I'll bet you've forgotten more about cars than I ever knew."

"No way! I couldn't ever hope to know what you know . . ."

I stopped because he started to cough. That's the first time I really noticed his cough. It was so bad it doubled him over and turned his face red. I reached out and touched his shoulder, noticing that it was shaking with effort to breathe.

He waved me off. "Shut it down. Let's talk."

I shut off the engine and took him inside my office to sit down. I watched him sit there, searching for words, until I couldn't stand it anymore.

"Dad, tell me what's going on."

He coughed a little more, clearing his throat loudly to cover it up. That's when I realized that he'd been sick for a while. He had been covering that cough for so long that he didn't even realize he was doing it anymore. When he looked at me his eyes were hollow and tired.

"I wasn't supposed to be out yet, Bobbie. I was supposed to serve another two years." He shook his head and almost laughed. "They let me out on 'good behavior,' you know. But I really wasn't that good. They just didn't want to pay the medical bills, I think."

I was suddenly frightened. "Don't, Dad. Don't tell me. I don't want to know."

"I have to. I left you without warning once. I won't do it again. I'm dying, honey."

"No. No, no." I shook my head, knowing even as I did it that it wouldn't do any good. I could see it in the sick color of his skin, his tired, hollow eyes.

His voice grew stern again. "Yes, I am. I've known for a long time. It's cancer, Bobbie. It's in my lungs. There's nothing anyone can do."

"There's got to be something . . ." I trailed off. I wanted to deny it, to convince myself that it wasn't real, there was some mistake. But I could see it in him. I saw it in his eyes, in the thinness of his once powerful frame. I noticed that the lines of age and worry could easily have been lines of pain. Why hadn't I noticed it before?

Dad smiled at me. "You're wondering how I hid it from you. It really wasn't that hard. You only saw me once in the last couple of years, and you expected changes in me. But I can't hide it if I see you every day. You'll see it as clearly as I do."

He coughed again, not as bad as the first time, but bad enough to make me cringe. When he caught his breath again he continued.

"I've done everything I could to make my life better. Not longer, longer doesn't get you anywhere. Time doesn't matter. Quality does. I won't go down in a deathbed, surrounded by equipment." He curled his top lip in disgust. "I'd rather drop in a footrace. Quick, that's what I want."

I closed my eyes. "Dad, I can't. Don't do this, please. I can't talk about this now, I can't handle it."

"Yes, you can. You're strong, Bobbie. Just look at what you've accomplished!" He motioned with his arms to show the shop and everything in it. "You've made it. Against the odds, you've made it. You have had to fight every step of the way, but you won. Those old movies were right. You got the car, you got the girl. You're winning the game. Don't quit just because it's time for me to drop out."

"Oh, Daddy. How can I keep going without you?"

"You can, and you will. You've come this far without me. And I'm so proud of you. I love you, Bobbie McGee. I love you."

I sat down beside my father and we held each other while I cried. He never spoke again about dying, or about his illness. And, after I talked to Agatha about it, I didn't speak of it again either.

But I spent all the time I could with my father, from that day on. He spent a lot of time with me at the garage, when he could. When he couldn't, we spent the time at home, mostly with Stella. I wanted her to know him before it was too late.

And we talked, Dad and I. We talked for hours, I wanted to know everything about him. And he told me as much as he could. But he wanted to know about the time in my life when he was gone.

I won't say that I lied to him, I didn't. But I didn't tell him everything, either. I didn't tell him about the times when I was persecuted, the times when I was beaten. I didn't tell him about the long nights of desperation, all those that I spent praying that it would all just end. I didn't tell him those things that I thought would hurt him. I didn't want him to feel guilty for not being there for me. I thought he had suffered enough.

I told him about the cars I'd worked on. That Hemi I'd dropped in Sara's Barracuda. That I went out a lot, that I had had girlfriends. I told him about camping trips with friends, long nights of stargazing. I told him all the good stuff I could remember.

So, was that lying? I don't think it was. In fact, I think I had already forgotten most of those details of my life, those things that happened before Stella. Put them in that little box, locked them up tight, and buried them somewhere in the deepest part of my mind.

Not long after my father spoke to me about his illness, the world began to change rapidly. I mean *change*.

Suddenly, it was cool to be gay. Clinton was in the White House, and people began to crawl out of closets all across the country. Everybody was coming out. And for the first time, women seemed to be in control of it all. It was the peak of the gay days. It was amazing, confusing, exhilarating. The country was in yet another uproar. Or maybe it was the same old fight, just under a different name. Equal is equal, right? I don't know, it seemed the same to me.

Yes, the world around me was changing. That was when Sheryl Crow just wanted to have a little fun. The Eagles were telling us that hell was freezing over. Aerosmith was "Crazy." And my father died.

Chapter Twenty-two

My father never did get a place of his own. He stayed with Howard and came to visit at our house daily, until he became so weak that he couldn't anymore. Then we moved him into our spare bedroom. I spent his last remaining days by his side. We talked a lot, when he could. When he couldn't, I just stayed there, being with him, hoping I was bringing some comfort. When it got so bad that he needed to be in a hospital, he didn't go. I remembered him telling me that he didn't want to go down that way, that he wanted to go quickly, he didn't want any machines to keep him longer. As much as it hurt, I respected those wishes.

When you watch movies, or read stories where someone is dying, there are always some prolific last words, something so revealing or comforting for those left behind. I don't know if that ever happens in real life (I tend to think it doesn't often), but it didn't happen with Dad. I would know, I was there.

I remember sitting there, by his bedside, on that Tuesday afternoon, waiting. Back when I was young, it was called a death watch. You took turns, sitting there in shifts, so that the person wouldn't die alone. And we did all take shifts, Howard, Agatha, me, even Stella. You sit there, all of your heart wishing and hoping against all hope that the person lying there will open his eyes, smile at you, get better. But a tiny part of you just wants it to be over.

That's what I was feeling as I sat there, watching my father die. My mind kept insisting that it was for the best, that he was going to a better place, that I should be happy for him. But my heart was slowly ripping in two.

I sat there and watched him take his last few breaths. I held his hand, and I remembered. I remembered everything I could, from my childhood to the last few months that he was with me. I heard his voice in my head, singing to the radio, telling me how to fix a car, telling me that he loved me. I felt the warmth of his smile, the gentleness of his rough hands as he held mine, or picked me up and twirled me around. I tried to recall every word he'd ever said to me, from the most important things down to the simple hellos.

When my father let out each breath, I waited for him to draw another. After the last one, I waited. I sat there, I don't know how long, until Agatha came in and took my hands from his. She led me out of the room and I followed her on numb, wooden legs.

Okay, I know what you're thinking. You're thinking that I sound cold and heartless. That I didn't mourn the loss of my father. You're wrong. I did. Believe me, I mourned him. My heart broke. And it broke again, every time I heard a man's footfall, looked up, and realized it wasn't him. Every time I started to call his name and he wasn't there. I don't know how I would have made it through it at all if it hadn't been for my family. I think a little piece of me died right along with him. But I didn't die. I couldn't. My family wouldn't let me.

My family. Howard spent so much time with me those first few days following Dad's death. I don't think he said much, but his being there with me said everything in the world. And my sweet Maggie May. She held me when I cried, and held me when I didn't cry. She stood beside me through everything.

Just having her there made me feel stronger. And I knew, no matter how much a part of me wanted to give up, I couldn't. Because I had to be there for Stella. She was still a child, and she needed both of her parents. There's nothing like that kind of responsibility to make you get out of bed every morning.

And Dad taught me something those last few months he was with me. He taught me that I wasn't losing him, I had gained him.

That's my tenth Great Revelation. In this life you don't really lose anything. How can you lose something that no one promises you'll have? Something that not everyone has? You can't. No one ever promised me that I'd have a father, but I did. Twice. And I had Howard, too. I even gained a mother. No, it wasn't a great relationship that we had, but she was there. She was there when I was small, and she supported me, at least financially, until I could make it on my own. I'm sure she even loved me, in her own way. No one comes into the world with any assurance that they'll have anything, so when they get something good, it's a gain. Even if you don't keep it, you gained it for a while. And I've gained a great deal in my life.

And I've seen so many changes. Tolerance is growing. Tolerance for all people, but especially for gays. Is it because people are beginning to realize that people are people, no matter what label they are given? No matter what masks they wear? Or is it because there are so many well-known people out now? Entertainers, musicians, politicians. We even have positive role models on TV now, something I had never even hoped to see. Even long-dead historical figures are being outed. We truly are everywhere.

Or maybe it's just that more people are open-minded and accepting. I don't know. Maybe it's a combination of all of that. Whatever it is, it's incredible to witness, and I'm glad to see it.

As for me, not too much has changed in my life. Stella is growing up so fast, sometimes it's hard to keep up with her.

And my Maggie May. Oh, she gets more beautiful and amazing every day. And I'm still here, hanging on to this crazy ride, loving every minute of it.

But this is where I was supposed to be telling you why I'm spending all this time writing this down. Well, for Stella, of course. But Melissa Etheridge really started it. I'm sure she didn't mean to, didn't even know that she did. But you see, she put out a CD that made me think. Made me remember.

I think I mentioned that my life felt divided. It's really almost a straight line through my past, cutting off everything that happened before Stella was born. Or maybe before Agatha and I truly became lovers. Somewhere in there anyway.

I guess I just put all that stuff behind me. I didn't mean to bury it, but it got buried in the day-to-day. After things have been a certain way for so long, you forget what they were like before. At least, I did. It's like being a parent, or being out. After a while, it's so much a part of you that you can't imagine what it's like to be any other way. You were once, but you forget about that.

I guess that was where I was. I was settled in my life, used to the way it was. My favorite radio stations started becoming called "classic rock," or even (God, must I say it?) "oldies" stations. And, like most parents, the things I did when I was young sound so dangerous to me, now that I have a child of my own. So, again like most parents, I pushed them out of my mind. Buried those memories. It got to the point that I couldn't even recall what it was like not to have Stella in my life. I couldn't fathom what I did before her, or how I could go do something without thinking of her.

Right up until that CD played.

It was close to Christmas that year, I guess Stella was about eleven. The Rock and Roll Hall of Fame Museum had opened in Cleveland. Women were really making it in rock and roll. Tracy Chapman was about to make a *New Beginning*. Jewel had her first hit and Alanis Morissette was pushing more envelopes than anyone thought one song could push. And Melissa Etheridge had yet another hit on the radio.

I knew who she was, of course. I mean, I'm a music lover, and a lesbian. I think I *have* to know who she is. It's a law, isn't it? Maybe there's a rule book that it's in? It's written somewhere, I'm sure.

So of course I knew who she was. I even had her CDs. But I never really thought of her beyond that.

I was sitting in the living room with Stella, putting something together. I don't remember what exactly it was, something broken we were trying to fix. Stella wasn't the mechanic I was, but that girl could figure out electronics like you wouldn't believe.

So, there we were, working away, when Agatha came home. She stepped in the front door and looked at us, sitting there in the middle of the floor with broken bits of . . . whatever it was all around us.

"Hey, Bobbie McGee!"

I looked up at her. She had only started calling me that in the past year, since my father died. And then only if she had something I didn't know about that she found amusing. She tossed me a CD.

It was *Your Little Secret*. I looked at it and back at Agatha.

"What's this, Maggie May?"

"Something I think you'll like."

She deliberately gave me one of her secret smiles, slower than usual. Like she used to give me, back when she was only a fantasy to me. Then she walked out of the room. I shrugged at Stella and put that CD in the stereo.

Stella and I went back to work, at least for the first couple of songs. Then something about the music caught my attention. Something unexpected, yet . . . subtle.

Suddenly, there was an explosion inside my mind. That little box that I had stored all my memories in, all those memories I'd forgotten, that box that I had buried deep inside my day-to-day, suddenly burst open.

And all those memories, or rather, fragments of them, flew out everywhere.

Without any warning at all, I was back, in my mind, to that little town I had left so long ago. I was looking down a dusty road, searching. Searching for the missing part of my life.

And I was sitting on the warm hood of a car, seeing the shadow of an old rusty boxcar blotting out the stars.

I was pulling my bike into Agatha's garage, against all common sense, knowing I shouldn't be there. Knowing it was the wrong thing to do. Knowing it was right for me.

Then I was standing on the corner, under a broken street-light, waiting in the darkness for one more ride, one more chance.

And I was on the roof of my old one-room apartment, staring into the rolling darkness of the river, wondering where she was, reliving those memories again, trying to explain to myself why.

And I felt the rush of the wind as it lifted my hair and cooled my face.

I listened to those songs, and they took me back to those places, back to those times. I listened to them again and I tell you, I felt the wind in my hair, the steering wheel in my hands, the night on my skin.

I saw Agatha's eyes, reflected in the glass as she turned her face away from me. And I saw Sara's face as she laughed in the sun, hanging her arms out the window as if she were flying.

And I *felt*. I felt all those feelings all over again, in such a short time span that I couldn't even separate them all, much less sort them out. I was flying from one emotion to another, and back again, and to yet another before I could grasp the first one. I felt so much anger, so much desperation, so much pain, so much joy and love. All mixed up in the words of those songs.

I sat there and listened, and when I pushed the button to play it again (the third time through) Stella looked at me.

"Mom, are you okay?"

I blinked hard and looked at her. My daughter. I was so lost in the memories that for just a split second I'm not sure I recognized her. I'm not sure I recognized myself. I jerked out of all those fragmented memories and overwhelming feelings and realized that I wasn't that person anymore. I was an adult. A *responsible* adult, with my own business, a child, a lover. I couldn't reconcile the image of me with that younger image that I had just been thrust into. I shook my head.

"Yes, honey, I'm all right."

Agatha came in and put her hand on my shoulder. Stella looked up at her and back to me. The little worry furrow showed between her eyebrows, just like her mother's.

"You sure? You look funny. What are you thinking?"

I reached up and put my hand on Agatha's. I opened my mouth to speak, then closed it. What could I say? Where would I start? How do you explain what a song can mean, especially when it feels as if the singer crawled inside your head and put your life to music? How do you tell your child about the feelings that are flashing through you so fast that you can't even grasp them? All those feelings you had as a confused teenager? How do you explain, and justify, all the stupid mistakes you made, all the things you did that you won't now allow her to do? It's not too hard to tell you, a stranger, but to tell my child? I couldn't. I didn't even know where to start. Or even if I could.

My Maggie came to my rescue. She smiled her secret smile down on our daughter.

"I think she needs to sort out some things in her own mind before she can tell you what she's thinking, Stella. I'm sure she can tell you later."

Stella looked at me and I nodded, still not trusting myself to speak.

Chapter Twenty-three

So, I listened to that CD and the memories blew up inside my head. There were all these fragmented pieces lying around, and I couldn't make any sense of them. I tried. I think I was pretty useless for the rest of that day. And the next. I felt all disjointed, like some insane Picasso puzzle.

By the third day, I had myself pretty much together. I started pushing those fragments back into the shattered box they exploded out of. They weren't back together, but they weren't foremost in my mind anymore. I was slowly getting them reburied.

Yeah, I was getting there, I was putting it back together by putting it behind me again. Then Stella put that CD back into the player. And all those shards of my past flew back out at me again. And this time I knew the box was shattered beyond repair. I knew I couldn't just put them back in there, just bury them again. I knew I had to face them.

Stella watched me closely. "Mom, what are you thinking?"

I looked at her, then at Agatha. "Help?"

Agatha shook her head. "I can't. I can't tell her what's inside your head. That's your job."

"Thanks." I looked back at my daughter. She was watching me so intently. Such a serious child! I sighed. "I'm thinking about . . . stuff. Things that happened a long time ago. Things that I thought I'd forgotten, until I heard that music."

"How can music make you remember stuff?"

"I don't know. It just makes me feel . . . just feel. I think the emotions in these songs are exactly what I was feeling a long time ago. I used to have this little apartment across town. And I used to stand up on the roof late at night and . . . think."

"What did you think about?"

I reached over and took her hand. She scooted over on the couch and laid her head on my shoulder.

"I thought about your mama. And I thought about a friend that I had lost. I thought about the bad things I'd done. And the good times I'd had. But mostly I thought about your mama."

"You weren't with her then?"

"No, honey. I wasn't with her until after I went through a lot of other stuff."

"But you said you met her in high school."

"Yes, I did. But we weren't together until a lot later."

"Then it wasn't love at first sight? I thought you said it was." So many questions!

"Well, yes. And no. I loved her, I just couldn't really love her. Do you understand?"

She shook her head. "No."

"Well, I don't know how to explain it any better."

"And this music makes you think of Mama."

"Yes, and some other things. I think this music just makes me remember."

"Tell me."

"I remember standing on that roof. I remember getting in fights at school because I was different. I remember when I used to take my friend Sara out driving, just staying out all day. And what it was like when I had no friends."

"But you just said you had a friend named Sara."

"That was after. And before. I didn't grow up with friends."

"Why not, Mom? You have friends now."

"I know, honey, but I wasn't the same person then."

"Who were you?"

I sighed. "I think I was someone that was scared and lonely. I think I was angry and bitter. I think I wasn't a very good person."

Agatha looked at me. "If you weren't a good person, I wouldn't have fallen in love with you."

I smiled. "But you really didn't know me. And there for a while I really wasn't good at all."

Stella sat up and looked at me. "Why not? What did you do that was so bad?"

"I wasn't always nice to people. Like people I dated."

"What were you doing dating people if you were in love with Mama?"

"I was . . . I moved away from Mama, and I was trying to make my own life. I loved her, but I couldn't . . . I don't know, I just was."

"You're not making any sense, Mom."

I looked back to Agatha for support. She shrugged. I sighed.

"I know, Stella, honey. I guess I just need to sort through some stuff in my mind. I think it needs to make sense to me before I can make much sense to you. Understand?"

"Sort of. Maybe it would help if you started from the beginning."

"Okay." Stella waited patiently while I thought for a minute. "I was living in a little town not too far from here, when your mama saved my life."

"How'd she do that?"

"By being my friend when no one else would. Everyone else hated me. But she was my friend, and that made all the difference in the world."

"Why did everyone hate you?"

"Okay, maybe that wasn't the beginning."

Stella shook her head. "You need to get your story straight."

I laughed. "Maybe I just need to not tell a story."

She suddenly looked worried. "Yes, you do! I wanna hear it, I really do!"

I shook my head. "I don't think so. I don't even know where to start, much less how to tell a story."

"But I want to know, Mom. I want to know about you and Mama. I want to know where I come from."

And that's what did it. I understood her wanting to know. After all, I had wanted to know about my parents not so long ago.

"Okay. I'll try to sort it out. I don't know how long it'll take, but I'll start sorting it all out. Okay?"

So I began to sort through all those fragmented memories, like the remains of a burned-out house, examining each piece and putting it aside. Stella would ask me every now and then, and that kept me working on it. And by the time I was through sorting out all those fragments, I began trying to puzzle them all together.

Now, that's been some time ago. The world has continued to change. More and more people are out now. More gay people are choosing to have families. Some like Maggie and I did, but some are even adopting. It's amazing how much progress has been made. I've seen so much of that, and even been a little part of it. And time keeps going by. My Stella is learning to drive now. I've watched the end of a millennium, the beginning of a new one. And still time passes.

It wasn't too long ago that Agatha and I were taking Stella on a camping trip. Stella slid that CD into the car stereo while I loaded up all the gear. We climbed in and headed down the road.

I realized almost right away that we were going straight through that little town I'd left so long ago. And, again, that music took me back.

I was so lost in the music and the memories, I jumped when Stella reached up and tapped me on the shoulder.

"Mom, what are you thinking?"

I smiled at her in the rearview mirror. "Just thinking. You know, about stuff."

"The same stuff you always think about when you listen to this?"

I nodded, knowing she wouldn't stop there. I was right. She sat back and crossed her arms for a few minutes, the little furrow between her eyebrows telling me she was deep in thought. Then she turned to Agatha.

"Mama, you tell me. She never will."

Agatha smiled. That secret smile lifting up one corner of her mouth and gliding across her face before lifting the other corner. It almost made me shiver.

"I can't tell you, Stella, she has to. It's not my story. I was only a part of it."

Looking back now, I think it was a conspiracy. Agatha knew where we were going. And she knew I hadn't been back there. Stella knew I'd get lost in those memories if she played that CD. I think they planned it out. Stella found her opportunity to find out all that she wanted to know, and she took it.

"Mom, tell me. Tell me why this music always makes you get that strange look on your face, and why it makes Mama smile like it's all some big secret that only she knows. Tell me the story."

I glanced in the mirror at my little girl. She was sitting forward, leaning on the front seat, looking back at me so earnestly. She had such an intense stare for a child. Although she's hardly a child anymore. She was nearly the same age I was when I met Agatha. Her blond curls were peeking out from under her baseball cap, and her blue eyes were so intense, so bright. I turned off the main highway and took a road going into the residential district of that little town. I drove down the streets until I saw the house, then pointed out the window.

"When we met, your mama lived there."

She threw an incredulous look at Agatha, who nodded. Then she watched as I turned down another street, slowing even more as I came up on my mother's house. It didn't look like anyone was home, but I pointed.

"That's where I lived." I tapped the window beside me. "And that window there used to be my room."

I continued down the street. Stella was quiet, like she was afraid of breaking whatever spell was cast to make me talk. I pointed to the spot where Agatha had pulled me out of the ditch.

"That's where I looked at your mama for the first time. When she scared off the boys that I was fighting with. I think she saved my life that day."

Stella's face brightened even more. "You were in a fight?"

"Lots of them."

"Did you win?"

"Not ever. But your mama saved me. She scared them off."

Stella looked at her. "She couldn't scare anyone off."

"Sure she could. Back then, kids were scared of teachers."

Stella's mouth fell open. "Mom! She was your teacher? Mom!"

"I told you we met in high school."

"But you didn't tell me she was your *teacher!*"

"I know, I know, it sounds bad. But it wasn't. It was simple and . . . I don't know. Things were different for me than they are for you. Your mama was the first person that ever looked *at* me. She didn't look *through* me or *past* me. She looked *at* me. And she saw me for who I was. She saw the *real* me. No one had ever seen me like that before."

Agatha reached over and squeezed my hand. "Sure they did. Sara did."

I smiled at her. She had read my thoughts faster than I had. I found that I was turning into the park. I pulled up by the old railroad tracks, now completely grown over. That old boxcar was no more than a rusty frame, and part of that had disappeared. There was a chain-link fence around it, I guess to keep the kids out. But I could see it clearly in my mind, the grass growing up around the wheels, no fence to block the view, just as it had been so long ago.

Stella looked out at it and wrinkled her nose. "Where are we now?"

I took a deep breath. "Nowhere." I smiled. "I brought your mother here a long time ago. And I used to come here with Sara. We used to sit on the hood of that old car of hers, drinking and talking all night. This is where I came to dream my dreams, to feel the night air. This was where we went when there was nowhere to go. This is my nowhere."

Stella looked out at the old tracks. "It doesn't seem like much of a place to dream to me. It looks like a place that needs to be cleaned up."

That's my Stella, always environmentally conscious. "I guess you had to be there. You had to know where we were coming from."

"I want to know. I've been trying to find out for years."

"I know."

She turned and took my hand. "Will you finally tell me, Mom? Tell me your story."

And I tried. I talked about almost everything. I got a lot of it out of order, and I left some things out completely, but I told her what she wanted to know. I talked all weekend, the whole camping trip. I tried to explain everything.

Then Stella asked me for one more thing. She asked me to write it all down. She asked me to keep it all in order (I think I have, mostly), and to be honest. That's been the toughest part, the honesty. But I've tried. And I think I've done it. I didn't think it would take long to write this, but it has. I guess that's not the first time I've been wrong.

Now Stella has this crazy idea that someone out there might want to read this. I don't know why, but she thinks so.

So there's my story. If you expected a big bang at the end, I guess I'm going to disappoint you. If you're reading this, you might think I've had some rough times. Maybe I have, but I don't look at it that way. I don't think it's been any worse than anyone else has had, and better than a lot. And I think I've been blessed. Gifts have been given to me all of my life, from simple kindness done just for the sake of kindness itself, to the greatest gift I could ever receive, my child. My love gave her to me, and I'll treasure every moment with her, just like I do with her mother. Not every moment is good, but I treasure each one. It's still work.

But I go to bed every night knowing that it's been worth it.

Maybe that's my eleventh Great Revelation. This *is* Happily Ever After.

Then again, I'm still here and kicking, so I guess it's not really over now, is it?